SOLDIER
HERO THIEF

By NS Austin

Table of Contents

Note to readers:

Soldier Hero Thief is fiction. Any resemblance to a real individual or actual events is purely accidental. During the wars in Iraq and Afghanistan, several brave women received medals for valor. Marnie is not based on any of these women. She is a completely original composite of all the bold and plucky women with whom I've had the honor to serve and of the women who agreed to speak with me regarding their service during war.

Prelude Iraq
Seven Years Earlier

Marnie shifted positions on her cot and tried again to nap. She'd become accustomed to a cacophony of sound, and the commotion no longer prevented sleep. In the background, the white-noise hum of generator systems was punctuated with the pounding of boots on wooden pallets or the crunching of gravel when someone chose a shortcut off the pallet walkways. Rumbling vehicle engines in the distance competed with the whop-whop-whop of helicopter rotors that passed near the base. Occasionally, the shrieking of military jets could be heard overhead as they went about their deadly business. A symphony of activity all played to the drama of men and women engaged in war. To be heard, a chorus of voices rose above those wartime notes. Added to the volume set on high at their base in Iraq were anonymous shouts of "Get your butt over here, now!" or "Edwards, find that tire pressure gauge," or "Make sure you have the extra load of ammunition!" or even "I'll be back for chow by 1800."

The unremitting racket was comforting to Marnie. Silence was the real adversary in this foreign place. Whether for vigilance or vigil, nothing good happened when a hush descended over their base. A sudden stillness normally meant all senses were on high alert to locate and deal with an enemy, and Marnie's heart, like a caged animal, responded by beating wildly against her chest. It was also in silence that she choked back tears while the dead were grieved and honored for their sacrifice. Aside from silence, Marnie was most undone by the heat and the dust. She would never become accustomed to sweat-soaked clothes and a light film of dirt on her face. Today the temperature was already above 100°F.

Zeke was sitting near on a folding chair and held an open bag of Gummy Bears. She startled when he said, "Want some, Marnie?"

Her brown eyes sprang open. "Oh, hell no. I ate two bags yesterday. Any word on the mission?"

"SFC McCray said the MPs have three prisoners ready to move, but they're still coordinating transportation."

"I'm too hot to sleep," Marnie croaked from a dry throat. "Why don't you go to the mess hall. I'll cover till you get back."

Zeke grinned. "You're speaking my language. They're serving pulled-pork sandwiches and fries for lunch."

"Yum, stringy pork and greasy fries. Nice accompaniment to a quart of bears. Get going then."

Marnie watched Zeke's long, skinny backside hustle from the tent toward the dining facility. That boy was always hungry.

"Good grief, will it ever cool off?" she mumbled to herself. Marnie despised this sweltering tent almost as much as she loathed the desert. It was her team's week in the hopper—their week to be bored senseless, waiting for grid coordinates to retrieve the next batch of prisoners.

As she gulped tepid water from a bottle, Marnie thought again about how she'd ended up in this godforsaken country. The Army had informed her that she was smart. Smart enough that they agreed to send her to Monterey, California for language training. The day the official language notification letter arrived, Marnie ripped open the envelope before she'd even stepped away from the mailbox. Brazenly bolded and in all caps, **ARABIC**, the majority language of Iraq, stood out on the page like a cruel omen—any schoolgirl dreams of a European posting were crushed under the boot of the U.S. Army.

Mac slid through the netted tent flap. A man of few words and surprising stealth, he stood behind her, and Marnie jumped when he said, "We're a go. Where's the beanpole?"

"Darn it, Mac. Can't you knock or something?"

"Right." The corner of his eyes pinched in amusement. "You had that look you get when you travel to la la land."

"Beats this place—and Zeke's where he always is, eating." Marnie smiled, perhaps her first of the day. Even dusty and sweating, Mac's broad, muscular shoulders and the sight of his dark eyes under a Kevlar helmet never failed to ignite a tiny shiver along her spine.

"Catch any winks?" he asked, quickly glancing at her Army t-shirt and the breasts underneath.

Marnie returned a knowing grin. This thing between them was a game they played from a distance. Mac was the team leader and senior in rank. That meant any relationship between them was strictly forbidden, and Mac was the kind of man who earnestly followed the rules. Other than the occasional yearning peek, he didn't offer much encouragement. She had once overheard Mac mention to Zeke that he preferred big curvy girls— not fat, but substantial. At five feet, ten inches tall, wide shouldered and hipped, with a tight muscular stomach, Marnie guessed she might fit Mac's description of preferred.

"Nope," she answered. "I couldn't get comfortable."

"Yeah, it's gonna suck out there today. I'll get Zeke. Grab your gear, Marnie, and meet me at the MRAP. Gun crew escorts are already here." Mac disappeared as quickly as he'd entered.

Marnie didn't really care if the arm's length relationship between her and Mac was a figment of her imagination. She needed something normal to cling to and get her through the alternating fear and monotony that was Iraq. She was sure they had chemistry, and that alone was an oasis in an otherwise parched existence.

She finished donning her uniform, slung her weapon, hefted the rest of her gear, and trudged to the MRAP to wait for Zeke and Mac. Their MRAP was nearly new, its desert sand paint showing no signs of wear from the dust-infested Iraqi terrain. When Mac had mentioned they'd be fielded with one of the first of these boxy, ungainly looking vehicles, she'd been elated. MRAP was short for "mine-resistant armor protected". Armor plating along the underside and body went a long way toward improving soldier survivability against improvised explosive devices, commonly referred to as IEDs, and ambushes. The day their new ride arrived, Marnie thought it was the most beautiful, ugly thing on wheels she'd ever seen. The guys were all excited about the technology MRAPs carried. They were loaded up with all the finest communication and intelligence gathering gear the Army had to offer lowly soldiers just trying to do their job and stay alive.

Their driver had already powered up the communication systems, and the squawking of situation reports pounded in her ears. One of the MPs from another crew offered his take on the mission as he passed on the way to the lead MRAP. "Convoy briefing in five. Should be an easy one, Marnie. Not much traffic in the area."

"Let's hope," she answered. She pulled a sweat rag from a pocket in her trousers and wiped her eyes and forehead. *Only five minutes into this mission, and I'm already sweating like a pig.* Examining her clean sweat rag, the soft cloth was already streaked with reddish-brown dust. *The hits just keep on coming.*

She looked up and smiled when she saw Mutt and Jeff ambling her way. Fair, freckled, tall, and rail thin, Zeke towered over Mac's squat muscular build, his coloring in complete contrast to Mac's dark hair and eyes.

Zeke gave Marnie a lopsided grin. "You ready, Freddie?"

She rolled her eyes. "Waiting on you, Betty Lou."

Pushing away from her leaning spot, Marnie joined the others to gather around the convoy commander for a mission and safety brief. When the signal was given, the group wasted little time loading into their four-vehicle convoy.

The desert whizzed by Marnie's perch in the back of the MRAP. Hardscrabble, bleached landscape interspersed with misshapen trees spread before her in a monotonous symmetry. The destination for the evacuation point purposely avoided small villages, away from prying eyes and, more importantly, the danger of ambushes and roadside bombs. Still, her pucker-factor meter always notched upward as the convoy moved away from the safety of their base.

A weird roiling in her gut gave Marnie pause. "Oh, please no. Not now," she moaned. If not for the burping of the radio, someone else might have overheard her plea. She straightened her gear, stretched, and willed the discomfort to disappear.

Laden with equipment for all sorts of unfortunate contingencies, she smirked thinking about her props: a medical bag and accompanying insignia. Prisoners would be in for a world of hurt if they waited for her to save them, since the nurse getup was merely a disguise. Her job was to listen. The hope was that mid-level value prisoners would be fooled into thinking a brown-eyed, blonde nurse couldn't speak their language and carelessly share information the good guys could use.

Unfortunately, most of the prisoners came to them wrapped and bound tighter than a frozen Thanksgiving Day turkey. When the prisoners talked at all, they normally used the opportunity to make rude comments about Marnie's anatomy. Her team's intelligence gathering mission, a great idea in theory, didn't pan out in practice. But they would keep doing it, at least until some other officer came up with a better idea.

As the convoy jerked to a stop at the meet point, another pain, this one sharp and insistent, wrenched Marnie's gut. "Sergeant Mac, I gotta go. Right, now!"

"Crap Marnie, you know the rules. You can't leave the safety of the convoy."

"Mac, we'll all live to regret those rules if you don't let me out, and soon. Go with me to guard. The trees over there will work," Marnie pointed, sweat beading on her pale forehead.

13

Mac sighed. "Okay. Zeke, tell the MPs we're taking a short bathroom break."

Already running toward a copse of meager trees, Marnie ducked behind the first that offered any modesty and groaned. Standing to her front, Mac laughed, his M4 at the ready. "I warned you about Zeke's bears."

She spat a curse in Mac's direction. After a cornucopia of embarrassing grunts and with as much dignity as the circumstances would allow, Marnie turned away from the convoy to zip, tuck, and reposition her gear, stepping forward as she buckled the last latch.

A hollow clunk echoed under her boot. Shocked and immobilized, she stood on that spot like a frightened rabbit reviewing its last moment of existence. It was five excruciating seconds of adrenaline-filled agony before Marnie realized that the sound she heard couldn't be a landmine.

Trembling, she crouched and scooped dry soil, then whisked sand to the side with the back of her hand to reveal metal plating.

"Come on, Marnie," Mac called, still facing away from her observing the convoy.

"Just a minute. I found something." The metal plate expanded as Marnie continued to brush sand. Her fingers felt a circular inset under the dirt. She tugged a hand grip centered on the object, and a rectangular door screeched open a crack.

"Marnie, they're signaling. We have to move out."

"Almost done!" Marnie slid a flashlight from a pocket and switched it on. She pulled the hatch with all her strength, gaining barely enough clearance to wedge the flashlight underneath.

Lying on the sand, she peered inside the mysterious hole.

The beam reflected off metal stairs and the gloom beyond. Dust particles swirled in the sunshine filtering through the slim opening, as if the air inside had been sleeping, and the intrusion had awoken some timeless energy. Dim illumination exposed the joining of a side wall and the ceiling, supported by a stout wooden beam. "Holy moly, there are stairs. It's gotta be big," she whispered in astonishment.

"Marnie, what the hell are you doing? There's a new meet location. Come now, or I'm dragging you back!"

Marnie ran after Mac and went quiet when safely aboard the MRAP. All thoughts of intestinal distress were gone, buried under desert sand. Something else was buried in the Iraqi desert. Something someone didn't want found. *Treasure? Gold?* Something important for sure. *Why else would someone hide an underground cavern here?*

"What did ya find, Marnie?" Mac asked.

"Nothing," she answered. "Just my vivid imagination."

Chapter 1
Waiting Room

I rubbed my eyes and wondered if I could ever share what had happened to me in Iraq. That the locked vault where I kept my secrets might be pried open a tiny bit to allow in fresh air. My chest tightened at the thought. *Nah, probably not gonna happen. Not today. I came home from Iraq with PTSD, a medal for valor, and a pocketful of priceless jewels. How can I ever explain that?*

As always, I was early. The usual assortment of wounded warriors was already trickling in for our group meet. Nubby, taupe draperies covered floor-to-ceiling indoor windows, which darkened the Veteran's Administration waiting room and contributed to an overall aura of gloom. I assumed the point of the window coverings was to keep the other hospital goers from peeking in at the crazies. Not that in one way or another, those on the opposite side of the bulky draperies weren't just as crazy as me.

Like the waiting lounge in any second-tier commuter airport, gray upholstered chairs were all bolted together, and tattered magazines littered tiny faux wood tables connected at the ends of each row. The feng shui in the room was so off-kilter, I'd recently placed a refresh plea in the VA suggestion box. The only attempt at making the space more than dysfunctional was a vase of fresh flowers at the reception desk.

My groupmates sat in the same chairs each week, evenly spaced so that no one was required to talk with each other. Instead, we nodded, acknowledging the presence of our brothers and sisters still fighting a war from the inside. We saved our social energy to talk once we crossed the threshold to the meeting room. To share our experiences and emote, and in doing so, somehow those shared insights might help to make us whole. I was doubtful any amount of emotional bloodletting could fit the pieces of my soul back together, enough that a new version might resemble the old, but I was still here.

My seat at the far-left corner allowed my back to hug the wall away from doors and windows, a covetous position for the battle hardened, and the reason I came early. Cell phones were forbidden in the VA hospital, and reception was crap anyway, so I read on my Kindle. Without that diversion, I'd be prone to analyzing my groupmates as they entered. Most wouldn't appreciate the attention.

Seven veterans and two service dogs comprised our group, all men except for me. Four had visible war injuries, and the rest of us were good to go on the outside. As I've come to learn, there was little difference in terms of trauma treatment whether war wounds could be seen by the naked eye. The only difference—the ignorance of the rest of the world. For those not in the know, it was simply easier to connect the dots when a veteran possessed a missing limb, limp, or physical scars. Exterior injuries equaled trauma—a veteran who appeared whole, not so much.

Like a mother hen, I took attendance in my mind. Watching for each of my partners in therapy, I ticked their names off the list as they entered.

Pete, an almost bald, broad-chested, thick-necked man had arrived before me and secured a seat in front of the muted T.V. Even now, he waited with his arms crossed and hands tucked under his armpits. When Dr. Santori passed around the clipboard for signatures during group, Pete couldn't keep his hands hidden. His fingers on the right were missing to the second knuckle, and the nails on the left were chewed to the quick and caked with scabs. It was as if the good hand deserved punishment for the offense of not matching the other.

Already here as well, Trevon's place was in front of the reception desk with his dog, Silky. A tall skinny dude, his huge forearms were heavily muscled to support a missing leg that he'd lost not from an IED explosion, but by being crushed with heavy equipment at a Kuwaiti supply depot. The circumstances of his lost leg were a constant source of pain for him. He'd often raved that when anyone was brave enough to ask about the circumstances of his absent limb, they were disappointed with the truth. "You've got to be kidding me!" he said. "My leg is every bit as gone as the truck driver blown to kingdom come by a lump of metal on the road. What they want is a gruesome story. Assholes!"

Infantry in Afghanistan, Tommy had lost his left arm and the bottom of his right leg in a firefight. His story was everything Trevon's story could never be. I checked his name off my mental list when he strolled through the aisle on a prosthetic leg to take a seat against the wall, three down from mine.

And then there was Marco, a handsome Cuban from Miami with one eye missing from an actual IED. He entered and took a chair near the door. Why Marco routinely chose that place to sit was still a mystery.

Continuing my reading, I waited for the next arrival. Finally, Alex and his dog, Princess, made an appearance. It was Alex I most worried over. Some days, the poor guy had difficulty framing a coherent thought.

Only Dan was still missing.

I thought back to that terrible morning— remembering was the only way I braced myself for another session. That fateful morning when I'd woken up covered in puke on the backseat of my SUV, a cliché hangover throbbing in my temples, and no memory of the night before. If not for my phone and GPS, I wouldn't have had a clue where I was, and I sure as heck didn't know how I'd arrived at Fulsome State Park, sixty miles from home. My loaded revolver had been lying on the floor behind the driver's seat.

Most folks who know me wouldn't likely describe me as a sweet, normal girl, but I'd never been known as a quitter. I decided that day in the state park that it was high time to buck-up. I needed help. I planned to stick to that decision even when I didn't want to. Unfortunately, I didn't want to about this same time every week.

For the first four years after my return from Iraq, mental health providers had handed me pamphlets and delivered sermons, harping that my behavior symptoms were indicative of post-traumatic stress disorder. Some of them were darn pushy about it. I kept telling myself that with time, my issues would all fade away.

That label, P-T-S-D, stuck like tree sap and was an epithet I didn't want to wear. Once the disease was annotated on your medical chart, there was no hope of washing it away. I knew if I accepted the VA's "help" I'd be forever resigned to carry that bag of burdens on my shoulders. My family and friends mumbling under their breath about Marnie's problem. Employers always wondering if I might be dangerous or could one day become postal at imagined slights. Me knowing I wasn't strong enough to hang tough.

It was nice to have a catchall name for every little thing that went wrong, collecting complaints and petty grievances like flowers from a garden, placing them tenderly in my PTSD basket of woes. The timing was wrong, but maybe I could even stick the big lie in that basket and forget that most of my issues were my own doing.

When I'd finally signed up for this group, a young redheaded nurse had asked if I minded being the only woman. Her large, blue, empathetic eyes had searched my face for trauma. "Well it's not like I was raped or anything. They're soldiers, marines, airmen and sailors like me, aren't they?" My voice had taken on that high, abrasive quality I hate. "Why would my issues be any different from theirs? Why the hell would I mind?" By that point, I'd been nearly yelling. And yes, my issues included an inappropriately short fuse.

Appearing hurt by my outburst, the nurse had penciled me in for Group C, meeting Tuesday afternoon at 1330. I'd offered a lame smile in recompense for my over-the-top response.

From the corner of my eyes, Dr. Santori's dome of curly grey hair floated behind the reception counter as she walked into her office. She would call us in shortly. Dan simultaneously opened the outside door to enter the waiting room, furtively looking around the room for a seat.

Everyone was now present. Curiously, his gaze landed on me, the first time I'd known him to meet my eyes. Dan beelined to the chair next to mine and dropped into it.

He was sweating profusely, as if he'd run miles in the humidity to attend this group session. His legs and hands in anxious motion, he focused on the floor by his feet. I tried to be casual. Surreptitiously stealing glances, the rest of our group had turned toward our location, as surprised by Dan's unusual choice of seats as me.

"Hi, Dan. How's it going?" I asked.

No response. Dan's fingers were doing a dance on his legs. I hate to admit it, but I glanced over to be sure he wasn't hiding a weapon somewhere on his person. *Darn labels*.

Finally, his head still bent to the ground, he said in a low, hushed voice, "Marnie, someone's following you."

My heart beat against my chest—and not from worry about Dan. For the last two weeks, this ominous, unshakeable feeling of being watched had frayed my last nerve. More like an itch than a tickle, each time I'd felt that intrusive lurking sensation, my head had whipped around to the source only to discover exactly nothing. A couple of times, I'd caught sight of a brown van that seemed to be tailing me. After placing my concerns and worries in the "probably anxiety" PTSD basket, I'd ignored these sightings and bad vibes as best as I could, but I'd still lost more sleep than normal. Over and over I'd asked myself, *Why now, seven years later?*

"What did you see, Dan?"

He looked up as I found his eyes. "When you came in, I was scoping the lot. A guy in a brown

21

van drove in behind you, sat and watched while you entered the building, and then pulled around to the access road. I crept up on him, but he saw me and sped off."

"Do you do that every week? Scope the parking lot?"

"Uh huh. Helps me stay calm."

"Okay, good plan. Did you happen to get a license plate number?"

"Only partial. He turned right before I had a chance to take it all in. Do you believe me then?" he asked.

Dan had nice eyes. Deep brown and sincere, his stare was completely incongruent with the fidgety demeanor. "Why wouldn't I believe you, Dan? You wouldn't make it up. But it could be something else entirely. Who knows, right?"

Dan shook his head. "Could be, but I doubt it. They were watching you. Any idea who they are?"

"None whatsoever," I replied, terror creeping up my spine. Dan continued to inspect my face. I had the odd sense he could smell my fear.

Reaching into a front jeans pocket, he freed a surprisingly uncrumpled business card and handed it to me like he was offering the Holy Grail. I guess reaching out to anyone was a big deal for Dan. "I might be able to help. I'm pretty good at this sort of stuff. Call me if you need me."

"Thanks," I said as I took the card. It was plain white stock with only Dan's first name and a telephone number on the front. Turning the card over, the partial plate number was handwritten in block letters.

Dr. Santori's assistant called from the door, "The room is ready. Please follow me." Dan sprang from his chair and didn't look back.

I was not big on sharing in group, but I was a good listener. These men had sacrificed so much they'd earned my rapt attention. Nevertheless, distracted the entire hour, I had a hard time remaining tuned in to the discussion. All I could think about was the hard, cold truth. Someone had found me out.

Resolving to catch Dan when the session ended and question him further, he must've been a big believer in the motto "last in, first out", because he blasted from his seat and down the hall the second Dr. Santori said, "That's all for today, folks. Have a good week." I was hot on his heels until an elderly gentleman in an electric wheelchair cut me off from an adjoining hallway. I made a snap decision not to attempt a running leap over the chair, which would've been a bad idea on multiple levels. Instead, I performed a skidding stop, skirted the slow-moving conveyance, and lost Dan.

I found myself sitting in my Mazda SUV with the driver's door open, clutching the steering wheel and shivering in the sticky August heat. The temperature in my dark upholstered vehicle was somewhere north of slow broil. VA patrons were coming and going in the parking lot, some eyeing me warily. One woman my mom's age saw me, stopped, and asked if I needed any help. "No thanks. I have a little fever. I'll be fine." She returned a doubtful look and moved on. *Everyone moves on but me.*

Chapter 2
Followed

I was on autopilot, my mind a blur of theories about who could be following me. If not for the bicyclist on my half of the road rather than their rightful place between the vividly marked cyclist lines, I wouldn't have braked immediately after turning right on Second Street. Checking the sideview mirror for another zoned-out driver itching to ruin the paint job on my pristine SUV, there it was, the van—four vehicles back waiting to make the same right turn. At least, I thought it was the same van. *Dammit!*

A honk, even a polite honk, might anger the bicyclist and only result in reduced speed as opposed to his movement into the cyclist lane. Whoever they were in that brown van, I didn't want them following me home. Slipping into the left turn lane, I warned the two-wheeled obstruction with a quick horn tap not to press his luck and scooted around him. The bicyclist replied with an obscene gesture.

Flooring the accelerator, I made a fast left at the next corner, blew through a four-way stop, turned right, and headed five blocks west to a gravel alley behind the Coffee Roaster, a coffee shop I frequented. I knew this alley was almost unseen behind overgrown bushes and unpruned trees. Buck, my dog, had often marked the territory as his own.

I watched the road from my driver's side mirror with a death grip on the steering wheel, my breathing rapid and shallow.

"There it is!" A newer tawny-brown Ford van flashed by without slowing. The van's windows were tinted, and the sun hit at an angle that reflected light back at me. There was no way to see who was driving. Pausing a few beats, I pulled forward into the Coffee Roaster's back entry drive, turned around, and crept forward to the road, searching for any sign of my tail. Goosebumps contracted the skin across my neck and arms. If I had any doubts that someone was looking for me, those doubts just sailed by in that van.

My breathing slowed while I held my position to ensure the van didn't double back. In some ways, this may be a good thing, I reasoned. The van was proof positive my issues had not progressed from anxiety to wild imaginings. I'd been waiting for seven years. Carrying my guilt for seven long, mind-numbing years on pins and needles, and all the while expecting at any moment to be found out. Knowing deep in my gut that eventually someone would come. It was almost a relief to discover the wait was over. Almost.

The van didn't come back, so I peeled out of the alley and headed home.

Buck slid under the garage door the second there was enough clearance, and after two long strides, sat alongside my SUV. "Good to see you too, big boy." I smiled through the window and opened the car door to allow him to leap over me into the passenger seat. He circled twice for comfort and then sat staring at me in that completely heartwarming and adoring way of his. I reached over to scratch his head and ears. "We aren't going for a ride now, Buck. Only in the garage." His tail thumped against the seatbelt harness. He didn't seem to mind.

Now that Buck was by my side, that creeping feeling of dread I'd battled all day leeched away like the release of an over-pressurized safety valve. I parked and pressed the garage door clicker to enclose us in the safety of home. The security pad by the door showed a steady green, a good sign my home was still secure. I let Buck in first. He'd know immediately if anyone had been inside during my absence.

Buck trotted from the kitchen to the bedrooms while I stood in front of the sink. He returned, rounding the corner, barked once to signal an all clear, and then headed to the stairs leading into the basement.

Back from his underground scouting mission, Buck nudged my hand with his snout. "One last thing buddy, and I'll let you go outside." I moved to the back door to check the fine string I taped from the frame to the door every day before I left. "It can't be!" A piece of tape was on the floor—the string now affixed to only one side.

Pounding my head with my fists, I thought back to my morning ritual. *Did I replace the string this morning?* A groan escaped my lips, and blood rushed behind my ears. A latent heartbeat signaled another anxiety response. I took a deep breath and slowly let air out through my mouth. After three repetitions the panic subsided.

Buck broke the spell of my Zen moment, whining to get attention. Prancing in a circle and barking, he scratched the floor by the back door, desperately communicating his need. "I'm sorry, sweet boy. Pull yourself together, Marnie." I let Buck out in the fenced yard and locked the door behind him.

Standing by the sink, I waited until Buck barked to say he was done and ready to eat. He didn't take long. He knew dinner would be served upon his return. After dumping dog food in a bowl, I plodded to my bedroom while Buck inhaled his dinner.

When I had bought this tiny house, there'd only been a few must-haves to my purchase: a fenced yard and a garage for Buck, and a closet that was large enough to hold my massive shoe collection and roomy enough to modify. A local handyman who advertised he was good with wood had agreed to make cedar wall linings for the sides of the closet. "Don't you want me to install them, too?" he'd inquired, confused.

"No, thank you," I'd answered. "That's the kind of task I enjoy."

One side wall and the back had been easy to install. After removing the clothes hanger pole, I simply pushed the perfectly cut panels into place. The last panel was a bitch. I must've watched fifty different YouTube videos to learn how to create a hinged, hidden door. I'd finally cut the last panel two thirds the way up and made a lip at the top of the door portion where belts and scarves could hang. The job cost a fortune in tools I didn't own, but I was proud of the finished product and my workmanship. It would take a smart criminal indeed to discover the eight-inch deep, invisible pocket closet hidden on the left side of the closet.

I tugged a hook that held one of my favorite silk scarves and pulled the door open. Flipping the inside light switch, also installed by me, Marnie the

YouTube electrician, I studied the cavity's contents. Everything was in order. Inside was my dad's rifle and pistol, a taser that came with a storied history, ammunition, important papers, a few bottles of varied alcoholic beverages, and a lockable, fireproof box. That box was the reason for the modified closet. Grabbing the metal receptacle in both hands, I carried it to the bed and sat it gently on the comforter.

On my knees next to the mattress, I accidentally glanced at the decorative mirror on a far wall. As was often the case, my dishwater blonde hair hung lank, plastered along the sides of my face. If only the brown eyes returning my stare didn't appear to belong to someone else. The color and shape were the same, but a haunted expression had laid claim to my face. Those eyes couldn't be mine—the young woman who had once believed all things were possible if you never quit trying. That young woman had received an award for valor in the face of a tenacious enemy. The insubstantial visage in the mirror was someone else.

Buck saved me from descending into a self-absorbed pity session. He trotted into the room, having made short work of his meal, licked me on the ear, smelled my hair, and settled next to my side. Watching as I entered a four-digit code and opened the box, he yawned, probably bored and uninterested in the contents. It didn't smell like food, and he'd seen me check the box before.

Loose emeralds, diamonds, and priceless jewelry pieces from some unknown age of antiquity filled the steel vessel and glittered in riotous colors. A mammoth, deep-red gem stood out from the fruit salad hues and sparkled in the ambient light. I plucked the ring from its companions and touched its smooth face.

Sliding the ring onto my little finger, the only digit petite enough to display this amazing piece, I straightened my arm to view it from a distance. "Superb."

I ran my fingers through Buck's ruff with my other hand.

"Buck, have I told you lately that you're a truly amazing friend? I don't believe I've ever seen a finer looking German shepherd." He stared up at me, his big chocolate eyes filled with compassion, his tail swishing methodically on the carpet. "Your awesomeness aside, I'm afraid I may have a serious problem. A problem that's all my doing, and in no way your fault, but since you live with me, I guess by default it's your problem too.

"I'm sorry I've dragged you into this mess. I really tried to keep it all to myself so no one else would be hurt by my bad judgment and poor choices. Except that when they offered you up as a therapy dog, I couldn't turn up my nose at their overture to meet you. That would have been rude. Then when I saw you, I just couldn't say no.

"It was love at first sight, Buck. I always wanted a dog, and you were the best dog I'd ever laid eyes on. Anyway, you're a truer friend than I could've imagined. I just wanted you to know that in the event my life becomes a shit show."

First things first, though. I have to figure out who's following me and what they want. It could be nearly anyone: the government, Iraqis, a terrorist group, or even a third party I haven't considered.

I didn't have any idea how to begin or where to start looking.

Chapter 3
The Yard Troll

The microwave hummed as I warmed some leftover chicken enchiladas that I bought from a specialty store near one of the schools where I work. When the scrumptious goodness was piping hot, I added more cheese, the salsa I make from mi tia Veronica, my Mexican auntie's recipe, and a dollop of sour cream. I wanted a beer but settled for sweet tea.

Buck was under the table waiting patiently for his chance to wow me with a beseeching stare. I'd tried to keep up on his training. The handler had cautioned when she gave him to my care, "Marnie, just like people, dogs develop habits. It's up to you to make sure he keeps the good ones and steers away from the bad." Buck even came with an instruction manual the thoughtful trainer had prepared herself.

I had trouble religiously enforcing the rules because some of those habits she'd been referring to were so darn cute. When Buck begged for food, he often performed a repertoire of tricks. He'd roll over, give me a high five, or bring me one of his toys in trade. Who could deny him a tiny morsel?

Unfortunately, I could no longer take him with me to group. He developed a bit of a crush on Princess, one of the other dogs that comes to our sessions. There'd been an embarrassing incident, and I now fully grasped the trainer's warning about bad habits.

Placing my empty plate on the floor for Buck's pre-wash, I cleaned the kitchen and then prepared myself for work the next day. The woodsy smell of my cedar-lined closet greeted me for the nightly selection of an outfit. I laid a pair of deep blue, narrow-bottomed, ankle-length pants on the bed first and arrayed three tops, two pairs of shoes, two belts, and a scarf near the pants. I decided it was going to be too hot for the scarf, put it back, and chose a long, beaded gold chain instead. I mulled the colors, decided not to try anything on, and made a final selection in less than fifteen minutes.

I thought back to my five-year Army stint, wearing mostly ill-fitting, camouflaged clothing and brown boots, and shook my head. Little gave me more confidence than beautifully draped fabric in a fashionable design, complimented by a fabulous pair of shoes. I reminded myself, yet again, to restrain from clothing excesses or be forced to downsize to a cramped apartment with a tiny closet.

Checking the locks and security system one last time, I settled into bed with my Kindle. Buck was on the floor next to my side, cuddled in an old bathrobe. I'd bought him three different doggy beds, but he preferred a ratty, velour relic that held my scent. Pushing down any thoughts of the brown van, I fluffed pillows for the perfect prone reading position. Reading was right up there with Buck in terms of my therapy.

My imagination took flight into space—a recent reading craze. In this novel, the aliens sported pointed horns, and a bull-like creature gored a desperate humanoid trying to board his ship. I must have drifted off because instead of a humanoid fighting for his very life, I was on a dusty planet not like earth. Looking through a lavender haze toward a shadowed ridge, a fearsome animal was braying. The demonic racket of an unknown predator became louder as it drew near.

My eyes jolted open. Buck was at the backyard window, barking—really barking. Not the bark precipitated by the occasional cat or rabbit wandering into his kingdom, but the mixed growl, air chomping, hackle-raising bark of a real threat.

Before Iraq, I'd had difficulty rising from a deep sleep. Now in one motion, I was up, sliding into my shoes, and reaching for the 9mm Glock that I left on the nightstand next to my Kindle. To say my pulse had rocketed to jackhammer proportions would've been an underestimation of the strength of adrenaline flowing into my limbs.

Buck noticed me out of bed and must have felt free to leave his protective post, his dark fur a blur as he dashed out of the room. I followed holding the Glock with both hands, keeping the pistol pointed to the ground. If someone was in the house, Buck had already found him. I was more worried about accidentally shooting my dog than tussling with an intruder.

Wreaking havoc on the kitchen door by throwing his front paws at the wood, Buck growled menacingly as he attacked the barrier, desperately craving pursuit of whatever menace awaited outside. My back hugged the wall of the dining area as I slid forward toward a window. I wanted to stay concealed while I peeked outside. Sweat was already forming on my forehead, a liquid grip in my hands.

The motion light over the patio was switched on. A plastic, thrift shop table and two folding chairs looked more forlorn than normal in the glare of the slightly blue fluorescent light. Beyond an illuminated circle, the perimeter of the yard was in shadows. I allowed my eyes to remain unfocused on any specific place, giving my vision over to movement rather than color and shape. Using a learned ability to hear over Buck's insistent warnings, honed by spending twenty-four hours a day with a dog, I slowed my racing breath and listened.

Buck stopped, looked to me, and went still as well, his radar ears standing at full attention, seeking the smallest noise. A minute passed, more, and then the three-minute motion light switched off. I saw the shape of a man at the same time Buck heard him. The intruder was making his move. He'd been hiding in plain sight next to the thick trunk of a maple. I raised my weapon and prepared to fire a warning shot if he headed toward my home, and Buck went completely crazy barking, growling, and hurling himself at the kitchen door.

The intruder's ensemble was basic black with matching face cover. He was shrouded in shadows as he traveled along the fence line searching for egress. In a flurry of movement, he jumped, grabbed the top of the chain link, then planted a boot midway up the fence and swung himself over.

I ran to the bedroom for my phone and yanked it free of the charger. Dialing 911 as I turned on the outside lights, I finally gave Buck the release he desired.

The 911 operator repeatedly demanded that I stay on the line and ensured that I did so by asking a litany of questions. I pressed the mute button on the inquisition to yell out the back for Buck to come, and the operator must have believed my absence was a sign I'd gone rogue. "Are you still there, Ms. Wilson? Please remain with me at all times."

Giving up his backyard search and sniff fest, Buck came to sit by my side, panting from the recent excitement. "Yes, I have a weapon," I told the operator, for the second time. "I understand. When the officers arrive, I will inform them of the weapon and lay it on the floor in front of me. No, I saw the intruder scale the fence to leave, and I don't believe I'm in any danger now. Yes, I'm fine. And I'll remain on the line. By the way, I have a dog too. Yes, I'll put him on a chain. He's a well-trained service dog."

I don't enjoy being treated like an overwrought, teenage girl, and I rolled my eyes at Buck. He seemed to catch my drift. Finally, strobe lights filtered through the front windows. I was glad the police chose not to accompany their arrival with sirens. I didn't need the neighbors thinking of me as someone prone to police visits at 2 a.m.

As the doorbell rang, I yelled through the door that I had a gun and a dog and that I'd place the gun on the floor. Even though Buck was excited again and barking, I shouted through the door that he was on a leash. By the time I pulled the door open, Buck was sitting from my command, and the weapon was on the floor a few feet to my front. Both officers were standing away from the house with their own weapons drawn but down. Couldn't say I blamed them. There were lots of crazy people out there—but still, the officer's attitudes bothered me. I was, after all, a veteran and on most days only mildly plagued by issues.

An African American with a close-cut scalp and nice smile said, "Ma'am, the drawn guns are standard procedure when a caller states they possess a weapon on their person. Please remain calm."

"I understand. Come on in," I urged.

He introduced himself as Officer Jones and his partner as Officer Murphy. I took an immediate dislike to his partner. Sometimes that happened when a stranger reminded me of previous acquaintance that I found unsavory. It wasn't fair, but once I made an association, it was hard to let go. Officer Murphy could have been a doppelganger of Sergeant Tiffany Billings, the supply sergeant from hell.

Murphy was almost as tall as me, but wider through the middle. Her police belt strained and creaked as she bent to retrieve my Glock and release the magazine. As she pulled the slide to clear the chambered round, she looked me in the eye with a frown and asked, "This weapon registered?" as if I was the criminal she'd been ordered to find.

Meeting her stare, I answered. "It is indeed, even though in this state registration is not mandatory." If there was one thing I'd learned in my thirty years of living, it was that showing weakness around the Sergeant Billings of the world was a monumentally fatal error.

They might, just for fun, send a young private to a senior commanding officer for an unnecessary signature approval on 83 sets of earplugs, all while the first sergeant was breathing down the young private's neck, threatening death by dismemberment if said private didn't obtain said 83 sets of earplugs by close of business. Or, if the mood suited them, the Sergeant Billings type could enjoy hours nitpicking the cleanliness of a weapon some young private needed desperately to pass inspection, so they could finally go home.

My Sergeant Billings experience in the Army wasn't my last with power-starved, minor bureaucrats who populate all government institutions, big and small. The key to interactions with a Billings was to never, ever, break in the face of relentless scrutiny.

"That dog under control?" Officer Murphy asked.

"Yes, most definitely. Buck is a highly trained service dog."

"Service for who?"

This answer could be tricky. He was in truth a therapy dog, but any mention of my issues and I'd be convicted without trial of mental instability. "Me. I have hearing loss in my left ear." Truth, but not the reason for Buck or his intended purpose.

"Do you believe the assailant is still on the property?"

"He didn't actually assail me. I saw him in the yard. He jumped over the fence to leave when he heard Buck and the motion lights went off."

"Uh huh. Get a good look at him?"

"He was wearing dark colors and something over his head, so no, I couldn't give a description. And as I said, the motion lights went off, and it was dark in the yard."

"Probably just kids." In three words, Officer Murphy dismissed my concerns.

"Nope. Wish that was true. He didn't move like a kid. But also, someone's been following me."

Officer Murphy glanced wearily over at Officer Jones, who was glued in place, watching our exchange. Undoubtedly, as a partner of a Billings, he'd seen this routine before.

"Marcus, why don't you go check out the yard while I take Ms. Wilson's statement?"

I directed Officer Murphy to the tiny two-seater table that had cardboard under one leg to reduce the wobble. My extensive wardrobe didn't allow spare change for furniture. "Would you care for anything to drink? I have sweet tea."

She hesitated before declining. A jolt of sugar at two in the morning was always a welcome respite, but she probably thought accepting a kindness might give me a tactical advantage. Officer Murphy's attention wandered to the only picture on my wall, a nicely framed 16 by 20 blowup of me, Mac, and Zeke, sharing Gummy Bears. She stood and lurched closer to get a better look. "That you? Where was this taken?"

"In Iraq. That's me and my best buddies."

"You were in the Army," she stated more to herself than to me. "I did six months in Afghanistan with my National Guard unit, the 562 Military Police."

I took a chance. "Did your deployment suck as much as mine?"

She didn't turn. "More than you know. My husband left me three months in."

"Yeah, that happens a lot."

Her shoulders dropped, and she sighed. "We weren't doing great anyway, but that deployment was the final nail." When she sat back down, everything had changed. The club of shared misery, shared service, often overtook other priorities. I'd seen this phenomenon repeatedly, and I called it the foxhole effect. Somehow, no matter how diverse or different—in attitude, profession, education, background, religion, or ethnicity—it was a bond that said we shared something important that others didn't know. We'd been in a foxhole together—not literally of course, but we could've been. A loyalty that binds us and offers the benefit of the doubt. As an example, had I known Murphy was a vet, I would have likely withheld the Billings label and allowed her to prove it to me.

"Okay, Ms. Wilson. Why don't you tell me everything? What the heck's going on? And please, I really could use that sweet tea."

"Call me Marnie."

"Tiffany," she smiled. I swallowed the hysterical laughter dying to be released, which manifested itself instead as a choking cough.

By the time they were ready to leave, it was nearly four in the morning and only two hours until wakeup call. Tiffany handed me her card on the way out and instructed Officer Jones to give me one too. "Marnie, I don't know if I can do anything with this partial plate number, but I'll try. You call me personally, ASAP, if you see that brown van again. If you see it, don't engage, but try to get the last three numbers. Also, be mindful of your physical security."

"I will, Officer Murphy," I replied, showing the appropriate respect. Also, to use the name Tiffany required that I swallow giggles. We shook hands. "Thank you for your time. I appreciate anything you can do."

I could tell Tiffany wanted to hug me. Thankfully, she restrained herself. Hugging relative strangers has never been comfortable for me, even more so since Iraq.

The minute the door closed, Buck whined and trotted to the cabinet containing his dog food. "Buck, it's only two hours till breakfast. I don't want you waking me up before then to go outside." His mournful brown eyes conveyed that he was on his last ounce of energy caused by an extended period of starvation. I gave him a dog biscuit.

"On the glass half full side, Buck, I think we've enlisted one ally. We're going to need more."

Chapter 4
School

Ever watchful for the brown van, I gulped coffee and blinked my tired eyes. I started the morning commute with an upbeat music set, the same one I used for running, but the head-bobbing tempo conflicted with my pensive mood. Reaching to my cell, I tapped another group and lost-love country and western crooned from the speakers.

Who was behind this sudden interest in me? For so long, I'd conjured up images of an FBI swat team pounding on my door, my face pushed helplessly in the dirt as they cuffed me while animal control dragged away an innocent Buck—or being grabbed by hard men in a parking garage, whisked away to a hidden location by Iraqi Intelligence, and tortured until I gave up the location of their precious historical jewels. Day by day, year by year, those musings became more like an action/adventure story. I played the always-one-step-ahead, hunted protagonist, saving herself in the nick of time by grit and determination.

I lived in two worlds. In one—the real one—I held dangerous knowledge. Dangerous to me and anyone else who might reside in my orbit. Too many players, who for greed or political reasons, might want to ensure I never talked.

It would've all been so easy in the beginning if I'd done the right thing and come forward, taking whatever punishment was doled out, and moved on with my life. Sure, I had plenty of mitigating circumstances. Who could blame a barely legal

Marnie for her confusion, for her embarrassment, for her grief? It was me who blamed that fool girl. She'd made a mess out of a promising life.

In the other world where I spent most of my time—the one I created to help me live with the weight of past sins—my secrets were my salvation. In that imaginary dream, I used what I knew to set the record straight, and in doing so, I was freed forever from the responsibility of my mistakes.

As we used to say in the Army, *this is where the rubber meets the road*. My worlds had collided. Reality met whimsical thinking, and I didn't have any idea what to do next.

Merging onto the slowing right lane to exit, Saint Mary's Catholic School was a block ahead. It occurred to me that if I didn't have this job, my group, and a dog, I wouldn't have any social contact at all. Quite a sad state of affairs.

I thought about calling Dan—at least to learn what he meant when he said, "I'm pretty good with this stuff." Still, I didn't want to place him in jeopardy. *I'm so freaking stuck!* My anguished scream filled the recesses of my SUV.

I didn't merit a parking spot at this school since I wasn't full time. I pulled into the visitor's lot to the beehive hum of active children in the distance. For the first time today, my spirits lifted.

Grabbing my mega bag of stuff, I hotfooted it across the already steaming blacktop to the mobile trailer where I taught English to native Spanish speakers. Several elementary school children were already waiting for my arrival to unlock the door. Two dark-headed sisters watched from the steps, and as always, serious expressions gave way to smiles when they noticed my arrival. Three boisterous boys were engaged in a game of football, without a ball, and romped across a grassy area where weeds and hard-packed dirt had overtaken any notion of grass. Tomas raised his fist in triumph, obviously scoring the winning goal in a big game.

"Ms. Wilson, Ms. Wilson!" Tomas shouted. "I'm the big star!"

"Indeed, Tomas! That was some pretty incredible footwork."

"Ah, it was nothing. You should see me play with my older brothers. Mi papi says I have a gift. Where's Buck?"

"Your father is obviously a wise man, and Buck was tired. I let him sleep in," I winked. "Let's get going children. No time to waste."

The children filed in, fourteen in total and two missing today. I always worried that something had happened to them when they didn't show. Some of these youngsters lived nomadic lives not conducive to their educational welfare. On a whole, they were happy, joyous kids, and they gave me a piece of their joy when I was in their presence. I stayed away from the politics surrounding the program that allowed me to engage with bright young children four days a week at seven different schools. I loved the kids, and that was all that mattered to me.

As the two-hour session wound down, the school principal stopped by, which he often did, finding one excuse or another to say hello. Yeah, his interest in me was not completely professional. He was a nice man, but a little too needy and soft for my tastes. Today's pretense was a book he'd just read that he wanted to share. "Marnie, have you read *The Martian*? I just finished it. The protagonist was delightful. I think the novel is one you'd enjoy."

"Actually, I did. I loved it! The title leads you to believe it's alien oriented. I kept expecting something strange to grow out of his potato farm."

His smile turned down a notch in disappointment, but not because of the potato farm. "Should've known. Hey, where's Buck?"

"I had a little incident with someone prowling my backyard last night. Wanted him to stay and guard the homestead."

"Marnie, that's terrible. If there's anything I can do to help, just ask. I'm more than willing to come to your aid. Anytime. Seriously."

"Thanks, Kevin. It was nothing. The cops think it was just kids."

"Well, okay. Let me give you my personal cell number. You never know."

I whipped out my cell phone. "Got it, already saved. I really do appreciate your concern, but I'm fine."

"I imagine someone with your background can handle herself."

Nodding, my lips formed a tight smile. "Oh crap, I have a dental appointment. I'd better get going."

He must've watched me from the steps of the mobile until I reached my car because he waved when I turned—a little creepy, but probably not meaning to be. He was harmless. Also, I didn't want to alienate the principal. I responded to his overtures as politely and as elusively as possible. If I ever got to the point that I depended on Kevin for my safety, I'd be well and utterly screwed.

Dan's offer of assistance kept nagging me for attention. After I was sure Kevin had left for the main building, I removed Dan's card from my wallet. The simple design, with only a first name and number, could be either a good or a bad sign. I wasn't sure which.

A text ping startled me out of my ruminations about Dan.

Officer Murphy: *No luck on the license plate number, yet. I have a friend that knows some shortcuts. I'll get back to you if he can do anything. Stay safe Marnie.*

Nice of her to follow up, but I was still at square one in my quest to determine who might be after me. My gut clenched, and my pulse accelerated. I used a few breathing exercises to calm down and studied Dan's card one more time.

Chapter 5
Dan

Dinner was a meatless salad, piled high with red leaf lettuce, tomatoes, avocado, olives, and chopped cucumbers, lathered with my salsa. To ward off hunger again in an hour, I added a paper plate brimming with local corn chips and then poured my last coke in a glass over ice.

Buck was fidgety. He didn't like to be left at home alone, and today was the second day in a row we'd been apart. Maybe a ghost memory of the night before was making him anxious. He paced the kitchen, stopping to stare at my food occasionally, and then resumed his prowl. A neighborhood stroll and some ball playing in the backyard before it got dark were in order. I hated even thinking that—that I should be inside by dark because some nefarious, unknown bad guys could be lying in wait.

I needed a clear head. Fantasizing about my current problem, remaining immobilized by fear, and ignoring the possibility that I was in present danger were counterproductive activities. *Start with the facts, Marnie*. First, someone was following me and lurking around my home in the wee morning hours. It didn't take a rocket scientist to recognize these events were connected.

But if someone wanted to shut me up, and knew what I knew, why bother with all the lurking? There were so many easier ways to take someone out. *Ugh.* The pounding behind my ears was back again, my pulse raced, and dinner was a churning miasma threatening to revolt. *Breathe.*

Buck was poking at my arm with his snout to go outside. For a therapy dog, he lacked a certain awareness of the tools and techniques for self-calming, often rousing me from a peaceful trance. I wearily rose from my chair and immediately wanted a drink, something filled with carbohydrates, but not sweet to the palate. Shaking off my craving, I opened the kitchen door for Buck and forced myself to start again.

They had to be either looking for the jewels or for information. The only other person in the entire world who knew about the jewels was dead, so their intent must be to get information. But if they had learned about my involvement, they already had the information I possessed. It made no sense and I was stuck. G*o on to the next issue, Marnie. Who?*

Only someone affiliated with the government could possibly have my number. If the government was searching for me, wouldn't they just come to the door? Have me hauled in for questioning? Homeland Security or the FBI? The CIA? Contractors working for the government?

I chewed the skin around my nails since the nails were long gone. Even miniscule growth was gnawed off at the first opportunity. *I'm the one who needs more information.*

I picked up my cell to try Officer Murphy. Maybe she'd heard something about the owner of the brown van. Stopping in mid-dial, I ended the call. Dan's card was lying face up on the table like a blinking sign. It took a few too many beats for cell towers to complete their mystical handshake. He answered at the first ring.

"Dan here."

"Dan, it's Marnie. How's it going?" Silence. "Marnie from group?"

"I know who you are." Silence again.

This was getting weird, and I was already regretting the impulse to call. Unfortunately, I couldn't just hang up, because I saw him each Tuesday at 1330. "Yeah, I thought about what you said, about the possibility you could help me identify who was following me." I waited. When Dan didn't pick up on my train of thought, I continued. "Anyway, last night I had a prowler in my backyard, and I'm really concerned. The cops came, and I gave them the partial plate number you gave me to see what they could do. So far they haven't come through."

"They won't help."

"You mean the cops? One officer was a vet and she seemed to believe me. I think she'll try." *I'm not sure why I'm defending Tiffany, but I am.*

"Your kind of problem is way beyond their pay grade."

I was flabbergasted, speechless, frightened. "How would you know that, Dan? What would you know about my kind of problem!"

"I tracked it."

"The plates or the van?"

"The plates. Told you already the van got away. I have a buddy that's so wired in, he pumps blood through his system by copper tubing."

I didn't understand his metaphor, but if he knew something, I needed to know it too. "That's excellent news. Mind sharing?"

"No."

"No you mind or no you don't?"

"I don't. Meet me, and I'll lay it out."

"Not something you can tell me now?"

"I don't like phones. Too many people listening."

I had a brief visual flash of Dan in boxers and a tin foil hat, lazy boy lounging in an airless room where every window was blackened. Nevertheless, I needed to know. *I would take Buck along with me.* "Name it. Tomorrow is my free day."

"That works. Meet me at 1100 hours at Marco's favorite joint. Later, Marnie."

He clicked off as I was yelling, "Wait, what joint?"

I spent most of the evening trying to remember anything Marco had said in group about a favorite joint and considering an outfit appropriate for a clandestine meeting. The correct location came to mind after Buck and I returned from our walk. If the meeting was a bust, the perplexing restaurant puzzle challenge had at least kept me from whiling away several hours fretting over my predicament. The intriguing Marco trivia hadn't, however, stopped me from recounting the events that had led me to a walk out on a tightrope without a net.

Chapter 6
The Deli

I searched the street for parking when the little lot outside Ricky's Cuban Delicatessen was full. The only empty space was several blocks away, and I had to dig for quarters to feed the parking meter. Buck sat on the passenger seat waiting patiently until I signaled that he could join me outside the SUV. In the back, his dog cage was empty and unused. His instruction manual stated, "Dogs must be confined at all times while travelling," but locking him up had always seemed wrong. I was responsible for the morale of my partner, and he liked the front seat.

Deciding on a professional appearance rather than attempt something clandestine, for which I had little experience, my hair was up in a French braid. I wore straight black silk pants and a mid-hipped, sleeveless white blouse with little pearl buttons starting just above my breasts. My sandals were flat and plain, other than a smattering of gold embellishment on the strap across my toes. Feeling confident, I opened the door and led Buck into the deli.

My eyes wandered discreetly to the four corners of the eating establishment. Every table was full, but Dan wasn't sitting at any of them. I debated waiting outside, but a delectable mixture of spice smells, and sizzling meat caused my stomach to rumble and lured me forward to study the posted menu. Deciding on the deluxe sandwich Cubano, I moved behind a man at the cash register placing an order. Before the man had paid, Dan was standing behind me.

I stepped back slightly to join him. "Hey Dan, glad you could make it. You gonna eat?"

"Hell yes. That day in group when Marco mentioned this joint, I was already hungry. I came here on the way home. Food's great."

"It took me a while to remember what you were talking about with Marco's favorite place."

Dan responded with a shrug, and the conversation lagged. Glad for a diversion, I ordered and stood waiting to nab the first table while Dan made his selection. Buck and I took a seat against a far window with our line of sight facing the door. *Perfect.*

Dan joined me and pulled his chair around closer to mine, so he could also keep the door in sight. Old habits, especially survival habits, died hard.

He seemed different today—not so jittery. He wasn't an entirely unattractive man. Just a little taller than me, Dan was still fit and wore his curly dark hair shorter, the beginnings of silver above his ears and temple. Thus far, I'd never seen him smile with his teeth. I wasn't sure if that meant he had a gnarly set or that nothing was amusing enough to engage his full self.

"You seem different today, Dan."

"How so?"

"More centered. Less nervous energy."

"Yeah." He paused, maybe waiting for the right words. "You only see me at group. I'm not big on the whole sharing thing. Makes me uncomfortable, mostly."

"Why do it then?"

"Same reason as everyone else." He sighed. "Hope that it'll help."

I'm pretty sure one of my eyebrows raised. I do that unconsciously when I'm curious or confounded. "You haven't actually shared much, Dan. I don't know anything about you other than you were in Delta."

He smirked. "Give me a break. I've only been in the group for two months. I'm working up to sharing. And I'd say you're in something of a glass house there, Marnie. All you do is listen to everyone else and wear that miserable, 'I know what you're feelin' brother' expression."

His words stung like a slap. Sure, he was probably right. I didn't share either, but I resented the "miserable" description. He was already beginning to significantly irritate. Thankfully, the food came, and I had a chance to cool my jets.

We ate in silence. Dan broke first. He asked, "Can I give Buck a scrap? I'm sorry he can't come to group anymore. He's a great-looking dog and always seems to be happy. I like that."

I thought that statement might be Dan's way of getting back in my good graces. Remembering he'd offered to help, I softened. Besides, being nice to Buck was always a conversation starter. "He's a great dog, aren't you, boy?" I cooed and started again. I needed to know what Dan had.

"So, you said you were going to lay it out about the van?"

"Right. I have a friend. He found eight vehicles with a match to that partial plate. None of them were brown vans. He also checked for stolen vehicles and didn't come up with anything matching the van. My bet is the plates were stolen from a long-term parking lot and the brown van is either stolen too, or not. The owner of the plates will eventually figure it out. Then we can determine where the plates were stolen, but that may not tell us anything useful."

Nodding, I was wondering why he couldn't have shared this over the phone. "Guess it's a dead end then."

"For now. Thing is, someone was following you and they went to the trouble of stealing plates, and quite possibly, also attempted to break into your house. Do you have an angry ex or owe someone something?"

"No. Really no. My life isn't that interesting. Since Iraq I keep mostly to myself. I pay my bills. I used to drink too much, but I've never used drugs. No way."

"Anyone bothering you online, weird friends on Facebook, strange calls, anything like that?"

"Nope. I don't use Facebook. No stalkers, no phone calls, nothing."

"The MO doesn't fit a nameless stalker, but I wouldn't rule it out." Dan stared a hole through me. "What are you not telling me, Marnie?"

The heat behind my ears grabbed me before I could gain control of my temper. "I didn't come here for an inquisition, Dan. Don't you think I've wracked my brain about the same thing? You said you thought you could help, and you have. I don't know who could be following me. If it'll make you feel better, I'll make something up like the government, the Iraqis, or maybe the freaking CIA! No wait, it was probably the Russians!"

Standing to leave, I was quaking in anger. *How dare he?* I didn't ask him to pry into my life. I knew this meeting was a bad idea. Buck padded to his post by my left side.

I grabbed my knockoff Fendi bag from the extra chair, and Dan placed a hand on my arm. "Hold up, Marnie. I'm sorry. I'm just worried for you. Please, sit down."

If he'd have said calm down, I would've bolted. Nothing pissed me off like being told to calm down. Still fuming, I sat. When the heat behind my ears drained away and my heart slowed, I asked, "Why should you worry over me, Dan? You don't even know me."

"True. Maybe it's that miserable expression I mentioned, which was a jackass comment by the way. What I should have said is that expression tells me you truly care about the guys in group, guys that you don't even know and barely speak to. Maybe I think someone should care about what happens to you too. Maybe I appointed myself to the task when I saw someone following you."

Dan shrugged again. He had completely taken the wind from my angry sails. Buck didn't know whether we were staying or going and finally dropped to the floor by my chair with a groan.

"Here's the deal. I'm available most of the time. If something happens, anything, call me and I'll come. No questions asked. If you don't need my help, great. If you don't want my help, I'll understand. No harm, no foul."

"You don't even know where I live."

"I have the internet, Marnie, and my friend. Anybody can get that info."

"Don't you have to work?"

"I consult part time outside the country. I won't be called again for at least four months. Why don't you stop on the way home and purchase a prepaid cellphone? Use the number I gave you and that phone to contact me. Then I can talk."

"Do you really think all this drama is necessary?"

"I couldn't say. I hope not. Oh, also, please memorize the number I gave you and destroy the card."

With a piercing stare, Dan was back to boring a hole through my head. I asked myself why he was so strident about helping me and whether he was just paranoid or maybe wanted to get in my pants. We were, after all, both enrolled in a VA war-related trauma program. But no, in person there was nothing about Dan that screamed tin foil hat—just the opposite. His eyes said he was totally tuned in and focused. Also, if it were my body he wanted, he would have led with some inane compliment or equally lame, suggestive innuendo. A more thoughtful man might even have tried to share some of his life in the belief that his vulnerability could open a gate and entice. I wasn't getting any sexual signals.

Hoping he meant what he said, and that the motive was simply one soldier caring for another, I rubbed my eyes and nodded. I left Dan sitting with a half-eaten plate of ropa vieja.

Chapter 7
The Opportunity

Buck and I stopped at the dog park on the way home. In the middle of the afternoon, the only other critter in the enclosure was a geriatric golden retriever that trotted with unexpected enthusiasm after a ball thrown by its master. Approaching ninety degrees, the humidity was so thick the air was like a wet blanket on my skin. When I pulled his tennis ball out of my bag, Buck backed up, his head high and alert with his hind haunches bent slightly, ready to rock and roll. His tail waved back and forth in anticipation.

After fifteen minutes of ball chasing and fence marking, he was panting hard. I poured water into a bucket from the cooler the park service provided, and when he had drunk his fill, I linked his leash to his collar. He snuffled in disappointment that we were leaving so soon. We drove to a trail that was mostly shaded for a walk. I needed to think. My mind was a numbing loop of questions without answers, and mostly, I was sad and lonely.

Sometimes I led myself down misery lane, reflecting on all the people that I'd loved who were now gone and how I'd quit trying to fill the void. Right after Iraq, I had this manic search-for-a-man phase, taking one after the another into my bed, hoping to dull the pain. If they hadn't picked up on my seething anger and left quickly, I'd shoved them out the door. The longest of these relationships had been four weeks and some change. He was a decent man, and it's still hard remembering his face when I told him to move on because he was too nice and that I'd only hurt him. He'd winced and said, "Maybe, but I'm willing to take a chance on you."

I may have some issues, but that didn't mean I enjoyed hurting others in a futile effort to force a real connection. Not long after I'd stopped seeing men altogether, my dad had a heart attack during his morning run. My dad, retired Master Gunnery Sergeant Phillip D. Wilson, gone in the time it takes for the heart to explode. He'd been the only man left in my life and one of the few I'd ever trusted enough to count on. He was not around much during my childhood; my mom had divorced him with the realization that she'd married the Marines too. After the second move in three years, two short deployments, and scores of late nights and weekends, she'd given up and moved back to her home in San Antonio to live with her half-sister, Veronica.

No matter what my mom did to keep him away, my dad hadn't been a man who could ever let go. Every week he'd called. No matter where he was, what he'd been doing, or how difficult the task, he'd found a way. It was quite the source of pride to have been the only little girl in the neighborhood who'd received post cards and trinkets from far-off lands, many of which I'd proudly carried to school to show my friends. He'd never forgotten a birthday or a holiday, and when I was old enough and his Marine duties had allowed it, he'd sent a plane ticket for me to spend the summer with him. The first time, I'd been ten and hadn't wanted to go, afraid he'd be more a stranger than a father. But Tia Veronica, who'd been impressed by his fortitude, forced the issue.

In Spanish, she'd said, "He's your papa. Learn something new. Not so many kids get to fly to Virginia. Give him a chance."

That summer was the best summer of my childhood. Outgoing, always laughing, and with seemingly limitless energy, my Marine father had been a stark contrast to mom: a dour, normally tired, and silent woman. I didn't realize back then how much energy it took to work two jobs and raise a kid, even with the help of Veronica. Unfairly, I'd painted mom as uncaring. By the end of that first summer with my father, I'd wanted to stay with him, but his Marine duties made a permanent residence impossible. Mom wouldn't have allowed it anyway.

Three summers with dad had given me the bug to get the hell out of San Antonio and see the world, which was part of the reason I'd ended up in the Army in the first place. That and the uniform. When dad had arrived home from work at the end of each day, even then he'd looked ready to take on the world. Hair closely cut and neat, his broad shoulders and trim figure in that uniform had made me feel safe.

Now, he was gone. Him, my beloved Aunt Veronica, Mac, Zeke, and my high school best friend, Jessica, who got into drugs after I left for the Army. Mom was still around and willing, but as often as not, her bitterness crept into our conversations. She had no capacity to help me with my issues when she had so many of her own.

I have no one except a police officer named Tiffany, whom I've only known for two days, an ex-Delta guy who may or may not be paranoid, and a kind but clueless school principal who mistakenly believes I may be someone he could love.

Pathetic, Marnie. My reclusive lifestyle had come home to roost. The VA counselor had warned me about isolation—how I had to proactively cultivate people in my life or pay the price when I found myself too alone. I told myself to get out in the world, form some friendships, but every time I'd thought about making the effort, there'd always been a million excuses to delay. I was turning into my lonely, distant mother with the added enhancement of PTSD.

Buck had stopped sniffing. He was staring up at me, probably because I'd quit walking and was now anchored on the running path. I wasn't sure how far we'd gone or where we were. Kneeling, I buried my face in his ruff. "Thank God I've got you, Buck. It's earlier than usual, but let's go home. We won't even stop at Rosie's Take 2 Designs."

* * *

The smell of curry made my mouth water. Buck and I had decided on something besides Mexican and made a stop at Pho You for carryout on the drive home. I loved the restaurant—for its name and the food. I couldn't explain it, but no matter what happened in my life, I still had a healthy appetite.

I was almost to my house and ready to pull into the short driveway when I noticed the side door to the garage didn't appear to be fully closed. *That's odd.* I couldn't even remember the last time I'd opened that door. My foot was pressing the brake, but my heart was pushing hard on full acceleration. That garage door wasn't very far from the side fence. *Maybe it had only looked like it was open.* I steered my SUV to park next to the curb in front of my home.

"Buck, we may have a problem. Hopefully not, but I think we need to check." I gathered my automobile emergency protection, a .38 caliber pistol, from under the seat, opened the box that held it, and conducted a quick check to verify the gun was loaded. I tucked the pistol and my cellphone in the pockets of my silk pants and took a long slow breath to slow my racing pulse. With the knowledge that the first step in these situations should be to call the police, something deep within shouted, "Do not make that call!" If anyone was inside, an opportunity existed to find out who the hell was after me.

On shaky legs and with Buck by my side, I moved rapidly from the SUV to the garage. I kept my back against the garage wall and slid forward until I was closer to the entry. Just as I thought, the door was slightly ajar. I knew the frame wasn't square and the door stuck if it wasn't slammed with some force. Someone else, perhaps in a hurry, hadn't slammed it hard enough. Pulling the door open, I jumped inside the garage, my pistol up. The garage was empty. I searched for the comforting green light on the security pad near the interior door, but no lights were visible, flashing or otherwise—my security system was down for the count. Someone was either in my home or had been.

"To me, Buck. Heel," I whispered. "We're going in together."

Buck was so wired he was quivering. "Silence," I said under my breath, scurried to the entry, and turned the knob to enter my home. Standing on the second step, I pushed the door open a sliver and waited while listening. Buck whined. I lightly trod three steps inside and waited again, sternly eyeing Buck to communicate he must stay with me.

The electronic hum of my router and the clunking of ice from the freezer icemaker were the only sounds in the kitchen. One cabinet door stood partially open. I never accidentally left cabinet doors open. Panting from my mouth, the recognition that this situation was no game slammed me. *If you're going to do this, you must be all in, Marnie,* I cautioned myself. I steadied my shaking hands and gritted my teeth.

With my Smith and Wesson in a two-handed grip, I pointed to my front and tiptoed to the basement door, motioning for Buck to sit and stay. "Guard," I mouthed. He gave me a dirty look but padded to the place he was needed and sat. He'd discourage anyone in the basement. His position at the head of the basement steps kept him away from the possibility of gunfire—to be more specific, the possibility of my gunfire.

I crept as silently as possible down the hallway toward my bedroom. Stopping momentarily to conduct a visual sweep at the open door of the extra bedroom, I led with the weapon and glided into the room. The closet door that was always shut was open, just like the cabinet in the kitchen. Whoever this intruder was, he lacked some professionalism. That knowledge gave me the confidence I badly needed right now. Or so I told myself.

Three more steps to check the bathroom. Nothing. Everything appeared as it always did. As I backed out and turned, I had a better angle to view the master entry. That door was shut instead of open. *What was up with this idiot and the doors?* Someone was in there now, in the place where I slept.

Like pulsating lava, the heat behind my ears was building, spreading from my head to my limbs. *How dare they? How dare they enter my home and go through my stuff?* I didn't try to contain my anger. I could see the black-clad man from the night before in my mind's eye and imagined his face contorted as I strangled the life out of him.

My breathing steadied, ready for a fight. I moved in front of the closed bedroom door, which I never closed, and prepared to fling it open and jump inside. The master bedroom window squeaked. Someone was getting away! I rammed the door with my body and burst into my sanctuary. Legs and feet were flying out the open window in a mad scramble. I doubted I could make it across the room and out the window in time to keep up. The man already had a lead.

"Buck, come!" I screamed, and he was there in a couple of heartbeats. He smelled a path to the window, and before I could ask him to do so, his brown and tan fur jumped out after the man. Choosing easy access instead of the window, I tucked the weapon in my pants and ran through the house, bursting into the backyard from the kitchen. Buck sailed over the back fence at nearly the same time as the intruder. I was a decent sprinter, but any man running from a large dog was going to be hard to catch. Buck would get him before I did. Fear that the man would try to shoot Buck sent my legs flying across the yard. Grunting, I performed the best high jump of my life over the fence, rolling on alley gravel and back up to my feet without stopping.

Buck was already at the man's heels, snapping and growling. Wearing loose pants and a grey t-shirt, the man lifted a boot-clad foot. He shot a lightning-strike kick at Buck's head, missing my dog by the barest of margins. He kicked again with considerable force, only this time he landed the thrust dead center of Buck's chest. Buck yelped. He was wobbling and stunned, shaking his head as if he'd been stung by a bee.

If I was angry before, that emotion paled in comparison with the rage guiding my hand to the weapon tucked into my pants. *He just kicked my dog!* I took aim and howled, "Stop where you are!"

He glanced at me, his return stare wary but also defiant. Probably in his late thirties, well-defined features and a strong jaw left the impression of a capable man. His face was a stone-cold replica of faces worn by warriors everywhere.

My trigger finger wanted nothing more than to rid the world of this dog-kicking, house-lurking enemy. I might've pulled the trigger, except there was something familiar about him. I knew him from somewhere.

In the fraction of a second that I considered where I'd seen him before, he bolted from the alley and made a left on the sidewalk out of view. Somewhat recovered from the impact of the man's kick, Buck was on his feet and pointed in the right direction to resume his pursuit. Then the unmistakable *whomp* of two grunting bodies colliding, and seconds later, an unpiloted skateboard tooled along the sidewalk past the alley where I stood.

Chapter 8
The Key Fob

Running from the alley after Buck, I found my nemesis lying prone on his back halfway off the sidewalk, obviously unconscious or dead. Blood was pooling under his head and soaking into the roots extending from a thick sycamore tree. That tree and the beefy teenager on his knees in the sidewalk had finished the job Buck and I had started.

Perhaps still angry about the kick, Buck continued to bark and growl, darting around the man's comatose form until I commanded him to heel. I turned my attention to the dazed teenager, his face a mass of scrapes. He stared at me obviously in shock. "Cool dog. Is that guy alive?" he asked while pointing, but keeping his eyes diverted from the body on the ground.

"The dog is Buck. Give me a moment to check this guy, and I'll be right with you."

Leaning over the intruder, I felt for a pulse. He was still breathing. Quickly, I ran my hands over his legs and arms, patted his pockets, and checked his boots for a hidden weapon. Buck had torn his pants but hadn't gotten any flesh. A key fob in a pants pocket was the only thing on him— no phone or wallet. I turned with my back away from the teenager and stuck the key fob into my bra.

Buck had lost interest in the man who'd kicked him, and he was now attempting to entertain the shaken skateboarder, grinning for all he was worth. The teenager listlessly scratched Buck's back. The boy glanced at the bleeding man, and then looked away quickly, mumbling about how much trouble he was in. I clicked on the safety and hid my pistol under the band of my pants in the hollow where my waist and the swell of my hips met. The loose shirt I was wearing covered the bulge. Even though I had a permit to carry, there was no point making my pistol an issue.

"He's alive. Are you okay?" I asked the teen.

"Uh, I don't know. I don't think I've broken anything. My shoulder and my face hurt though."

He was trying to stand. I grabbed him around the waist and helped him to his feet. He yelped once from what I thought might be a dislocated shoulder. The arm was dangling at an odd position.

"You have a cell phone on you?" I asked.

He reached across his body with the good arm and pulled a phone from his pocket. I called 911.

While waiting for the police and an ambulance, I learned he was fifteen and named Trevor. He lived on the corner of my street a few houses down. He never quit talking once he started, a good sign he hadn't suffered head trauma.

Animated he said, "I don't know what happened. The man like came out of the alley so quick, I couldn't skate around him. When he hit me, he went flying. Must have hit his head on the tree. My parents are going to be like so pissed."

"Well, you can tell your parents I chased him from my house when I caught him robbing my place. That's why he was moving so fast, to get away from Buck."

"He did?"

"Yep, tell your folks you helped nab a criminal. Look, he's wearing latex gloves."

"You're right. Nice!" Trevor nodded, obviously impressed. "Great dog, by the way. You said his name is Buck? Hey, are you like married or do you have a boyfriend?" He realized almost instantly that his question sounded strange and blushed. "I only asked 'cause I do stuff around the neighborhood, like mow yards or carry things for people. If you ever need any help around your house, I'm your guy. I can even feed or walk Buck if you want me to. I'm really good with animals, and I'm like reasonably priced too."

"Thanks, Trevor. Good to know that and you. I think Buck's already smitten. Sorry our first meeting is under these circumstances. I'd better check again to see if sidewalk man is still breathing."

Sirens blared throughout the neighborhood. EMTs rapidly loaded the unconscious man into the ambulance and left. A police officer took statements from me and Trevor, and another cop remained in his patrol car, talking on a cell. Apparently, an unconscious man, skateboarding teenager, and woman with her dog didn't appear threatening enough for both officers to survey the scene. By the time a second ambulance arrived to attend to Trevor, he'd contacted his mom, and she joined us on the street.

"Hey Mom, I'm a hero! I stopped a robber— accidentally," he yelled to her.

"That so," she said with a dubious smile. I nodded in agreement with Trevor, as she went in for a hug with her big, teenaged man-boy. I was left alone with a police officer to finish the interview as the second ambulance ferried Trevor and his mom to the hospital.

Officer Jennings, a no-nonsense, mid-height, stocky, and dark-haired man, wanted to investigate the robbery right away because he was already onsite. I convinced him Officer Murphy had a prowler case open from the night before and that she would want to handle my break-in.

"She doesn't come on shift until later," Officer Jennings warned.

"Fine by me. I need a chance to see what was stolen. She told me to call her if anything else came up."

"He didn't have anything on his person. Doubt he stole anything. But have it your way. I'll leave her a message. She'll also want to follow-up with the alleged thief. He didn't have any identification on him."

"Really? Weird that he had nothing on him. I'm not sure 'alleged' thief is the correct term though since I chased him from inside my house. But *have it your way*. Thanks for your quick response, Officer Jennings, and have a good day."

He gave me a scowl and a verbal slap. "Please don't chase robbery suspects in the future. If he'd been armed, you might be in an ambulance too. Not smart."

Mind your mouth, Marnie, I thought. "You're right. Dumb idea. I was just pissed."

He looked me over to be doubly sure I wasn't the criminal, and then got back in the police car with his partner. Waiting anxiously for him to leave, I was shifting my weight from foot to foot as Officer Jennings typed a novel into the vehicle's onboard computer. The key fob and a search for an auto that matched the device was calling to me. Buck and I remained rooted in place until police taillights disappeared into the distance.

Starting our quest close to my home, I hit the unlock button every twenty-five meters, hoping to hear the familiar refrain of electronic mating. We travelled down one street and then another, further and further away from the scene of the crime. I wondered if the battery on these fob gizmos ever ran out of juice and decided I was being paranoid.

The sky was changing from a peachy orange to slate, and my frustration meter was pegging toward bright red. If I'd retrieved my phone, I could at least check neighborhood streets to see if I'd missed any. I kept walking and Buck continued to mark every pole and tree along the way. I jumped when a push on the fob finally yielded a bleating reply. A deep blue SUV parked near the alley of the Coffee Roaster was unlocked and awaiting my inspection—the very same alley in which I'd hidden from a brown van. *Karma, or something more sinister?*

In the SUV I found a wallet, a cellphone, a Sig P226, a rental car agreement, and a mostly finished Monster drink that might be valuable for DNA testing later. With the bottom of my shirt, I wiped my fingerprints from the SUV and the fob. Since there was no reason I could pinpoint worthy enough of retaining the fob for later, I threw the key inside the car onto the driver's seat. After tucking the intruder's weapon in my pants, my waistband was tight from holding two pistols. I prayed my pant snap wouldn't give way until I returned home. More frightening than a broken snap, if I had another encounter with the police right now, carrying not one but two loaded weapons, I could be in serious trouble. As casually as possible, Buck and I ran home.

I checked my cell first when we arrived home—three messages from Officer Murphy. The last one, five minutes prior, said she was on her way with an ETA of fifteen minutes. I didn't have time to scour the burglar's phone and wallet for clues, so I hid everything except the recovered weapon. While we waited for Tiffany Murphy, I fed Buck and then inhaled cold pho.

The doorbell chimed exactly on time. I liked punctual people. "Hey, Officer Murphy, thanks for coming. Please come in." Tonight, Murphy was alone, and she entered my house as if she were involved in a criminal conspiracy.

Her curly brown hair was frizzy from the humidity; the style like an old-time afro. Red cheeks on a round face nearly hid her gorgeous, bright-green eyes. "We had a little interagency dispute about who'd investigate your robbery since the department has recently set up a burglary task force. The number of break-ins in this area has reached epic proportions. Also, Officer Jennings said you seemed suspicious." Tiffany smiled. "Anyway, I won because I thought your case might be something more than a burglary, and because I responded to your first call. If it turns out this is a simple steal stuff scenario, I'll have to give it back to the task force."

"Okay. Suspicious you say. More like I can't keep my mouth shut."

"Yeah, I noticed," she responded with a wry smile.

"Do you want to sit and talk or look around first?" I asked.

"I'd like to sniff around first. Just stay here and chill, Marnie. Then we'll sit and talk."

Twenty anxious minutes later, Murphy joined me at my little table. I was working on a sleeve of crackers. When I offered to share my dinner appetizer and sweet tea, Murphy gladly accepted the tea but declined the crumbly saltines.

"I heard the alleged thief had nothing on him, so I won't bother asking what he stole. I also stopped by the hospital. He's regained consciousness, but they won't let me question him until tomorrow. I know the head nurse from a previous case. She allowed me a peek into his room to see if he might be someone known to police. He sure didn't give me the impression of a garden variety house burglar."

"I know! Hey, before we talk more, he left a gun." I got up and retrieved the 9mm Sig wrapped in a dish towel and laid it in front of Murphy.

"Did you handle it?"

"I did, before I thought, sorry."

"Nice piece for a burglar, yes?"

"Uh huh. I would think so."

Murphy pulled an evidence bag from a pouch on her belt and placed the weapon inside. "What made you chase the man rather than just call me?"

I had thought through some of my answers between the time of my first police interview and this one. They sounded believable in my head. Murphy seemed to have a capacity just like Dan to know there was more than met the eye with my situation. I needed to tread lightly.

"He escaped out the bedroom window, and Buck followed him. I was worried about my dog."

"Yeah, okay, I can see that, but you've got a security system. Didn't the keypad warn you someone could be in the house?"

"I must have forgotten to arm it."

"Right. After being followed and a prowler, you forgot to arm your system. Somehow, you don't strike me as someone all that forgetful."

She had me there, and she was staring at me with laser like focus, just like Dan had done when he'd asked similar questions. I could get mad again, but the highs and lows of the day had left me so tired I couldn't work up the energy required. Instead, I rubbed my eyes and shook my head. "I don't know what to tell you."

"How about the truth? Your place looks like it was a searched, not robbed. The person of interest and his weapon lead me to believe he's more than a burglar. Why don't you let someone help you, Marnie? If you're in trouble, or you caused trouble, it's better and safer to trust the police."

Why does everyone think I should trust them? And why does everyone suddenly want to help me? How can they possibly understand how embarrassing it is to talk about my choices? How humiliating it is to know I received an award for bravery, and all along it was me that was the garden variety thief—that I received a medal when better men did not? How can I tell anyone what I'd done, and what I'd hidden for seven long years? Part of me wanted more than anything else to let it go, to give my bag of shit to someone else to sort out, even knowing it would be at their peril. The anger was returning.

"I can't explain it. Turn my case over to the burglary task force if you want, Officer Murphy. I can't give you what I don't know."

Tiffany sighed. She didn't believe me, but she wasn't going to press it further. "I'm going to get someone over here for prints. I'll also try to find ownership info from this weapon. Think about what I said, Marnie. Sometimes it's more dangerous to keep a secret than to share it. I'll be in contact."

I didn't respond and was certain the grimace on my face said, "Leave me the hell alone."

"And Marnie," she added, "Watch your physical security. Whatever they're looking for, they didn't find it. They'll probably be back."

Chapter 9
Buck-up

Alone at last with time to sort through what had happened, and I found myself crashing. It was invigorating to do something, to take the first step toward resolving a problem I knew was drifting at sea like so much flotsam. As secrets often do, mine got caught in a current and had finally washed up on Marnie's beach, stinking like rotten garbage.

Sitting at my little kitchen table with my head in my hands, I fought the urge to drink. Oblivion was calling me. I knew I should force myself out of this chair. The mess some nameless jerk had left in my home needed to be picked up and decisions on what to wear to work tomorrow were necessary. I also needed to form a plan—now more than ever I needed a plan, but I was so tired. Buck was snoring on the family room sofa, blissfully sleeping off what a dog probably called an exciting day. *If only*.

With my last ounce of energy, I grabbed the prepaid phone in front of me and texted Dan.

Me: *Hey*

Dan: *I'm here*

Me: *Know anyone who can find electronic listening devices?*

Dan: *Probably. Now?*

Me: *No. Too tired. Work early. 3 tomorrow?*

Dan: *K*

I almost replied with thumbs up or a smiley face, but Dan would think me a lightweight.

Deciding I really did need that drink, I remembered that I'd hidden from myself all the libations in the house truly worth the bother. If that bastard dog-kicker had left electronics while he was sifting through my personal possessions, opening the hidden pocket closet to get at my alcoholic beverage stash would be an awe-inspiringly stupid idea. They hadn't found the jewels yet.

Moaning, the tears started. I didn't want to cry and go to work resembling a pathetic, puffy-eyed loser, even though right now I felt every bit the pathetic loser. The first tears were always the best, pouring like a faucet to release pain that had no other outlet. Waterworks in full bloom, I roused Buck for a last bathroom break, armed the security system, and staggered to my lair.

I ranted and cried as I piled clothes onto the floor; the clothes that had been left carelessly on my bed during the invader's search. Wearily climbing in, I called Buck to join me. The next tears were the ones I wished to avoid. Those tears clogged the nose, puffed and reddened the face, and leaked saltwater and snot onto my pillows. Still they came, remorselessly.

The dream was back. I knew it was the dream, the one I'd had many times before. I tried to wake, but the nightmare had its grip on me.

I'm running in the middle of a formation.

Mac is calling a Jody. His voice drawing me forward, he's singing a cadence in time to each footfall. Left, then right, then left.

> Sittin' on a mountain top, beating my drum
> Beat it so hard that the MP's come
> I said MP, MP, don't arrest me
> Arrest that leg behind the tree
> He stole the whiskey, I stole the wine
> All I ever do is double-time

My legs feel like they're hobbled with extra weight, each step forward a monumental effort. I can't get my breath, and my lungs burn; I'm struggling to take in air to continue. If I could just get out of the bodies running around me, push past the others pressing closer and closer. I can smell their fear sweat.

If I falter and fall, it will mean my death. The other runners won't stop running. They'll trample me with their feet while they continue their mission. There are so many of them, there's no escape. I look ahead and then glance behind at the rows and rows of bodies running in time to Mac's singing.

Everything hurts. My arms and legs are so tired I try to take a deep breath, but it seems like the other runners have consumed all the oxygen. I inhale nothing.

Mac's singing is getting louder now. He's singing over the pings and rattle of weapons fire. I hear screaming all around, and my face burns from the smell of blood and an acrid burning odor. I want to stay inside the safety of the other people, *and I want to quit running. The choice is not mine to make. In the chaos, the other people disappear. Only Mac is left. He has stopped singing and is lying on the ground. I must help him.*

No longer scared, I'm angry. He's covered in blood, and I don't know why. The deadly whizzing noise of bullets is everywhere, yet I run to him. There is nothing but him. No cadence, no bodies, just me and Mac. The weight holding my legs is gone. I grab and pull—pull him to safety.

I want to help him, to make the blood go away so he can stay. His eyes plead with me to stop. "No, no, no!" he finally screams. "Buck up, Marnie! Save yourself and the others first."

I pick up my weapon that is somehow next to me. I want to kill them all, so I can help Mac. I feel the heat of it against my chin as I aim and fire.

Gasping, I jerked awake. I normally cried and shivered from the dream, but my reserves of salt and water were all used up from the night before.

The dream was so strange, bits and pieces of what really happened intertwined with symbols that made little sense. If I were ever truly free to talk about my issues, that dream would be the first thing I'd ask about. Maybe an outside observer could make sense of my confused inner world.

When Mac had been wounded, and I'd pulled him to cover, I'd believed at the time he would make it, or maybe I'd convinced myself he would. Whenever I was in the dream, I knew that he wasn't going to survive. During the dream, I held him in my arms with full knowledge that it would be the last time I heard him speak—the last time I held his watchful brown eyes with mine, two souls joining into one—and still, I couldn't change the pattern of my sleeping imagination. Each time the dream had come, I'd picked up that damned weapon to shoot.

Having him near, even if for only a moment, filled me with a sense of joy I couldn't explain. And as always, I woke up, and he was gone all over again.

Buck was lying next to me, his nose close, and his eyes locked on mine. He whimpered, and I snuggled closer to him and his comforting dog scent.

Daylight filtered in the room. My cell informed me I still had over an hour to sleep. The dream, or variations of that same dream, had never included Mac's last words. I remembered his words, of course, but the only meaning they held was my failure to save him and Zeke.

Scooting back, I propped myself against the headboard and spoke to Buck. "You know, I never thought about why I named you Buck. That name was the first thing that popped into my head. But maybe my mind was playing tricks on me, and I was only trying to remind myself of something else."

Mac had died on an emergency evac flight not a full day later from too much damage and blood loss. I smiled to myself thinking about how his last words had been so totally Mac. We'd have all been lost if he hadn't spurred me to action. He'd often told me that you can't save anyone else if you didn't save yourself first. His final order had been a selfless act, meant for my welfare and the welfare of the other soldiers in the convoy, and what had I done with that? Had I created a big wonderful life because I survived? Nope. I've pissed it away by hiding and grieving and holding my secrets.

The Mac I knew wouldn't have abided my bellyaching for long or understood my inability to move on. Without complaint, he'd always watched over everybody else with a stern prodding if necessary. He was this sexy, hands-on, get-it-done, do-the-right-thing, and move-on kind of guy. So solid. So male. Even when I'd told him three months later about the cavern I'd found in the desert, his first response had been to do the right thing.

On the day I'd made my mad dash into the wilderness, Mac had asked what I'd found. I'd lied and said, "Aww nothing. Just my vivid imagination." At the time, I hadn't wanted to tell him. I'd believed that underground room was my discovery, and whatever treasure waited within that dark space was my treasure. It seems almost laughable now to remember the Marnie who'd convinced herself Aladdin's lamp had been hiding just under the sand, like a lottery ticket you purposely hide in your wallet because if you don't check, it's still a mega winner.

I'd surprised Mac with my treasure trove find a full three months after my discovery. We'd been sharing dinner in the dining facility after a full schedule of meaningless scut work. Mac had swallowed a big bite of his cheeseburger and said, "My dad just emailed me. The bank is going to foreclose on his auto repair shop."

"Crap, Mac, I'm so sorry. I know you were hoping to go into business with him. I thought you were going to cosign a loan to help him out."

"Tried. He has a lot of other debt, and it's hard from Iraq to convince bankers to make a loan.

Couldn't get anyone to bite. I'm more worried about my folks. This is going to be hard on them."

The knowledge of the hidden buried room and my inability to investigate further had been driving me crazy. I'd known then if I didn't tell Mac, I might never be able to revisit that place. "What if you found treasure in Iraq, Mac? What would you do?"

Mac had looked at me with his mouth open and then started to laugh. "Marnie, damn you're random. I suppose I'd sneak the treasure out of the country to sell on the black market, and then when the MPs caught me, enjoy a cozy retirement from the inside of Fort Leavenworth."

"I'm serious."

"So am I." Mac's chuckling died as he studied my face. "What are you trying to say, Marnie?"

"You know that day when I had that gastric event and you had to guard me when I left the convoy? I really did find something. There was a huge room with stairs and everything, covered by a metal door. I couldn't see what was in it, but it seemed like no one had opened that place in some time. What if there's valuable stuff down there?"

Mac's mouth hung open. "Are you sleeping okay, Specialist Wilson?"

"No Mac, really. I found something."

"That was three months ago. Why didn't you say something then?"

"Because you'd have just told me to report it."

"Well, yeah. There could be weapons in there or something worse. No, I take that back. There are probably weapons in there or something worse."

"Maybe and maybe not. Why don't we find out? If it's something bad, we report it. If not—if there's something else—we decide then."

"How the hell do you propose we get to that location again without a convoy in tow?"

"Exactly my problem so far. But that area is no longer considered high risk. If we could find a reason to go in that direction, we could stop and check it out. See what's what. Simple. Please, at least think about it, Mac."

"I think that's crazy talk, Marnie, but another day's wait probably won't matter. I'll mull it over. Don't get your hopes up though. My gut says it'll be trouble."

"That's all I'm asking. Wouldn't it be better to report more than just a hole in the ground?"

"Maybe."

"And I really am sorry about your dad's business. I know you were counting on it for later."

Mac had given me one of his trademark narrow-eyed smirks, probably believing I'd been resorting to manipulation, and he'd have been right. My grand plan at the time had been to be with Mac after Iraq—to ride off into the sunset with him and our Aladdin's lamp. That younger, naive Marnie was so certain she'd known him, even though we'd never even shared a kiss. Maybe later I would have thought him boring, or dull, or too controlling. Instead, his memory as the ideal man was stuck in my heart, and I couldn't find it in me to replace him with anyone else.

"It's time, Buck. Time to get off our asses and take the fight to them—to make Mac's sacrifice mean something. Not that you've been sitting on your bum, Buck. That was meant as more a reminder to me, but since you're along for the ride, I said we."

Buck was standing on the bed taking in my words, his big tan ears cocked forward. He probably just needed to go out, but I wanted to believe his focused attention meant more.

When I flipped on the bathroom lights, I was witness to the devastation of last night's crying jag. My eyelids were thick and red, and they contrasted nicely with the dark bags under my swollen eyes. I applied heavy makeup and then chose a colorful summer outfit to draw attention away from my head as I contemplated how to follow the trail of my pursuers.

The intruder's face came to mind. *Where have I seen him before?*

I ran into the kitchen, dug for my finds in a drawer, and opened the wallet I'd taken from the house invader's SUV. I'd been so busy feeling sorry for myself last night, I hadn't searched through the man's belongings for answers. Some detective I was.

A familiar countenance stared back at me from a Virginia driver's license. It was the same tough-guy mug I'd seen bleeding on the ground. The name that went with the face, Pitch Daniels, gave me nothing other than a clue that a name like Pitch Daniels probably wasn't real. If I'd seen him somewhere before, I didn't know him well enough to get a name. The rental car registration showed Pitch had also rented the SUV.

Palming the recovered cell next, I swiped, and was asked for a password. Since my recent investment in a similar device, I recognized the man's phone as a burner. As could be expected from all worthy burglars, thieves, and ne'er-dowells, he'd taken the time to ensure the cell was password protected. Another dead end unless Dan knew someone who could hack the phone.

Sighing, I breathed in slowly and fought the urge to panic.

Chapter 10
Bugs

I was holding back the urge to restore my place to order, aware the mess might give Dan clues on possible hiding places for listening devices. Clicking on the text message from Officer Murphy again, I hoped a second read would say something different. Something other than Pitch had snuck out of the hospital during the night, and no one had taken his fingerprints. I should've kept his keys to allow Tiffany to get prints from the SUV, but that would've required me to tell her what I did.

Marnie's dance—one step forward, and two steps back. I could complain about police inefficiency, but what good would it do? Tiffany would probably say they didn't have the resources to guard a burglar for a full night, particularly one who hadn't stolen anything. I knew Tiffany was trying to help.

With little sleep and after completing three classes at two schools, I had more energy than could be expected—something had changed. Somewhere between the crying binge last night, the dream, and the revelation about Buck's name, I had reached a decision. One way or another, I had to put my secret to rest.

Gulping a caffeine and sugar-laden coke, I waited at the kitchen table for Dan to arrive for our meeting. Going off half-cocked could mean placing someone else in danger. I had to be smart—way smarter than I'd been before.

Buck heard a knock first and ran to the door barking. I opened the door to Dan who was dressed better than I'd seen him thus far. His faded designer jeans, black polo, and expensive running shoes almost looked like date attire. Surprisingly, Marco was standing next to him.

"Marco?" I asked with my customary, one-brow-lifted expression.

Dan answered. "Yeah, Marco was an electronics wizard in the Navy. He knows more about listening devices than me, and I hoped you wouldn't mind if I pulled him in."

Marco smiled and peered at me with his left eye. The other was a good replica of an eyeball, but as a useless prosthesis, it never moved from staring straight ahead. "I brought along a device that can locate RF signals," he said in a deep, sensuous voice.

Even with one eye, Marco was smoking hot. It was hard not to notice when I ushered them into my humble home. About my height, I took him to be a bit older than me. He had a lean body—the type of body that hid six pack abs under a Miami Dolphins t-shirt. Thick dark hair, almost black eyebrows and eyes, and a clean-shaven face already showing a five o'clock shadow, was all right up my alley. I worried for a moment my "what's the point?" celibacy was resulting in hormonal spikes, but there was nothing to be done now other than to control any urges to act like a flirtatious fool.

They followed me into the bedroom. Having two men I barely knew enter my sanctuary was uncomfortable. I was restless as they surveyed the residue of a curious house burglar. Their gazes wandered over my possessions. I'd left open the drawers the house intruder had searched, and some of the mess was still stacked in one corner.

Marco said, "This isn't good!" and Dan gave me a knowing glower.

"He was looking for something, Marnie," Dan whispered.

"Really, Dan? I hadn't noticed. Where do you want to start, Marco?"

Marco put his finger to his lips and thumbed a note on his cell. He passed the phone to me to read the note he'd typed. *Don't talk about it out loud. Likely hiding places—bedroom, kitchen, garage. Dan said you were followed, need to check vehicle for GPS tracker.*

I nodded, and Dan waved me toward the kitchen door. Buck and I followed outside.

"This where you give me the third degree, again?" I asked.

"Would it do any good?" Dan returned.

I didn't answer. I sat in the most dilapidated of my outdoor chairs, saving the newer one for Dan. I pushed it with my foot to signal it was all his. We were both squinting from the sun.

"So, tell me," he said.

I laid out the events of the previous day. How I'd found someone in my house when I'd returned home. How he'd escaped out the bedroom window, Buck followed, and then I'd chased them both. The skateboard collision and the intruder's key fob, the matching SUV and the evidence. How the police had the weapon, and how the man had slipped out of the hospital during the night.

"You still have the phone, ID, and registration then?"

"I do. The phone's password protected, and I was hoping you might know someone who could hack it. I think the ID's are fake, but maybe you could check."

"Marnie, someday you're going to have to trust someone. I don't know what you've gotten yourself into, but there's an escalating feel to it. You may be in real danger here. Why don't you give it up? Let me really help you."

I winced. "Officer Murphy mentioned they'd be back."

"She's right! Maybe you should share what you know with the police. I haven't found local police to have the resources to do much with something like this, but who knows."

"Something like what, Dan?"

"That appears to be the germane question, Marnie."

After that, we sat there sweating in the summer humidity, swatting flies drawn to the yard by Buck's presence. Marco came bursting through the door carrying something in a dish towel.

"Got em! One in your bedroom and one in the kitchen. Also, a tracker on your car. You were right, Marnie! What the hell's going on?"

Marco laid the dishtowel on the plexiglass topped table. "See those?" He pinched a device no larger than a small pea between his fingers. "These aren't cheap Amazon 'I want to catch my significant other in the act' listening devices. They're sophisticated, expensive technology. Someone is serious as hell about listening to what you have to say."

I stood quickly on shaky legs, both men staring, probably concerned at my expression. I knew I was in deep, but those tiny bugs were proof positive I was dealing with the big leagues, and all my bravado about taking the fight to them was so much bullshit.

"Let's go inside so I can give you the phone and ID stuff," I said. Buck, sensing my fear, clung to my side as I wobbled to the air-conditioned safety of my home. The familiar rushing behind my ears was present as I entered. A panic attack was in full swing by the time I turned to get the goods for Dan. I couldn't catch my breath, my heart trying to knock its way out of my chest.

Marco caught me as I was melting to the ground. "Whoa, bella dama." In Spanish, his alto voice soothed. "It's gonna be all right. Do you have any medications that help? I know, Marnie. It'll be okay."

I whispered back in Spanish, "I know you do, Marco. Thank you," and then I passed out.

When I woke up, I was lying on the sofa, with Buck draped across my feet. Marco was kneeling on the floor next to me. Dan was sitting in a chair across the room. He was tapping his foot and scratching his head, as if freaked and uncomfortable. Most of us in trauma groups understand that the trauma syndrome includes momentary blips in our ability to deal with what life hands us. Some, like Marco, are simply better at dealing with the effects when witnessed in others. I didn't judge Dan for his discomfort.

I tried to speak and coughed. Swallowing, I tried again. "Crap. How long have I been out?"

"Not long, Marnie. Do you have a doctor you want me to call?" Marco asked.

"No! That won't help." I sat up. "I'm good now."

Marco appeared doubtful, but thankfully, he didn't argue. "Dan, how quick do you think you can get that phone hacked?"

"I don't know, but I'll do everything I can. Please, Marnie. Don't fight this alone."

"I'm not. Really. You've both been very helpful." I stumbled on spastic legs into the kitchen to finish what I'd started, pulling open the drawer with the phone and wallet. I reached behind cereal boxes for the Monster drink can, also in a baggie, and handed everything to Dan.

"What's this?" he asked, turning the can around in his hand.

"A partially full can from the man's SUV. DNA?"

Dan shook his head. "Above my pay grade. I think that's TV investigative stuff. Removing DNA from a can takes some real knowhow. Even if you knew someone who could collect the DNA, you'll need a warrant or a cop to match it. I'd just throw it away."

He handed it back. "Think about it, Marnie. I'll do all I'm able, but without anything to go on, my hands are mostly tied."

"Wish I could give you something more to go on, Dan, but I can't. Marco, thank you for everything. I feel better already knowing someone isn't listening in. And Dan, you have my eternal gratitude."

Marco gave me one of his sexy, concerned stares. "I can stay for a while, if it'll help. Get you some dinner."

I gave him my "I'm fine" smile. "No, Marco. You've already helped, and I'm good. I need to clean up this mess. I'm sure you've got something better to do with your day than hang with a crazy woman."

"Not really," he responded and chuckled. "You aren't no crazier than the rest of us."

"True that, I suppose." I herded them out the door. Taking my cue, Buck hustled behind the two men in his own guiding maneuver. I watched from the living room window as they pulled out. *Alone again*.

Chapter 11
TGIF

Why wouldn't people leave me alone? What I wanted more than anything was to be allowed to put everything away, eat, read, and go to sleep. Starving, I'd just finished leftover Thai and was working on bacon and eggs when Mom called. Standing over the skillet with a spatula, I pressed speaker phone and prepared myself for one of our conversations.

"You haven't called me in a while, but thanks for picking up this time. Are you doing okay? What's that noise I hear in the background?" Mom had an amazing ability to be whiney, concerned, and nosey in three short sentences.

"I'm cooking bacon. How're you doing?" I returned.

"I'm fine. I just worry about you when I don't hear from you. You know, if you had a Facebook, at least I could see what you were up to. Everyone else has one."

"You know I hate Facebook, Mom. Sorry I haven't called." I overcooked my over-easies while attempting to keep the conversation brief and pressed the call end button after only ten minutes. I knew she meant well, and that she loved me in her own way. I'd never shared my issues with her, but she couldn't stop digging for what her motherly instincts perceived but didn't know. Besides, she believed me to be crazy. I'd seen her looks when I visited.

After eating rubbery eggs and bacon, I gave Buck his slice. He smiled and raised a paw in a high-five, begging for more. Washing the plate and skillet, I placed them in the drainer and then had a hankering for Thin Mints—one box was still left over in the freezer. The doorbell rang when I was pouring a glass of milk to go with a sleeve of my favorite cookies.

It was Trevor, the neighborhood skateboarder. Much more welcome than a call from Mom, he stood at the front door with a tangled mass of unruly brown hair, his scabbed face beaming at me as if we'd been friends for life. Buck obviously believed Trevor was likewise a lifelong friend, because he went to the teenager in an ingratiating display of fawning.

"I just wanted to tell you my shoulder is fine. It still hurts, but once they popped it back in, it was much better. No reason I can't do your lawn sometime or like take care of Buck."

He looked around me into the house, waiting for an invitation.

"That's great to hear. I've been thinking about that very thing. Would you like to come in and give me your contact information since we didn't have time yesterday?"

"Sure." He wandered inside, taking in everything while Buck, the infatuated therapy dog, vied for his attention. "You have anything to drink?" he asked.

Chuckling as I went through my slim menu of beverage offerings, he settled on the milk already on the table. Trevor took a seat and immediately eyed the cookies. "Please help yourself," I added.

"Hey, did you hear about the dude I plowed down?" Trevor asked.

"I did. He survived and was good enough to escape from the hospital last night."

"No kidding! That's good to know. Even though he was a criminal, I'm glad I didn't kill him."

It was easy to talk with the teenager since he had absolutely no inhibitions. The fact that Buck really, really liked him was a good sign. I'd noticed in my short time as a dog owner that Buck possessed a keen intuition about the heart of people.

Trevor volunteered most of his history—high school, sports interests, recent girlfriends, and dreams for the future. The fact that I didn't have to say or ask much to keep the conversation flowing was most appreciated. I really, really liked this young man. I promised I wouldn't rain on Trevor's entrepreneurial parade and would find him some work.

"Hey Trevor, I'm bushed. I didn't get much sleep last night."

"Yeah, me neither. The shoulder and all. Guess you want me to leave now."

"I'm glad we had this chance to talk. How's about I call you this weekend after I decide what I can afford to pay you to do around here? There's plenty of work."

"Thanks, Marnie. And thanks again for making it sound like I was a hero. My dad was only mildly pissed because of the hospital bills."

When the door closed, Buck snorted. I think he wanted to keep Trevor. Only one cookie was left in a torn cellophane wrapper. Someone, probably his mom, had trained him not to eat everything. I really, really liked that kid.

As if the fate gods were toying with me, I was thinking about peace, quiet, and sleep when the phone rang. "Hi Marnie, I just wanted to check-in," Officer Murphy's loud voice boomed over the cell speaker. "The report said the intruder was wearing gloves, but we checked for prints on the weapon anyway and got nada."

"Not surprising," I replied. "You working tonight?"

"I am. It's a full moon, hot, and a Friday night so I'm expecting a shit storm. I'm off this weekend, thankfully. How are you doing, Marnie?"

"I could complain, but who'd care to listen."

"Yeah, that's the truth of it. So, we're still checking where the weapon was purchased. It may take a few days."

"I figured. Appreciate anything you can do."

"Listen, if you come down to the station, you can go over our mug books. I'm doubtful your man will be in there, but it's worth a shot."

"Why not? When would be a good time?"

"I'll get back to you. By the way, I've got an errand in your neck of the woods this weekend, and I'd like to look around your place again. You up for that?"

"It's your weekend, Tiffany."

"I know, but it's fine. Sisters in arms as they say."

"I think that was brothers, but good by me. What time?"

"Noonish Saturday?"

"That works. I'll have some sweet tea ready. It's supposed to be a scorcher."

"See you then." She clicked off.

Buck smelled every portion of the back fence during his final, nightly pit stop. I made my way to rearm the security system, wondering if I needed outdoor cameras and longing for sleep. It was only

8:30, but who was there to question my choice of an early bedtime?

Oh my God. The doorbell was ringing, again. It was almost six weeks from the time I purchased this home before I knew I had a doorbell, and that was only the mailman delivering a large package. How had I gone from a near recluse to social butterfly?

Buck was barking as I squinted through the peephole. I held my Glock by my side. *Marco!* My heart skipped a beat. *Down girl*, I cautioned myself. My pulse raced at the sight of him on my doorstep.

As I swung open the door, Marco's smile was not as effusive as Trevor's, but far more disarming. My earlier assessment was spot on—he was a fine man.

"Sorry to drop in unannounced, but I didn't get your phone number when I was here before. Mind if I come in for a moment?"

"Of course. I'm out of milk and cookies though."

He returned a wry, curious look, said hello to Buck who appeared disappointed Trevor had not returned, and then sat at the table I might have as well renamed the conference zone.

I didn't offer refreshments. Marco appeared uncomfortable for a moment, which made me nervous. He smelled good too, and a fleeting lightheadedness overtook me.

"Marnie, ah, where to start. I think you have some secrets."

My eyes widened in alarm, and Marco held up his hand. "Hear me out. We've all got secrets. It's not for me to judge. I won't ever pressure you to give up your secrets since I know from personal experience, it isn't always easy to let them go. That's not why I'm here.

"You seem to have big trouble—dangerous trouble. And I believe you when you say you don't know who's chasing you, even if you may have some idea on why. That's where you must start. Find out who has need to cause you trouble.

"I did some research this evening and called my cousin. He works in IT for the Office of the Armed Forces Medical Examiner. I thought he might know something about DNA because the repository for armed forces DNA falls under that agency. You remember, Marnie, we all had our DNA taken to identify our remains if the worst case were to happen or if our bodies were not found until much later."

"Yeah, I remember. Go on."

"Part of what Dan says is correct. It isn't always easy to get saliva samples from a glass or cup, but it's possible. My cousin confirmed a warrant is required to compare DNA from a possible suspect to the Department of Defense repository. He also warned it all takes time, sometimes a lot of time.

"I was thinking, if you could convince this police officer you know to get her forensics folks to extract the DNA from the can, maybe I could convince my cousin to do something slick and check the DNA against armed forces data."

"That's lots of ifs, Marco. I appreciate the thought. Why do you think we should be considering the armed forces for suspects?"

His eyebrows raised. "Just a guess. I can't imagine you're involved with the criminal underworld. I do know you were in the military. Veterans populate the government and companies

94

with the know-how to cause you the kind of trouble you're having right now. I'm just calculating the odds, and I happen to have a cousin in the right place."

"That's the most helpful idea I've had in a while, Marco." I didn't mention I'd already arrived at the same conclusion. That the dog kicker and home invader must be someone I saw in Iraq.

He nodded and tapped his hand on the table. "Good. We have a plan. A plan based on many ifs, but still a plan in lieu of nothing at all. I'll let you get some rest. You look like you could use it."

It seemed as if it was raining helpful people these days. The skeptic in me asked if I should be careful about bestowing trust too quickly, and then the lonely woman inside told the skeptic to *shut the hell up*. After I showed Marco to the door, I stood watching until his car disappeared down the road.

For some reason, I was even more alone and afraid. He'd inadvertently reinforced my worst fear. I was up against some powerful people.

Chapter 12
Officer Tiffany Murphy

A dreamless night, no break-ins, and two days off for the weekend. My barometer for what constituted a good day, or what I called my joy-o-meter, was set to the lowest possible expectations. I was looking forward to cooking dishes to freeze, stopping at my favorite resale stores, exercising Buck, and even a visit from Tiffany.

I had set to work early Saturday morning on a spicy chicken tortilla soup, the pot simmering nicely when Tiffany arrived. Her first words when she came across my doorstep were, "That smells great. I wish I could cook."

Buck gave her a greeting as Murphy sat herself at my little table. I delivered a sweet tea in a tall narrow glass filled with ice, a wedge of lemon, and a paper umbrella adorning the lip.

"Delux, Marnie!" she said as she twirled the little umbrella. "Where's the fancy straw?"

"Sorry, fresh out. I thought in honor of your weekend, still doing the public's business and all, you deserved something special."

Sergeant Murphy somehow managed to look like a cop even in civilian clothes. Wearing boxy, khaki trousers that were probably man's cut, and a dark green, short-sleeved polo, her lively green eyes, round cheeks, and untamed hair conjured images of a cop that worked part time as a fairy godmother. Murphy had totally upended my negative associations with the name Tiffany.

"Before we delve into war stories, here's where I'm at so far on your investigation. The weapon left at the scene was purchased in Pennsylvania by a man named Donnie Meeks. He's a collector, and Mr. Meeks said the weapon was stolen during a gun show in Richmond. His record is clean. No reason to believe anything other than what he says, even if I have my doubts.

"Unless you can identify a familiar face when you review our mug file, which by the way is on database, not in a book, we're at a dead end. I want to look around again, particularly under your bedroom window where the perpetrator escaped, as well as the fence and alley area, just in case we missed something. I see you've put everything away." She glanced around at my clean kitchen and living area.

"I did, and I found something else in the process of cleaning."

Tiffany's eyes scuttled back and forth over the rim of her iced tea as she swallowed a sip. She waited patiently while I retrieved the baggie with the can and placed it in front of her. She picked it up, studied the contents with tight lips, and then said, "What the hell, Marnie? A probably professional wearing gloves searches your place, leaves his weapon and a monster drink he brought with him to the party? You need to tell me where this came from, or I'm done. I'll close your case and move on. Maybe even consider charges against you for interfering with an investigation. That what you want?"

Sighing, I dropped into the chair across from her. I'd convinced myself I could be casual and make her believe what I said. It wasn't Officer Murphy who was stupid; it was me.

"I'm sorry, Tiffany. I found a key on him when he was unconscious on the sidewalk. After the police left, I went in search of his vehicle. This drink can and the weapon were the only things in the SUV. After we talked later, I realized you could probably get fingerprints, and I went back, but the vehicle was gone. I know. I screwed up royally trying to do this myself."

"Ya think?" she huffed at me. "Marnie, you aren't trained for this. I'm trying to help you, but you can't go off on your own. I understand the need to do it for yourself, but in this case, you're not helping. Dammit, Marnie!"

I gave her a fully repentant expression and hoped she'd believe it. Whether she did or not, she moved on.

"Did you at least get the license plate number?"

"I did." Scampering to the drawer where I'd placed it on a note card, I handed it to her. "I'm truly grateful for your assistance, Tiffany."

"Don't press your luck. Are you sure this is everything?"

"I am. What about the can? Think you can get DNA from it?"

"Absolutely. Based on current priorities at the department, we should know something in six months to a year."

"Seriously? That's exactly why I was trying to do it for myself. As far as the police are concerned, all you have is an interrupted burglary. One of my friends said if we could get DNA from the can, we might be able to run it against the DOD repository. Maybe I should've just paid a private laboratory, whatever it costs."

"Nope. You need a warrant and a chain of custody certificate before DOD will compare their database against any DNA. You've blown the chain of custody unless I lie, which I won't. Marnie, I need to know right now. Do you have some reason to believe the perpetrator was a veteran?"

"It's common sense. I'm not involved with anything criminal. In Iraq, I was military intelligence, helping with prisoner transport. The only thing I can imagine is I heard something or saw something that makes me dangerous."

"Hmm. At least that's something I can work with. Look, I have a friend at the medical examiner that owes me a favor. Actually, it's my ex, but that's a story for another day. I'll ask if he can do something fast with the can. Don't hold your breath though. He owes me, but his record of paying up is spotty."

"Thank you, thank you! I'll owe you one too. How about a partial payment with some soup? I believe it's done."

The soup smoothed the edges of Officer Murphy's irritation with me. I felt bad about lying and withholding information on the wallet and cell phone. I was pretty sure the ID was phony and hacking a cell fell in the "bridge too far" category for local police. Funny—not ha ha funny—how one lie leads to another until they roll off your tongue without a second thought. It's only later, as the pile of lies grows to monstrous proportions, that keeping them all straight becomes a full-time endeavor.

After finishing her soup, Officer Murphy scoured my yard and the alley. Buck trailed behind her, sniffing each piece of ground for any additional clues. If he found anything, it remained a secret. Murphy didn't find anything useful either.

"My niece has a soccer game shortly, and I need to get going. When you have a second, could you send me the recipe for that soup?" Tiffany handed me her personal email.

"If I can get DNA, and that's a big if, I'll run it against NDIS, the National DNA Index System. We won't be able to use any matches for an arrest, but a match could point us in the right direction. I can't do anything about the DOD repository." She gave me a hard look.

"I have this sneaking suspicion you've identified a back door to DOD. I need you to give me your word, right now, that you'll share the results."

"I don't know for sure that I have a back door, but yes, I'm hoping."

She replied sternly, "And you'll provide the name of any suspects to me immediately, correct?"

"I don't want you in danger, Tiffany."

"Marnie, that's my job. Last time, correct?"

I nodded, but Murphy wasn't done. "I need to hear you say it."

"Oh, for Pete's sake. Yes! I will give you any matches, ASAP."

"Good," she smiled. "Don't forget the soup recipe." She gave me a hug like a big bear of a mom. The hug wasn't as uncomfortable as I thought it might be.

Chapter 13
Pandora's Box

After Tiffany's departure, I needed some me time. Buck and I headed into town for a little retail therapy. Our first destination was the best resale store in the area, a place called Labels. We strolled through the glass-paneled door, and a chiming bell announced our presence. A familiar sales clerk sitting behind the cash register looked up from her phone. "Marnie, Buck! Where've you been? We just got in some new stuff. It's in the back. There's some vintage bags and coats to die for. Can I give Buck a treat?"

"Absolutely. He's always down for a snack. How are you, Denise?"

"I'm well, thanks for asking."

"Just point me in the right direction. I haven't had a fix for a couple of weeks."

Denise was a giggler, so she giggled and then pointed to some racks at the far left of the store. Buck lingered at the counter with Denise for a bit. He always tried to convince snack holders he'd be willing to work for food. When he'd exhausted her patience or her snack supply, he joined me in the back.

One hanger after another, I touched, examined, turned, and methodically sifted through the racks while Buck sniffed. Imagining the people who'd previously donned these garments, it occurred to me that the clothing smells must be an exotic smorgasbord for a canine. No matter what resale shops do to cover it, there always remains a residual odor of things used and discarded.

I sucked in my breath, excited to find a tooled leather purse hidden under a folded sweater. When I opened the flap to examine the interior of the bag, a belt of a similar color with an interesting buckle was rolled up inside. My lucky day! Two unique and matching accessories at a price I could afford. I carried my finds to the cash register for payment.

"Oh, I love that bag!" Denise exclaimed. "It's like finding buried treasure, isn't it?"

Nearly gagging, my first thought was that *she knows*. Somehow this thrift shop matron knew about my stolen treasure. Part of me recognized the absurdity of my reaction, and the other part went ape shit and freaked out anyway. It was if I had no control over something deep inside that was always lying in wait to take advantage of my inattention. My breathing shallow, I clenched my fists—the worst possible response to prevent a panic attack. Buck leaned against me and whined. The clerk asked, "Did I say something wrong?"

Running from the store, I left the bag on the counter and a shocked sales clerk in stunned confusion. A block away, squatting with my back against the exterior concrete of a bank, I slowed my respiration as Buck looked on in sympathy.

Why? Why panic at the mention of buried treasure? *Because Marnie*, the sensible inner voice yelled, *that's where your life made a U-turn in the wrong direction*.

I regained control, at least enough to grab Buck's lead to walk. Walking helped. We wandered in the direction of a park. After a catastrophe, I believed it was human nature to

102

drive oneself to the brink of insanity to determine that point where unfolding events could have been changed—that exact moment on a timeline when one action or inaction sent life careening in the wrong direction. Even though it's a fruitless exercise, I still indulged in the "what ifs" of how things could have been different—what I might have done to change the trajectory of my messed-up existence.

But I was kidding myself. I already knew the place of my undoing. After Mac and I had talked about the buried room that evening in the dining facility, he hadn't said another word about the conversation for seven days. Seven days I'd waited, watching his face for any clues as to his decision. No answer had seemed better than the alternative, a big fat *no way*, or *Marnie, you're out of your mind*. His silence had kept my crazy dream alive, and for once, I hadn't badgered or cajoled.

* * *

It was a Tuesday morning. Zeke and I were playing a game on his PlayStation. Neither of us noticed Mac entering the tent, because our total attention was straining from the ensuing road race. "Marnie, get your gear. Zeke, report to MSG Williams at the TOC to assist with details."

Zeke's body was leaning into a turn, his fingers dancing a jig manipulating the controller. He replied with his eyes directed to the screen. "Just one sec, Sergeant Mac. I've almost got her."

"Now!"

Mac's harsh tone surprised us both. We dropped our controllers with the game at an indefinite conclusion.

103

"Where're we going, Mac?" I asked.

"Just get your gear and meet me at the MRAP in five." Without another word, he turned and left.

"What's up his butt?" Zeke wondered aloud. "Shit, last thing I wanted to do today was work for MSG Williams. He's a big believer in continuing the beatings until morale improves. See ya later, Marnie. By the way," he smiled, "I saved the game."

Hefting my load of stuff, I made a quick stop at the facilities and then jogged to the MRAP. Mac was on the radio sitting in the driver's seat when I arrived. He never got behind the wheel because there were always at least four in a crew. I didn't ask questions about the wisdom of leaving the base as a duo. I just tossed the extra equipment in the back seat and climbed aboard.

Mac was performing the normal security and communications business before departing. I whispered, "I can help," but he shook his head.

"Bravo Twenty-Three is departing for destination now. Over."

"Roger Bravo Twenty-Three, everything's a go. It should be smooth sailing. Out."

Mac finally turned toward me. "Colonel Jamison needs some high priority intel ASAP, and there's no one around to retrieve the package, so I volunteered."

"You volunteered? Not following your own rule to never volunteer?"

Mac didn't answer me. "You're going to need to man the .50 Cal. Better get to it. I've been assured the route is clear. It's only thirty klicks back and forth."

"Oh, goodie," I retorted. "No one ever lets me do the fun stuff." When I saw Mac's scowl, I shut my smart-assed mouth and climbed into the turret.

Mac drove with a lead foot, pushing the MRAP faster than I'd ever known it to go. As the desert landscape blazed by, I knew there was a possibility this mission was an excuse to check on the buried room. We were heading in the right direction, but when we zoomed right past that familiar stretch of road, I got scared. We were, after all, out here all alone.

I was listening to Mac check situation reports, as I scanned the way ahead for any threats. Suddenly, I thought about Zeke and how he manned the .50 Cal on almost every mission. I hadn't truly appreciated what the job entailed and the responsibility of operating our best means of defense. Zeke seemed to fill the role effortlessly. Responding to an awareness that failure could mean the difference between life and death, every muscle in my body was rigid. *My God*, I thought. *The focus necessary to be ready for a fight is freaking overwhelming.* Perhaps Zeke had become accustomed to the stress. Regardless, I had a new respect for that skinny kid. Zeke never complained about anything other than MSG Williams' details.

We arrived in record time at Fire Base Delta. Mac was in and out in record time too, carrying an envelope back to the vehicle. I made a quick pit stop and then leaned against the MRAP, flexing my fingers. They were still tingling from clutching the machine gun in a death grip during the journey. Only fifteen more klicks to go.

Mac finished the commo and security checks and asked if I was ready. "I'm good to go, Sergeant Mac," I shouted from my position.

105

"Stay alert, Marnie. I'm counting on you. Still clear sailing out there."

"Roger that, Mac. Let's hope it stays that way."

I was so involved in scrutinizing shapes in the empty desert and watching the road that when Mac screeched to a halt, my heart kept moving, leaping from my chest. Using my hips for leverage, I swung the .50 Cal around to meet the enemy with deadly force.

It wasn't until Mac yelled, "Ten minutes, no more," that I realized where we were parked. That group of bushes, the place of my intestinal release, was just to the right, exactly as it was in my dreams of lamps and riches.

Mac slung his M4, stuffed the classified envelope into his uniform, jumped out the MRAP, pulled a crowbar from a back-storage area, and ran like a deer, all while I watched him in shock. He turned and threw his hands up, like, "What the hell, Marnie?" I followed.

He'd already found the opening and pried it open enough to see inside by the time I caught up with him. Mac moved behind the opening and heaved to yank the metal grate open further. I stood beside him and we pulled together. The screeching of unlubricated hinges reverberated against low rolling hills like an audible beacon. If we wanted to paint a target on our location, we couldn't have asked for a better signal.

With enough room to enter the underground cavern single file, Mac urged, "Let's hurry. I go first, you cover my six." He went forward down the stairs, taking each tread carefully. I went in backwards and had to feel for each step with my toe before moving down to the next.

As we were creeping down the metal treads, I asked, "What if someone sees us? Don't they have drones in the area?"

"Marnie, did you think we could investigate without risk? We'll just say you had to go and we found it. The same thing that happened before except not the same day. As long as we get back safe, I might get an ass chewing, but it won't amount to much. The colonel was screaming for a courier, and MSG Williams was demanding bodies for a detail. What's a sergeant to do?"

The smell was off, cloying, something more than stale air. Bending and pulling my gas mask from its pouch, I placed the unwieldy thing first over my mouth first for a seal and then slid the hood and straps over my head. I knew chemicals that killed didn't have an odor, but given everything, wearing a filter against this malodorous environment was probably the right move. Mac noticed what I was doing and stopped to follow my lead.

Protective masks, with their big plastic fish eyes, always reminded me of the way the world bent underwater when snorkeling. Distances felt different, like my feet were closer to my head than normal. I ran into Mac's back after my toe made the last step to a packed dirt floor. Mac stood as still as a statue.

As I maneuvered around him to get a view of the arc of Mac's flashlight, my eyes bugged out and I quit breathing. Speechless, I gawked at a room so large that the back was not clearly visible. Dust motes swirling in the meager light, my visual perspective skewed from the mask, still, the gold bars lining the right side of the cavernous space reflected a soothing glow.

Stacks and stacks of gold bars. I couldn't even imagine what they represented in terms of real money. Mac and I turned to each other at the same moment, our eyes wide open and magnified by mask lenses. "Holy shit!" I screamed.

Mac didn't answer for several seconds. Finally, he said, "We'd better check the rest of the area and see what else is down here." His instructions were given in that neutral, sometimes maddeningly calm voice of his.

A five-foot clearance led through the space. The temperature was noticeably cooler here than above ground. Goosebumps blossomed from my sweaty skin.

The gold, neatly arrayed along the wall to the right, sat opposite one lonely pallet to the left. Nine or ten ammo cases were bunched together in the middle of the wooden pallet. Mac was already heading through the space to the back, while I was still stuck staring at the ammo cases, wondering what could be inside. "Marnie, please come here right now!"

Reluctantly, I followed the light to Mac, his flashlight directed to one barrel among many. A plastic label was taped to the side, and Mac was unsuccessfully trying to read the Iraqi inscription. "What does it say, Marnie? You can read it."

I bent and studied the Arabic abjad. I was much better at the written word than the spoken language. My expertise was unnecessary though because at the bottom of the label, in English, the lettering worn and barely legible, the word *SARIN* glared at me. "It's sarin, Mac," I whispered.

"I knew it! I knew the U.S. Government wouldn't send us here for nothing!" Mac yelled.

"Just like the president said, there are weapons of mass destruction in Iraq."

Mac was already moving quickly along the back wall. In the far corner, one other pallet was covered with sealed plastic boxes. Right on his heels, I bent and discovered the same thing as Mac. An imprinted bio-hazard warning symbol was displayed and nothing else. In unison, we both backed away. "It doesn't say what's in it Mac, but I don't plan to open a box to find out."

"Okay, Marnie. Now you know. Let's move out."

He was already at the steps heading toward the light. That was the moment when my world went to hell. I could have followed Mac, ran after him up those stairs to tell the world what we'd found. I had no doubt that was his plan—the honorable course. We'd be heroes for finding the illusive WMD and could've easily spun the story about how we'd found it. No harm no foul when you do a good deed. But no, my curiosity assumed control of good sense.

Like being drawn to Pandora's box, I cracked open one of those ammo cases and stuck my hand in. Cool stones swirled around my fingers. Faint light filtering from the open manhole cover, I drew a handful up in my palm close to my eyes. *Jewels. Huge, beautiful jewels*. Without breathing, I grabbed all that I could stuff into my pockets and ran after Mac.

One stupid decision followed by years of lies and secrets, and just like the compounding interest on a 401K, my life was irretrievably hosed.

Chapter 14
Monday Morning

Thunder woke me before my alarm. Gray skies and late summer rain were the perfect backdrop for the start of another angst-ridden week. I let Buck out, but he didn't stay long. He was kind of a wimp about rain, and thunder frightened him. He decided upon a place under the table, which allowed him to beg for scraps and be shielded from possible lightning strikes.

I sopped up over-easies with toast, sipped coffee, and scrolled through the news on my tablet. I'd never paid much attention to the state of the world until my return from Iraq. After that, it seemed important to follow world events at least enough to know whether someone had found the WMDs.

Logically, I didn't believe there was an Iraqi still living who knew about the cavern. There was too much wealth hidden in that hole; any Iraqi worth his salt and involved in hiding the fortune would have been back to retrieve it by 2007. I couldn't be sure, but the frozen hinges on the manhole cover indicated that the room hadn't been opened for at least a few years.

Even so, the possibility that the bad guys knew all along or that someone had accidentally found the WMD, like me, no matter how remote, made me physically sick with fear. Debilitating fear possessed me whenever I considered the possibility that if the war went against them, the bad guys might use chemical or biological weapons on American soldiers. Of all the horrible consequences of my actions, that would have been the worst. I'm not sure how I would've survived with more soldier deaths on my conscience.

My anonymous whistleblower call to the FBI with grid coordinates should have been enough. Why didn't the FBI find the room hidden under the Iraqi desert? Did they even look? The White House, in disgrace for a war based on WMD that were never found to exist, most certainly would've welcomed the information. The story of WMDs in Iraq, even a tiny amount, might have changed everything.

Weeks, months, and then years passed, and nothing happened until now. Why now? Finally, the troops were home. At least, I didn't have to fret anymore about our troops in Iraq and the possibility some evil madman would get the idea to kill indiscriminately with WMD. *Maybe that room is still out there unknown, filled with treasure and destruction.*

Dan had texted at 6 a.m. on my burner phone to let me know the ID of my burglar was fake—no surprise. Only ex-military would think to text or call that early. He also said he was still "working other angles" and would be in touch if something turned up. Tiffany had sent a more hopeful text at 6:30 on my personal cell:

> Murphy: *Great news! Ex says he'll attempt to get DNA from the can! I'll text if he gets results*
>
> Me: *Outstanding! Thank you!!!*

With the help of some new friends, I'd done everything I knew to do to solve the mystery of my pursuers. Time to get ready for work.

I really wished I hadn't run from Labels in panic; the outfit I'd selected for the day would've been perfect with that bag and belt. It made me sad to know that my embarrassing behavior made a return to my favorite store difficult. While brushing my teeth, the familiar refrain of my personal cell was ringing from the dining area. Who could be calling me this early? Maybe Tiffany.

I scrambled to the kitchen to pick up and noticed the unknown caller information after I'd already swiped. Expecting a pause for a telemarketer to be connected, I was surprised by an immediate reply from a deep male voice.

"Ms. Wilson. This is Special Investigator Russel Cook from the Federal Bureau of Investigation. My task force has been assigned to conduct research on an incident that occurred in Iraq while you were present in country."

I was dumbfounded and unable to speak. As if my precarious situation couldn't get worse, now the FBI wanted a piece of me. "Ms. Wilson, are you still there?"

"I'm here," I squeaked.

"Please, there's no reason to be concerned. We're currently conducting general background, and we've contacted many of the other soldiers assigned to your base during the timeframe of the incident in question."

Knowing I absolutely had to get control of myself or appear guilty before the first question was asked, I calmly responded. "Certainly, Mr. Cook. How can I help?"

"Would you have time today for an interview?"

112

Good golly no! "Sorry, but no. I teach English and have three classes at two different schools on my agenda today. I don't know how I'd squeeze it in."

"How about tomorrow morning then. Say eight tomorrow morning?"

"It depends on where you're located and how long you expect the interview to last. I have another class at eleven and a doctor's appointment in the afternoon."

"No problem. We have an office only twenty minutes from your location that we can use. Do you have something handy to write down the address?"

"Is the interview urgent?" *Keep the voice neutral, Marnie.* "How about later this week?" The FBI apparently knew where I lived. Concern gave rise to a gut churning of the four eggs and five bacon strips I'd recently consumed.

"Ms. Wilson, I'm betting you understand what it's like when your boss is breathing down your neck wanting you to finish their pet project. We've already interviewed fifty-seven other individuals. Since we approached the task in alphabetical order, and you're a 'W' for Wilson, we only have three people left to interview. So yes, there is some urgency."

"Give me the address." I held the sigh that was making its way through my lips.

After providing the interview location, Special Agent Cook signed off, thanking me profusely for my cooperation.

That I was one among sixty was a good sign. The interviews were a go fish situation, and I consoled myself that the FBI's interest could be about something else entirely. "Not likely," I manically laughed out loud. The "why now" question I'd asked during breakfast was beginning to take on new clarity. Something had happened. I had no idea what had changed, how, or why, but I knew with certainty I was sick of unanswered questions.

Chapter 15
Open Door

Tired from tossing and turning all night, I'd finally arrived at a decision as the sun was filtering into my bedroom window. I couldn't lie to the FBI. If they asked about an anonymous whistleblower call to the FBI hotline from Iraq, I would say yes. *Hell yes, it was me!*

It might not be wise to be quite so forthcoming about information I'd never shared, like my knowledge of entombed contents that lay underneath the desert sand. If the government knew about the hidden cavern and had finally followed the trail to the storage location I'd provided, what good would it do to the tell the story of me and Mac?

I wouldn't take the chance Mac's good name could be implicated in my thievery, especially since it was my fault that everything went to hell, and he's now buried in a VA cemetery in Salisbury, North Carolina. I would wither in jail forever before I'd allow that to happen. He deserved my total loyalty. It was partially my fault he never came home.

I'd tell them I accidentally found a hidden room on a foray into the wilderness to relieve myself. That I didn't have time to investigate the underground room, and at that point in the war, it was dangerous to linger. Every bit true. My answer to the FBI's next most likely question required significantly more finesse: "Why didn't you inform your chain of command?"

Seven years' experience bending the truth would come in handy to answer that question. I would emphatically reply, "I did! I told Colonel Jamison, but he didn't believe me, so I made a call myself." Colonel Richard Jamison, known as dickhead behind his back, was a heinous human being and a miserable leader anyway. He was the one who transferred us to those risky convoy security missions because I got Mac in trouble. He's the one that offered up our team for a mission we had no business being a part of. It would be my word against his.

After all, I had tried to tell Col Jamison.

* * *

Command Sergeant Major Williams demanded that Mac report ASAP only minutes after Mac and I had arrived back at base from our desert hole investigation. The sergeant major had caught wind about our two-person convoy. It was horrible to witness the aftermath of Mac's humiliation from the sergeant major's wrath, and all because Mac was trying to accommodate me.

Early evening after our WMD find, Mac returned to the operations tent with a hangdog expression plastered on his face. "Should I ask how it went?" I asked.

"Seriously bad. First he chewed off my ass and then started gnawing on my boney carcass."

"Did you tell CSM Williams about what we found?"

"He wasn't in any mood to listen. So no, I didn't tell him."

"Is he going to take any action against you?"

"If I had to guess, I'd guess no. They don't have enough NCOs as it is. His last words were something like, 'One more screw-up like this, and I'll make sure you never collect a retirement paycheck.' Marnie, I think we need to go to the colonel with the information."

"Speaking of dickheads," I added, to which Mac broke his frown and laughed. "Sergeant Mac, I'm really sorry I got you into this."

Mac rubbed his face. "Nah, it's okay, Marnie. I wanted to see what was down there too. You got to me. It was a good thing we found it."

Not two weeks after Mac's butt chewing, we were reassigned to dangerous convoy protection missions. And soon after that, Mac was gone.

I had to tell the colonel about the WMD. That's what Mac had wanted, and he'd never gotten the chance, once again because of me. I owed Mac that much and more.

Under the Open Door Policy, every soldier has the right to a direct voice with the officers in their chain of command, so I requested an open door audience with the colonel. Of course, it's also standard practice for the noncommissioned officers in that same chain of command to talk a soldier out of that choice. Soldier welfare was an NCO responsibility, and as such, NCOs endeavored to determine the soldier's problem and resolve it before the issue became further complicated by officer involvement. Nevertheless, in a culture like the Army, one that values strength, soldiers who had the balls to air their grievances with seniors deserved their shot. There was risk in an open door. If the complaint was deemed untrue, the soldier could be labeled as a whiner and slacker for the duration of their assignment. I wasn't worried. What I had to tell Jamison was the whole truth.

My first sergeant made the first attempt to change my mind. A good first sergeant, he was sincerely concerned, but information about a secret stash of WMD warranted senior officer ears.

I'd refused Command Sergeant Major Williams' advances as well. The command sergeant major was the commander's senior-most advisor on enlisted matters. Any decisions made by the commander regarding enlisted assignments were always coordinated with the CSM. Our mission change would have had to involve CSM Williams too, and I was angry with him. I didn't want his help.

My open door appointment was scheduled for 8 p.m., 2000 hours in military lingo. I knocked, and from inside his office, the colonel said, "Enter." Opening the door, I marched to the front of his desk. The only light in the colonel's office was a pale blue gleam of a computer screen that he was studying from a work station beside his desk. *Weird.* I waited for him to acknowledge me, and when he didn't, I came to attention and saluted. "Specialist Wilson reporting for my open door appointment."

The colonel continued his work as I held my salute for what seemed an eternity. I eventually dropped the salute and stood at parade rest, determined to have my say. Jamison was relatively tall and fit, six feet two or so. I'd seen him use his height to bully people, a sure sign of an insecure or narcissistic man. A full head of neatly trimmed, sandy brown hair and steel gray eyes might have rendered him handsome except for a small mouth and weak chin that had the effect of enlarging a bulbous nose. He was bereft of smile lines, and as I'd witnessed, even when he did smile it was a smug leer used as a tool to degrade or demean.

Colonel Jamison had no idea how stubborn I could be. I could wait at parade rest until the cows came home. Finally, he glanced in my direction. "Specialist Wilson. At last, an audience with the brave and courageous Specialist Wilson."

Completely confounded by that statement, I remained silent. He didn't offer me a seat. Instead, he scooted his rolling chair back to the throne position behind the desk and glared at me.

"I want you to know, I recommended disapproval on your award. As far as I could tell, the only thing you did in that convoy ambush was to save your own skin."

"I don't know what you're talking about, Sir," I sputtered.

"The Silver Star, Specialist Wilson. Don't act as if you hadn't heard from somebody."

"Sir, I sustained a concussion in the convoy ambush, and I've been on bedrest for the last week. I don't know or care about any award."

"*Pfft*," he exhaled. "The world has changed. The generals I work for are so convinced we need female heroes, they've lowered their standards and overturned my better judgment. Can you imagine, they even discussed upgrading the recommendation to a Distinguished Service Cross? I convinced them otherwise. A medal awarded to be politically correct? Revolting and unwise. So yes, Specialist Wilson, you will get your Silver Star whether you deserve it or not!"

"Sir, that's not why I'm here."

"Then why are you wasting my time?"

Wasting his time? He was spewing venom at me, even though he was the one who'd sent my team on that ill-fated mission that killed eight good soldiers. Projecting his ire at me? I only wanted to do the right thing for Mac's sake—a sample of the jewels lay heavy in my front top pocket to show him proof.

My blood boiling, my heart thumping, reason took another detour. The information I'd meant to provide came out instead as a furious question. "Sir, the reason I requested an open door is to ask why you approved that disastrous mission, and why you sent my team with the convoy? That convoy was neither trained nor equipped to deal with the opposing force that you knew was in the area."

Colonel Jamison began laughing—his pretentious, holier than thou expression making my hands tremble in rage. "You want to know why I sent you on that mission? Young lady, that's my job. In the event you hadn't noticed, there's a war going on. How dare you question my decisions. I am privy to information that someone at your level never sees. You don't have the experience or intelligence to question my judgment. If you weren't protected from punishment by politically correct bureaucrats, I'd consider awarding you an Article 15 for insubordination. Now get the hell out of my office."

Staring a hole through Jamison for a moment was the only satisfaction I could take from the encounter, and that was almost nothing. I couldn't share the information on WMD because Dickhead couldn't be trusted. Completing a snappy salute that was not returned, I performed an about face and strode out of his office, my hands clenched in tight fists. Command Sergeant Major Williams was waiting just outside the door. When he saw my face, he backed off two steps. Before he said a word, I growled, "DO NOT ASK."

* * *

Whenever I thought about Jamison and my one attempt at an open door, I became angry—angry that I'd allowed him to get under my skin. I'd known when I'd entered his lair that Jamison was a pitiful excuse for a human being. Everyone had known him for what he was--they didn't call him dickhead for no reason. Naïvely, I'd believed doing the right thing mattered, even to someone like the colonel. My best chance to do what was right for Mac, to talk to the colonel and spill the beans about WMD, and I'd blown it by becoming angry. *You're older and wiser now, Marnie. You can ace this FBI interview. Now get ready.*

Holding a jacket to my body, part of the outfit I'd selected for the interview, my reflection in the mirror admonished I was trying too hard. The subtle striped shell and paisley jacket with three-quarter-length sleeves matched perfectly, but the synchronicity of patterns was unlikely to impress FBI investigators. I placed everything away except the shoes and chose a more subdued skirt and jacket. The shoes were perfect. Four-inch heels lifted me to over six feet tall. I could wear those shoes with aplomb. Strong, confident Marnie, able to leap tall buildings in stiletto heels.

Chapter 16
The Interview

Calling to Buck, I snapped his therapy dog vest in place, and he followed me to the SUV. The fact that I owned a therapy dog might work in direct contradiction to the strong look I was going for, but screw it, I needed him by my side.

An insurance company, the magnet business in a seedy, seen-better-days strip mall, housed the FBI field office. Nestled between a yoga studio and a lawyer's office, the interview location was marked with only a suite number stenciled in white lettering. We were fifteen minutes early. I used the extra time to rehearse my carefully prepared statements and to get my head on straight. At exactly three minutes until go time and after a last check for mascara failures in the rearview mirror, I turned for a pep talk with my BFF.

"Buck, your only job today is to keep me calm. If you think I'm getting anxious, lean on my leg or put your head in my lap. Something, anything." Buck wagged his tail. *Good enough*.

The FBI office was one large room, a closed door in the back. An attractive woman about my age, with dark ebony skin and a short hair style that accentuated the lovely lines of her face, stood when Buck and I arrived. She confidently strode in my direction, her hand out for a perfect, firm-grip handshake. "You must be Marnie Wilson. I'm Special Agent Kiara Davies. Thank you for agreeing to meet us so quickly. My partner, who I believe you spoke to on the phone, is in the back preparing for the interview. And, who is this handsome creature?" she asked, glancing down at Buck.

"This is Buck." He wagged his tail, and his ears perked up at the sound of his name.

"Beautiful animal. I'm going to go help Agent Cook. Please take a seat, and we'll call you in momentarily."

Taking the only seat in the place, a wheeled monstrosity behind a lonely desk, I scooted the chair against the wall to allow visibility of both doors. Agent Davies' idea of momentarily turned into forty minutes. If these FBI agents were trying to put my nerves on edge by leaving me alone to my thoughts for an extended interval, they were doing a fine job of it.

I tried to read a novel that I'd started on my phone, but the words merged together into meaningless gibberish. I grabbed a Kleenex from my bag to dab the sweat on my forehead. The air-conditioning was set to meat locker cool. Sweating profusely while merely sitting in temperatures dipping toward sixty degrees would surely communicate that I was guilty of something. As a last resort, I tried calming breathing, and of course, just as the tightness in my chest and neck loosened, I jumped when a huge man stepped out from the back office.

"Ms. Wilson. Thank you so much for waiting." Agent Cook was totally bald and at least six-four. His shoulders were so wide, I wondered if he could get through the narrow office door without turning slightly. He smiled at me with good teeth, but it wasn't a warm smile. Like his partner, he wore a dark suit that fit well, but the generic fabric spoke to an agent on the lower end of the FBI hierarchy.

"Agent Russel Cook," he said, as he grabbed my hand. "We were just reviewing your military personnel file to have some context for today's interview. Please follow me."

Looking to Buck and nodding, we did our best attempt at a self-assured stroll rather than a perp walk to the gallows. My gait was hampered only minimally by shaky legs. Sometimes the breathing exercises really do work.

Agent Davies directed me to a seat on the other side of a conference table from her position. There was nothing but white paint on the walls and no windows. Another door in the back most likely led to the outside. If I didn't know better, I could almost believe they had placed me with my back to that door on purpose. Cook sat next to Davies and placed his gigantic hands on the table. Buck plopped on the floor next to my hard metal folding chair.

"I'll be leading today's interview," the woman started. "As Agent Cook mentioned on the phone, we're interviewing service members who served in Iraq during a specified period regarding an incident that occurred in November 2007."

I knew I'd placed my call to the FBI hotline about that time, but I honestly wasn't sure of the exact date. There remained three months of my life that to this day are still blurry. After the convoy ambush, Mac's and Zeke's deaths, and suffering from the lingering effects of a concussion, I'd lived life zombie-like in a painful stupor.

"This is only an interview, a fact-finding mission. We have no need to place you under oath. You are not the subject of an investigation. We only ask for your truthful answers and permission to record this session." Davies slid a permission certificate on a clipboard to me. I read it and signed. *Why the heck not?* I had a plan.

"Very good," she said. "Please, let's get started," she cheerily added, as she flipped a switch on a small recording device.

For over an hour, Agent Davies probed my background. She started with current information like where I lived and worked, living relatives, current education level, and whether I owned a home. She then transitioned to Iraqi history: job positions and responsibilities, chain of command, missions, and finally, the routes that had been used on various missions. Davies pulled a map from a briefcase and asked me to annotate with a marker those roads in Iraq where I remembered travelling.

Davies asked the questions and Cook watched, never interrupting or saying one word. At times, I would stare back at him trying to get a reaction, but he was good. He seemed to notice every nuance with barely a blink or a nod. It might have been easier to be hooked to a lie detector than to be the subject of Agent Cook's hypnotic stare. If he played poker, the man had a future.

Obviously dreaming, Buck made a whimpering noise as his tail thumped on the carpet. Even Cook cracked a half smile at the sound. That was when Davies used the Buck diversion to jab me with a question I wasn't expecting.

"Did you ever see anything unusual during your tour of duty in Iraq?"

"Unusual?" I stammered. "Seriously?" Unfortunately, my sometimes contrarian nature stood at attention and poked up its head up from the tedium of Davies' previous questions. "You mean unusual like seeing half the people in a convoy blown to bits and my team leader and best friend being shot and killed. Unusual like that?"

Buck startled and sat up to lean on my leg. *He was such a good boy.* Davies' eyes widened, realizing she'd just stepped in a big pile by her question, but Mr. Cool Cook batted nary an eye.

"Ms. Wilson, we apologize. Having reviewed your military file, we're aware of your involvement in an attack where you demonstrated courage and an exemplary devotion to duty. Agent Davies' question was simply an unfortunate choice of words. Let me be clear, and again, I sincerely apologize."

He allowed me a moment to lower my hackles, and he seamlessly assumed the mantle of interview lead from an embarrassed Davies. "Did you ever see any illegal activities in Iraq?"

I thought hard about that question. In a war zone, there was always the occasional bending of rules. Heck, even outside a war zone, soldiers were prone to improper carnal relations or the sneaking of alcohol into places where it shouldn't be snuck. Stealing pens, paper, and other office supplies was an illegal activity, but I wouldn't think that theft was of concern to the FBI. Military people lived within a multitude of rules and regulations and keeping those restrictions straight was difficult for everyone. When assigned to a hellhole, halfway around the word, breaking minor rules becomes almost sport for the disenchanted.

"Can you be more specific?" I asked.

Agent Cook must have intuited my momentary pause. "I was speaking of higher-level crimes, like black marketing, the sale of weapons, contacts with the enemy, that sort of thing."

"No. Nothing like that. To my mind there were some highly questionable decisions regarding missions on the part of senior officers, but I doubt you'd count that as an illegal activity."

"Did you want to talk about those commander decisions?"

"No, not really."

"All right then. That's all the questions we have. If you can think of anything else that might be helpful, here's my card." He handed me the standard government business card, and Davies did as well.

The smart move now was to leave. It wasn't my fault that they'd asked the wrong questions. I'd been ready to spill my guts about my whistleblower call, but they hadn't even asked. Maybe this interview was about something else entirely. "Agent Cook, I'm not sure how I can be helpful, because I've no idea what the incident you referred to originally was all about. The one in November 2007? Can you tell me?"

"No. We aren't able to divulge that information at this time. Please just be advised, we may call you in later for some follow-up questions."

Agent Davies saw me out. I sat in my car for several minutes wondering what the hell had just happened and what the FBI wanted. The timing of my pursuer's actions and an FBI interview in the same week meant there had to be a connection. I was more confused now than I'd ever been.

Step away from the emotion, Marnie. Think logically—like an uninvolved bystander. If I assumed that the FBI was now aware of the buried cavern, but they didn't know who had made the call seven years, the FBI wouldn't reveal any information about the secret room. They'd want to keep that information close-hold. And if the FBI was telling the truth and not trying to fake me out, the only reason to interview so many people was to find the whistleblower. Come to think of it, sixty was about right number of females on our base in Iraq. Everyone they interviewed was probably female like me, the real culprit.

I patted myself on the back for my most awesome power of deduction. More amazingly, I could probably cross the government off my list of possible suspects. If my interview was any indication, the FBI didn't know much. It was doubtful the government would be clandestinely pursuing me and interviewing fifty-nine others just to get to me. Not likely at all.

There must be someone else involved. A third party who knew or suspected I was the one that made the call? Someone who found the room? Maybe that's why the FBI asked about weapons sales and black marketing. Could the chemical weapons have ended up for sale on the black market? Were the gold and the jewels still there by the time the government found the stash? Certainly, that much wealth was a powerful motivator for anyone who happened upon the buried treasure.

Also, there remained the question as to why now and not seven years ago? Why didn't the government check out those grid coordinates then, when I gave them the chance?

To make my class on time, I drove through for burgers. Enthusiastically, Buck stood on his seat, smiling at the cashier in the window, begging for an appetizer dog treat. As sweet as I knew him to be, Buck failed to realize that a German shepherd's smile was sometimes misinterpreted as a snarl. The cashier seemed in a hurry to move us forward and threw my change and an aroma-laden sack in our direction.

We parked to gobble the juicy meat and cheesy sandwiches that I rarely allowed myself. I'm not even sure why I limited my consumption of burgers since they were relatively inexpensive as takeout. Generationally, it seemed the thing to do, I guess. They say you are what you eat. Did eating hamburger meat from a drive-through mean I was a chemical filled, fast food loving junkie with no concern for the plight of cows or a red-blooded American who consumed high-protein meals on a budget, or both? A question to be pondered when my life became something other than what it was right now.

Regardless, Buck had no such concerns. He swallowed his plain cheeseburger whole and then proceeded to beg for more of mine. As I studied his happy, worry-free face and chewed, I wished for a moment, I was a dog too.

Chapter 17
Mclean, Virginia

Richard Jamison sat behind an ultramodern desk and glumly surveyed his view of other unremarkable office buildings. He thought it unfortunate that to be a player, he had to park his company in the lap of the nation's capital—a place where hangers on and wannabees scrabbled for the fruits of the almighty tax dollar.

There were so many more interesting places in the world from which to toil. In New York City, his perch in a corner office might score a Central Park vista instead of the packed corridor of Route 123.

He asked himself again why he bothered. He had enough to take his young wife anywhere in the world and live life as a king. It would've all been different if he hadn't been born to merely a factory worker and secretary—if he hadn't been forced to attend the stifling Military Academy to pay for an education, or his first wife hadn't been such a nagging shrew. Maybe, if his beginnings had been more noble, he wouldn't have had this burning need.

It was cathartic when he realized it wasn't the money he craved, but rather, the power the money purchased. Once he was sitting on a pile of gold, he found himself needing more. In the most powerful city in the world, it was the dance of Titans that kept his blood flowing. The gold only a means to an end.

And now a silly girl threatened everything he'd built. He would simply not allow it. Pressing the administrative assistant button, he yelled into a headset. "Where the hell is my brother? I told you, I need to speak with him now!"

"Yes, Mr. Jamison. He's just pulling into the parking lot. He'll be in your office momentarily. I thought an in-person meeting would be preferable to a phone conversation."

"When I say now, I don't pay you to decide otherwise. Do it again, and you're done!" He clicked off, huffed, and threw a Montblanc pen at the wall.

Finally, Richard heard a light tapping on his door. "Come in, Goddammit."

His brother, as always, oozed danger. He moved into the room like a prowling panther, light on his feet, his every movement powerfully graceful. *It's a good thing I know in truth that he's a tender-hearted fool*, Richard thought. "What took you so long?"

"It didn't take long. I got here as quick as I could. I've been laid out in bed with a massive headache. That's why I couldn't respond on a moment's notice to your beck and call. Good to know you've been so worried about me."

"Well, you could have called."

"You know, Richard, sometimes you sound just like my ex."

"Tell me what happened."

"She got home early and snuck in while I was still there. That dog of hers chased me out a window. She followed the dog and me into the alley behind her house and was going to shoot me. In my haste to save my skin, I collided with a skateboarding giant. The next thing I know, I woke up in a hospital and had to sneak out. Someone must have taken my keys. When I finally got back to my vehicle, the SUV was unlocked, and the keys were on the seat. My gun, wallet, and registration were gone. My guess is she found the keys and then the car when I was lights out on the sidewalk. She must've taken them."

"Oh, for Christ sake. How could you have let this happen?"

"Here I am, thinking I got lucky. Never saw the police. The identification was fake, the weapon stolen, and I got the listening devices installed. Also, scared the crap out of her. If this doesn't flush her out, maybe Richard, like I've said from the beginning, she doesn't know anything. At least I'm going to live from my injuries. Probably no permanent brain damage."

"It's her. You'd screw up a one-man rock fight, Gerry. Do I have to remind you that you have as much to lose as me if the FBI identifies her as the one who called? She's the only one who can sink us."

"Sure, remind me again. It wouldn't do to have a day pass without your threats. You didn't have any complaints about my competence when I got the gold out of Iraq. Get a grip, Richard. Her house is bugged. We listen to all her phone calls, even though she never talks to anyone. The only person she speaks to is her mother a couple times a month. She has no friends. She has no money to speak of, and the money she does have she spends on clothes—quite a nice wardrobe by the way. It's been seven years. Don't you think if she knew anything she would have said or done something by now?"

"No, I don't. I think she's waiting to bring me down. When SFC McCray told me about what he'd found, he never mentioned her. Everyone knew they were always together. You think she didn't know about it? He was trying to protect her, that's all. She knows!"

"Maybe, but who cares? She has no reason to come forward now. I think you're paranoid and stirring up a hornet's nest for no reason."

"We've got to get rid of her. The FBI's interviewing all the females assigned to that base during the time of the anonymous call. They have different reasons to ensure she never talks, but they want to keep the stash a secret as much as us. They'll threaten her, and she'll break."

Gerry scoffed. "And what if she does? She doesn't know we went there later. No one knows but us."

"You're so naïve. If she saw what was in that buried room, don't you think she knows it was more than just the chemicals. She knows about the gold and the jewels. By the time the Department of Defense became aware of the hidden storage area, it was fucking empty except for the WMD. They'll ask questions."

"Once again, so what? She can't know we stole the gold, and why would they believe her anyway? She's just a nobody. Now that the Iraqi withdrawal is finished, the administration's running scared the news will get out that there were chemical weapons hidden in Iraq all along. That's all they care about. They'll threaten her and make her sign some secrecy pledge. We're safe."

"I don't think so, especially if she glad-handed something herself. The CIA was forced to turn over the whistleblower search to the FBI. Who knows what some moronic, self-righteous FBI agent will do when they find out that the underground room contained gold and jewels. Gold and jewels that are now gone. And lest you forget, she's a war hero. They'll believe her."

"Richard, I didn't find any evidence in her house. You're paranoid and wrong, but it's your show. I'll give it to you that she's more capable than we expected, but I've got a guy on the ground to help."

"Flush her out, Gerry. Sooner rather than later. Maybe we should ransom that damn dog or something. We need to eliminate the problem and tie up the last loose end. If you can't do it, I'll find someone who can."

* * *

As Gerry was descending on the elevator from his brother's realm, he saw in his mind's eye Marnie's hesitation when she drew her weapon. He was almost positive she'd recognized him. That momentary indecision had given him the second or two he needed to escape and probably saved his life.

He'd purposely kept that tidbit from his brother. If Richard knew Marnie had recognized him, he'd commission a hit contract on her before the elevator pinged giving notice of the basement parking garage. It was likely she remembered him from the dining facility during one of his regular visits to her base. The last thing he needed was for Marnie to make the connection between him and his brother.

That the family heist had come back to haunt them seven years later was the stuff of nightmares. Still, he didn't want Marnie to pay the ultimate price, and he was the only thing standing between Marnie and his sociopathic brother.

He and Richard were rich beyond their wildest dreams while Marnie had served well and had been rewarded by trauma issues and self-imposed isolation. His brother was an asshole, always had been and always would be. Richard couldn't have cared less about a beautiful woman and war veteran, just doing her best to keep her life together.

Gerry knew what Marnie had endured in Iraq and her resulting struggles. That sacrifice alone should be worth something, but maybe not. He wasn't going to rot in prison because of his brother and a woman. If she knew something, she might just be the most stubborn, tight-lipped bitch he'd ever encountered.

Chapter 18
The Pause

I'd been waiting so long for my transgressions to resurface, now that my secret had come back to bite me and was pushing my fate relentlessly toward some unknowable conclusion, I didn't want to wait any longer. What I wanted was to get the battle over with, fight the fight, and survive or die trying. That was where I found myself after the FBI interview—impatiently waiting. For what, I couldn't be sure, but the monkey riding my back confided it wouldn't be something fun.

So far, every lead into my mysterious pursuers had reached an impasse. Dan had just called to ask if he could come over to return the phone I'd pilfered from the slippery intruder's SUV. He didn't say what he'd learned, but his defeated voice indicated that the phone was another dead end.

On a brighter note, the hot, humid weather had finally released its grip on man and beast. I'd been remiss in my running regimen. Exercise was another of the techniques the VA recommended for dealing with anxiety. I donned running clothes and linked a lead on Buck. He didn't need a leash, and he'd diligently run by my side, but everyone else who spied a loping, ninety-pound German shepherd felt more comfortable knowing he was tied to me.

We set off on our pavement pounding trek. I had in mind an easy four miles to start. My lungs filled with oxygen from something other than stress, and my heart rate accelerated to pump blood to my arms and legs. There was nothing quite like the cleansing release of hard physical activity.

I'd purposely left my tunes at home today. Music in my ears with a righteous tempo helped me to establish a running rhythm, but if some treacherous bogeyman decided to take me, I wanted to hear him coming.

For the first time, I gave serious consideration to laying all my cards on the table face up, to make the FBI aware of my entire story. *Isn't that their job, to investigate?* The Cook/Davies team seemed more than capable, even though they hadn't asked the right questions.

There was one big fat problem with a tell-all plan. My concerns were completely different from that of the FBI. America was out of Iraq. The current administration had little interest in any publicity surrounding WMD hidden in Iraq all along. The government's instincts would be to muzzle anyone with knowledge of the existence of chemical or biological weapons in Iraq. The FBI was now searching for the anonymous caller to their hotline, little ol' me, albeit a full seven years later. My intuition said the FBI's play was to censor my free speech.

Moreover, the FBI couldn't keep me safe from the other guys now breathing down my neck, whoever they were, nor would they necessarily try. Both the FBI and my pursuers gained from my silence. Even if the FBI agreed to search for my nameless stalkers, wouldn't that result in an adversary even more determined to shut me up? So far, the bad guys had only broken into my home. The FBI, on the other hand, had failed me by not acting on my call. There was no reason to believe the FBI would do better now.

I need to know. To hell with them all. I had to know what had become of that stash in the desert. I'd found it, and in a way, that buried room was my responsibility. After Mac and I had investigated the underground room and our mission shifted, I'd always felt there were unknowable events swirling around in the shadows. I needed to make sense of the machinations occurring behind the scenes in Iraq seven years ago. My life might depend on unearthing those answers. For the moment, the best I could do was prepare for the worst. Be ready and follow Tiffany's warnings about physical security.

I was wondering how much three additional prepaid cells would set back my budget as Buck and I made the last corner. I didn't understand all the technical considerations dealing with bugged phones, but it seemed as if nearly anyone could listen in on phone calls these days. Dan's advice about listening ears was more prescient than paranoid. It was far better to avoid the possibility that I could become an easy target for snooping.

As if my thoughts about Dan's guidance had summoned him to my doorstep, his car was parked in front of my house. The man himself was waiting, leaning against the passenger door. I slowed to a walk to allow my heart to steady before I greeted him.

Dan was dressed like me in running attire. I decided Dan's legs might be his best feature and should never be hidden. His shoulders and arms weren't shabby either—just the right combination of lean, well-defined muscle. As I rapidly made a body assessment, his eyes failed to do the same to me. I'm guessing here—but it appeared his interest in me was purely on the up and up. I was torn between being happy about his indifference and somewhat insulted.

He said, "Hey, Marnie."

"Hey, Dan. Coming back from, or on your way to a run?"

"On my way. You know, I'm a little concerned with your physical safety out running alone. Are you practicing good situational awareness?"

"I'm not alone. Buck's with me, and I can't quit living. None of your business, anyway."

"I know. That was just a reminder. By the way, there's a kid with a lawnmower in your backyard that said you hired him. I'd thought to question him, but he gave up most of his life without asking."

"Trevor's the kid that ran into my burglar with the skateboard."

"Yeah, he told me."

"You want to come in?"

He paused and then said, "Nah, I need to get going." Pulling the stolen phone from his pocket, he handed it to me. "My buddy hacked this and fixed it so there's no password. Must've been just out of the wrapper. Only thing on it was a GPS location to the rental car company and your home. There's one number that was called three times, but no record of that cell number. Obviously, the calls were made to another burner phone. I wish I could give you more. Probably too late to fingerprint, but maybe you can give it to that cop to try."

I thought about what Tiffany would say if I handed her yet one more piece of contaminated evidence. "Nope, not a good idea. I appreciate the effort, Dan, really. You can't manufacture information."

"Oh, but you can. In this case, it just wouldn't be helpful."

"True that." I wanted Dan to leave before he inserted himself more into my life. It was weird attending group on Tuesday with two groupmates who now had personal knowledge of my problems. Also, even though Dan had tried, he hadn't been of much use. He identified dead ends, and that was about all.

Dan said, "If you're interested, I could probably find someone to install some nifty electronics to screen your fence and yard for threats. I might be able to do it myself. The backyard is the most vulnerable to incursion." Laughing to myself, it occurred to me only vets use words like incursion.

The lawnmower started up from the backyard. Knowing his new friend Trevor awaited, Buck left my side to paw at the gate between the garage and the house. "Great minds think alike. I've already given additional security some thought. I'll let you know if I need any help." Fearing it might hurt Dan's feelings, I didn't mention that I'd already asked Marco for his help securing my fence. "And Dan, once again, my mess is not your fault."

"Your mess. Marnie, are you sure there isn't anything you can tell me? If it's nothing recent, could this be something from your time in service? Is there anything at all you remember that I might track down?"

We stared at each other as I shrugged and shook my head. "If you think of anything, you know how to find me. Please just give it some thought." Dan walked around to the driver's side door, got into his car, and leaned toward the open passenger window. "It's messed up that a war hero should have to deal with this shit in addition to the normal garbage."

What? Dan had probably googled me and found the award orders, a write up, or something. That sort of snooping is commonplace when you want to know more about someone. Still, I don't like anyone rooting around in my life.

Chapter 19
Fortress

Marco was knocking on my door at 6:30 a.m. I'd barely had a chance to down three cups of coffee. After I'd purchased a new Marco burner phone and sent him the number, I'd asked if he could hook me up with something to provide early warning of intruders in my backyard, something in addition to a barking dog. He responded immediately and said he could lay hands on the necessary equipment that very night. Reminding me the sooner the better for extra security, Marco agreed to perform the installation before work the next day.

Thus, his cheerful, one-eyed face brightened my door. Buck seemed excited to have guests at barely daybreak and gave a halfhearted bark before wagging his tail furiously at Marco's arrival.

Dressed in work jeans and an old t-shirt with a Navy anchor logo on the front, he carried a tool kit and a large shopping bag stuffed full of electronics equipment and wire. "Hey Marco. You want some coffee before you start?"

"I'd love some, but I don't have time. This should be an easy installation, and I want to show you the app for your phone after I'm done. Maybe some coffee to go, then."

"Okey dokey. Buck will follow you around. It's what he does. I'm going to go get ready for work myself. Just yell if you need anything. I have lots of woodworking tools."

He gave me a curious look about the woodworking tools, and then smiled, and commented, "You're kind of random, Marnie."

Dang. Mac used to say that. I might be in trouble here. I headed to the bathroom to finish my morning routine. Buck's absence near my beautification station felt different and lonely. Normally he lounged between the commode and the sink, crowding me out so I could barely reach the mirror. My row of prepaid phones lay on a window sill, one for nearly everyone in my life, few as they might be.

I was wondering how to carry four cell phones and keep them all straight, when a text ping sounded from the cell sporting a piece of pink tape. Tiffany.

Tiffany: *Great news! Ex came through. We got DNA!*

Me: *You're a super hero! Can you send results*

Tiffany: *Yes, but don't share any more than required. Email? BTW, we got lucky. Plenty of spit*

Me: *No. Send attachment to this phone only!*

Tiffany: *?*

Me: *Explain later. Thank ex for me*

Tiffany: *Don't forget our deal*

Me: *LOL, got it!! More later*

I sprinted from the bathroom, down the hall, and outside to share the news with Marco. This was the first piece of good news I'd received. Marco was crouched in front of the corner of the fence, and Buck was sitting on the grass behind him watching closely, surely to encourage Marco's efforts.

When they heard the door slam, Marco jumped up and Buck came running, both probably assuming some new tragedy had befallen me.

"Marco, we've got DNA!"

His face went from concern to pride. "Outstanding!"

"I know," I said. "I'd almost lost hope there was any way to unravel my situation. Officer Murphy is going to send the attachment to my cell. Can I forward the DNA data to your cousin or do you want to do it?"

It wasn't a good sign when his face morphed again, this time into a sheepish expression. "About that. Anton didn't agree to run the DNA against the DOD database. I thought you could go with me to visit him. Use your womanly ways to help convince Anton he'd be helping a vet and a damsel in distress."

"I was afraid of that. How soon can we go?"

"How about after work today? I'll see if we can meet for dinner. Plan on it unless I find out Anton can't make it. What time can I pick you up after work?"

"I'll drive. Text me your address." If this cousin, Anton, didn't come through, I was probably dead in the water again, and if I was reading the tea leaves right, time was running out.

* * *

Already starving, I vigorously chewed one of those meaty, sticky energy bars that require extra energy just to get down. Using milk as a chaser and with my rumbling stomach satiated, I would probably survive until dinner with Anton and Marco.

Before departing for class, I'd selected a dining ensemble and did a quick change into skinny white jeans, a comely floral-print rayon shirt, and dangly earrings that set off the shirt. Choosing flat sandals and a new bag that I'd been eyeing for a while and had finally purchased at lunch between schools, I stuffed three burner phones into separate pockets within the bag. One phone each for Dan, Tiffany, and Marco. My smartphone was for everything else, including apps for my in-house and recently acquired backyard security systems.

Buck was still wearing his vest and didn't need to dress. I called him from the yard and engaged the deadbolt and lock on the backdoor. I left most of the inside lights on. Marco had disabled the timer switch on the outside flood lights with no regard for my electricity bill, a worry for a later date.

This meeting with Anton was Important— critically important. Convincing him to illegally run DNA and take a chance for a cousin's friend required I be on my best behavior. No blurting of sarcastic truths allowed tonight—*be nice, Marnie*, I warned myself. Buck's adoring gaze buoyed my spirits. *I can do this.* I had to.

After arming a multitude of electronic protection paraphernalia, Buck and I loaded up for our meet with Marco. Maybe tomorrow I'd consider a weaponized drone or two as a last-stand backup.

Chapter 20
Gerry

Gerry perched on a stool in Richard's vast kitchen. Miles of stainless steel and granite surfaces were spacious enough to feed a pro football team or even a small city. Gerry thought Richard's manse in Bethesda, Maryland, was over the top for two guys from the penniless side of the tracks. Of course, that was probably the point. Flaunting his wealth was the reward for Richard's abominable dealings.

Richard's young wife, Julie, was nice, if not the brightest star in the heavens. At least she had excellent taste unlike his brother, who on his own, might have decorated his living space to resemble a sultan's palace. Julie preferred modern, simple lines for the furnishings, natural materials, and esoteric paintings. Gerry couldn't have identified the artists responsible for the interesting works adorning the walls if his life hung in the balance.

Gerry was drinking a dirty martini that Julie had served up in an elaborate, crystal highball glass. The glass set was probably custom ordered and flown in from a small European country, costing more than a moderately used truck. Richard had kept Julie busy decorating the 12,000-square-foot behemoth they called home, but now that her work was mostly complete, Gerry wondered what Richard would do to keep her occupied. A young, gorgeous wife like Julie might become restless and develop wandering eyes. Other than money, Gerry couldn't imagine why someone like Julie would marry his brother. It was a surprise to him that she was still around, two years after her nuptials with Richard.

"Richard should be down shortly, Gerry. Did you want anything to eat while you wait?" Julie asked.

"No thanks, Julie. I'm good."

"Well if that's the case, I hope you don't mind if I wander up to my office. The control for the entertainment system is there on the coffee table." She pointed in the direction of a family area that was so far away, Gerry couldn't be sure where the designated coffee table was located.

"Have at it, Julie. If you could, please tell my brother I don't have all night."

She returned a feeble smile that said, "I have no control of what he does," and then turned her shapely ass around and sashayed toward the back staircase.

Gerry rubbed his eyes. He despised his brother. He wouldn't have used the word *hate*, but only because when he was young and didn't know any better, he'd wanted to be just like Richard. It wasn't until he'd followed in his brother's footsteps to the Army that he became fully aware of the true nature of Richard's character, hidden in plain sight by an eight-year age difference.

Sure, when he was a boy he'd seen signs of Richard's cruelty. When Richard had held him underwater in the bathtub to see how long he could hold his breath, his brother had taken a bit too much glee in the game. And then there were the equipment accidents—always Gerry's things— his bicycle tire inexplicably coming loose during a downhill speeding race with his brother, a Game Boy exploding in his hands, the brakes failing on

Gerry's go cart. Family cats had never lasted long either. It wouldn't be a year before they disappeared. Their parents had finally quit bringing them home. Gerry still wasn't positive those unfortunate events had been his brother's doing, but he was mostly sure. As a boy, he'd only known that bad things frequently happened when he was around Richard. He'd never even considered that these events had been a willful plot on his brother's part. *Ah, the innocence of youth,* Gerry thought.

Richard was a master at sounding like the smartest man in the room when it suited his purpose. Intelligent, street-wise, athletic, and persuasive, he had all the tools to be successful without resorting to murder and mayhem. Gerry believed Richard was born a psychopathic narcissist, and no amount of loving parenting could have made a difference. Certainly, their shared parents were the nicest, most caring, and most responsible couple any young boys could have asked for. Poor yes, but their parents had worked hard and had sacrificed everything for their children. If they'd only known what Richard would become, they might have considered drowning him in a sink as a baby to rid the world of yet one more monster

Gerry's dream, if he still had one, was a simple life—the life that could've been if he'd resisted Richard's duplicitous entreaties and avoided becoming intractably entwined with his schemes. In that normal life, Gerry would've completed an honorable military career, found a wonderful partner, and lived off the government tit comfortably until he was too old to care. It was too late to turn back though. The prospect of three hots and a cot at a federal penitentiary, perhaps while waiting for needle insertion day, was the only reason he sat in Richard's house now.

His brother entered the room with his trademark disgusted snarl, the one he reserved for underlings and those closest to him. It was those two groups that were most frequently witness to the face of Richard unplugged.

"I'm busy, Gerry. I hope you have good news."

"Does it ever occur to you that I'm busy too? Taking care of your dirty laundry is a full-time enterprise."

"My dirty laundry. Oh, dear brother, you're in the stink up to your eyeballs, too. Do we have to tread this same ground at every encounter? Must I remind you that our fates are linked as brothers, comrades in arms, and businessmen? Do you have a fucking plan?"

Gerry frowned. His brother was right no matter how infuriating it felt to be under his thumb. There was also the not-so-minor issue of his own safety from the whims of his brother. Who knew how far Richard would go? Richard believed Gerry was the only one besides himself who knew the whole story. If a time came when he wasn't still useful to Richard, Gerry wasn't sure an accident of birth would be enough to save him from his closest living relative.

"Yes, I do have a plan, and some good news. My source at the FBI said Marnie has been interviewed, and there were no red flags. She didn't say anything about making the anonymous call."

Gerry saw Richard's head bend slightly, as if he had a moment of doubt, but doubt wasn't a

150

state familiar to his brother. "I wonder what she's waiting for. Tell me the plan."

"Better that I don't. I assure you, if my plan doesn't flush her out, she doesn't know anything. Have you ever considered that her sergeant only gave her the grid coordinates? That she called the FBI, and for her that was the end of it?"

"No, because she does know more. Why else call the FBI rather than informing her chain of command?"

"Just a hunch—maybe because you're such an asshole, any soldier with a half a brain would go to anyone before you."

"She knows. I'll let you have this last effort. See what shakes out. It's better to know everything including whether she confided to someone else. Speaking of that, what information have you gathered from the listening devices, telephone, computer?"

Gerry didn't want to tell his brother that the listening devices were dead in the water. Marnie had made short work of his hard-won effort to listen from her home—the bugs had gone silent the very next day. "Nothing. I'm telling you, she's a hermit."

"If she's a hermit, there's a reason."

"Dammit, Richard, she's got PTSD. Maybe that's the reason for her lifestyle. What is it about this woman, anyway? Why are you so obsessed with her?"

Richard gave Gerry a steely gaze and didn't answer the question. "Find out what she knows. Then we'll deal with her."

"You know, Richard, so far I haven't had to kill anyone, and I don't plan to start now, especially a woman who may be clueless."

"I won't involve you when it comes to that. I wouldn't want to trouble your sensitive conscience."

"Screw you," Gerry spat back.

"I trust you know the way out. Update me when your plan unfolds. I hope for your sake the timing of this plan is immediate." Richard turned and departed with a stick-up-the-butt gait on the same set of stairs used by his young wife.

Gerry slammed the mahogany front door on his exit, and his shoulders loosened. At least Richard had believed him that he had a plan. Gerry was counting on his partner on the ground for one, and so far, his collaborator hadn't come through.

If Marnie were clueless, Gerry wasn't sure her innocence would matter, or that there was anything he could do to save her. Richard wanted her dead. And, as Gerry knew all too well, his brother was tenacious to a fault.

Chapter 21
Marco

I wound through narrow streets and over a multitude of traffic humps, separated by what seemed like mere yards, to find Marco's apartment buried deep within a sprawling apartment complex. He was waiting, sitting on a lawn chair just outside the sliding glass windows of his ground-floor unit. When he glimpsed my SUV, he gave me a wait sign, entered his apartment through the glass door, and then jogged to the vehicle from an adjoining stairwell.

He opened the passenger door to find Buck staring back at him. "Move it, Buck," I commanded. Buck tossed his head in indignation and then jumped over the center console into the rear seat.

"I don't think he wants to give up his position."

"No one ever does," I responded. Marco looked good, as always. I easily picked up his male scent over a pervasive fragrance of eau de dog. It had been a very long time since a human male had graced the cabin of my motor transport system. The effect of Marco's presence was a mixture of nerves and excitement. I really, truly needed to get out more.

"You'll want to take I-95 through Baltimore to Edgewood. Anton's meeting us halfway."

"You're the navigator. Just give me directions on how to get out of these apartments." After Marco guided me to a back alley that avoided most of the speed bumps, the conversation lagged. I wondered if Marco might be as bereft of contact with the opposite sex as me. Hard to imagine how even one-eyed he wasn't pursued by any number of attractive women. It wasn't until we hit rush-hour traffic outside of Baltimore that Marco spoke again.

"How'd you learn to speak Spanish like a native, Marnie?"

"My mother's half-sister, who mostly raised me, was from a small town in Mexico. Tia Vernonia's English was broken and difficult. The minute my mother walked out the door to go to work, she switched to Spanish. How about you? Are your parents first generation Cuban?"

"No, my grandparents. They were determined to make sure me and my siblings knew the native tongue. That way when we get the island back, we'll be able to speak to our lost relatives." Marco chuckled. "Anyway, I'm glad I learned the language."

"Me too." I paused, wanting more than anything to know Marco's story without having to give up my own. "So, you were in electronics in the Navy. You never said how you ended up anywhere near an IED."

"I didn't spend much time on a ship," he answered.

That statement hung in the air. The only people I knew in the Navy who didn't spend much time on a ship were stateside or operators. "Don't tell me you were a SEAL."

"Okay, I won't."

"Dang, you're a SEAL. I had no idea. Most of those guys can't wait to brag about how hardcore they are."

"That's because the ones who blab aren't really that hardcore."

"Yeah, I suppose you're right there. How many tours did you do?"

"I had three tours total in the suck. Two in Afghanistan and one in Iraq. You?"

"In the suck?" I asked.

"Yeah, just a term we used to describe any shithole deployment."

"Interesting, never heard that one, but it sure fits. I only had one tour in Iraq. And since we're sharing the hell out of this conversation, I'll give a little. I was in military intelligence."

"Language?" Marco asked.

"Yes indeed. Arabic, thus Iraq."

Talking waned again during the stop-and-go traffic, but I was on an unusual conversational roll. "Mind if I ask you something else?"

"Depends on what it is."

I thought Marco might be pulling my chain but continued. "You don't normally see operators like yourself suffering from PTSD. If they get through the first bit, they're mostly resilient. Why'd an IED knock you off your game? Seems like a sitting bomb is far less personal."

"That's actually a good question. My PTSD has to do with the disappointment involved in my inability to shoot worth a crap after losing an eye, and since the IED, when I hear loud, unexpected noises, I panic."

"Like how does it affect you? Do you panic bad?" Marnie asked.

"Pretty much. It's worse when I'm stressed. If I hear something close, like a glass plate shattering on the floor or maybe a door slammed shut from the wind, it's like some strange force takes over my body. My heart rate accelerates, I shake, and an uncontrollable fear paralyzes me for a minute or more, it all depends. The doctors have been working with me on different therapies. What sucks is how powerless I feel when it happens."

"Yeah, I can only imagine. I'm sorry, Marco."

"Hey, don't be sorry for me. I haven't lost hope that they'll fix me. I was the lucky one. The two brothers standing near me when that bomb exploded aren't around anymore to worry about panic reactions."

"Jesus. Do you miss it, Marco? The service?"

"Mostly, yes I do. I miss the guys I served with most of all."

"One last weird question, and I'll let it be. If you could choose whether to do it all again, would you?"

"Absolutely."

I pounded on the steering wheel. "Me too! What's that all about? For all the hell it brought me, I would do it all again. I'd probably change a couple of really bad decisions, but otherwise. . ."

Marco was staring at me. He might very well have wanted to ask about those bad decisions, but he held his questions. "I think I'd be a different person," he said. "And I believe a lesser person, if I didn't know what I know now—if I hadn't experienced what I did. That version of me would be a shallow boy compared to the man I am. That boy might have two eyes, but he could never see like me." Then he laughed at himself. "Whoa, that was pretty deep. Maybe you should be asking the questions rather than Dr. Santori."

"Well, in the immortal words of Dr. Santori, thanks for sharing. Your insights are a benefit not only to yourself, but to the other people in this car."

"Roger that, Marnie. Could we lighten up, please?"

"Agreed. Now tell me everything you can about your cousin, Anton, so I can convince him to help me out."

"First, he's a crazy smart nerd. He'll try to present himself as a laid back, artsy type with bad grooming habits, but don't be fooled. Behind that cloak of coolness is a brilliant mind that watches and takes in everything.

"We were good buddies when we were kids. I was better in sports, and he was better at school, so we helped each other out. I'd say just be yourself and present your case. He'll see right through any manipulation or insincere flattery.

"Also, Anton believes himself to be a protector of the downtrodden since he was bullied as a kid. I think he'll want to help you out if he can."

And I'll bet you saved him from those bullies when you could, I thought to myself. "I can work with that."

"Another thing you might be able to use: Anton believes the government is trying to control us all. He's into government conspiracy theories, which is laughable because he works for the government. I don't get it. He told me once it's good to keep your enemy close."

I stopped talking to consider what I'd do if Anton said no. I'd pinned my hopes on identifying the man who broke into my house using the pop can DNA. If Anton said no, the only thing left for me was to wait like a sitting duck for my pursuer's next move. "I'm pretty desperate here, Marco."

"I know. I picked up on that. As I told you, I won't ask about your secrets, and I'm over ninety-nine percent sure you know far more than you're saying. I feel like you must have good reasons for keeping whatever this is all to yourself. Thing is, sometimes when you concentrate on a problem head-on for too long, you lose the ability to really see it. That's why teams are good, because a fresh perspective can make all the difference. If you ever decide you could use that kind of help, I'll be here."

"I appreciate that, Marco, truly, but I don't want to place anyone else in harm's way."

"Yeah, I figured that was part of the problem. Just so you know, I'm the kind of guy who revels in harm's way from time to time."

I grabbed his hand and squeezed. We drove the rest of the way in silence.

Chapter 22
Cellphones

Anton wasn't what I expected. When Marco had mentioned a cool dude with poor grooming, I'd anticipated a man that looked like Marco but didn't try as hard. Anton was short, maybe only five feet five inches, and as wide as he was tall. The cousins gave each other a man hug, obviously happy to see one another. Anton was wearing glasses that were thick and of a shape that would never be considered cool. He asked the hostess for a table for three with room enough for Buck to lie on the floor.

We were seated in a booth in the back, and even so, a clamor of voices and sports shows assaulted me. The hearing loss in my left ear made it difficult to focus on close conversation whenever there was an abundance of background noise. The place, named the Brewery Stop, like so many other restaurants with brewery in the title, was focused on beer and sports, with little concern for ambiance. The food was average, and I had to turn down beer in favor of a coke.

Anton was funny in a dry humored sort of way. He and Marco spent the meal making fun of each other and recounting boyhood stories. I noticed that Anton slipped Buck meat scraps while he ate his meal. Buck had moved closer to Anton's side. I might not be making much of an impression on Anton, but he was making a good impression on me.

When the waitress ferried away our plates, Anton rubbed his hands together and began. "I've researched how I can run the DNA Marco sent against the database. It appears I can slip it in an analyzation batch and then pull out the results before a report is prepared. No one will even know it was there.

"What I need to know from you, Marnie, is why I should?"

I was caught off guard by Anton's frank question. If I didn't have this overriding secret, a simple answer would be easier to frame. I went with the most truthful response I could give.

"Someone's after me, and I don't know who. I have some ideas on why, but it's dangerous information to share. It all goes back to Iraq seven years ago, and no, I don't know why it took seven years for this thing to find me again.

"I'm no saint, and I made a couple of mistakes during my tour. As a result, I hold some dangerous secrets. Here's the thing—even though I screwed up, the guys that are after me, you can bet your ass they're totally bad guys. I tried to make it right while I was still in country, and I failed." I could feel blood rushing behind my ears. This was the closest I had come to fessing up, and it felt like I'd taken my finger out of the dike. I paused, waiting for the flood to wash me away.

"Neither the government or the bad guys want me to air my secrets. I have no one to turn to, and I must solve this puzzle on my own. Your help might be my last chance." If Anton was willing to risk his professional reputation to help me, he deserved some truth in return. I was hopeful my story, even though short on specifics, might classify me as among the downtrodden.

Anton's eyes were huge. He was leaning forward from his bench, taking in every word. "The 'man' is after you. Once they get their hooks into you, there's no option but to use their own methods against them. Very unfortunate Marnie, and your situation truly sucks. Yes! I'll do it."

"When?" I asked.

"It depends. There's no set schedule for the timing on batch runs. Could be a day or two, or even a week or more. I'll make sure I stay on top of it."

I was so excited, and even though my budget was badly blown by numerous cell phone purchases and a backyard security system, I yelled, "Drinks are on me!" There was a moment when I almost ordered a drink too. Any significant emotion could spur my longing, and it didn't help that we were in a brewery with a hundred different designer beers. I might have been even more tempted if I weren't the designated driver. My drunk, unconscious meandering into to a state park had scared me straight on that score.

Marco and Anton were fun. I'd nearly forgotten what it was like to simply enjoy an evening in the company of others. Riding high on expectation, at midnight I reminded Marco I had to work the next day. It was obvious he wasn't feeling much pain when he answered in Spanish.

"See? You did it, Marnie. We're going to find this bad guy and make him pay for causing such a beautiful woman so much pain and suffering. Right, Anton?"

"Right, Marco. You and me dude. And Marnie too. No way they'll get away with their reprehensible tactics!" Anton replied, also in

Spanish. *Must be a thing when Cubans drink,* I thought.

Thanking Anton for the tenth time, I grabbed Marco's hand to drag him to the SUV. He was leaning into me on one side as we walked, and Buck was on the other. After the *thunk* of disengaged door locks, Marco stopped me before I could open the SUV. He held my face in both hands and kissed me. A nice kiss. A really nice kiss. Sliding one arm around my back, he moved his other hand to cradle my head. He pulled back for a moment and murmured something in Spanish that I couldn't understand but was still sexy as hell.

Then the kissing got serious. At least until a beeping emanating from my purse, something that sounded like it could be a nuclear attack warning, interrupted a very nice moment. I rummaged through my purse, searching for a phone that was lit and ringing. My everything else cell phone glowed. I'd never known my smartphone to make such an obscene noise. The backyard security system app was alive and flashing red. I swiped and viewed a circle indicating an ongoing intrusion along the fence line.

In a matter of seconds, Marco went from a slightly inebriated Latin lover to the steely eyed warrior that most certainly still survived inside this man. "Call your cop friend," he ordered. "I'll call 911."

"Could it be a false alarm?" I asked, hopeful.

"Nope. It's a very reliable system."

I dialed Tiffany from the everything else phone because it was in my hand; I was too freaked to locate her phone. It went to voicemail, and I left a message. Marco was talking to the 911 operator. When he clicked off, he rushed to the passenger side of my SUV, yelled to Buck to get in, and said, "Drive Marnie. Fast but safe."

Chapter 23
Not Just Smoke

Two fire trucks, an ambulance, and several cop cars blocked my street. We stopped several houses down, parked, and walked toward my house. Flashing lights from emergency vehicles lit the night sky. I couldn't see flames. As we drew near, an acrid smoke odor put to rest any fleeting hopes that the fire trucks were called to the scene merely as a precaution.

I willed my mind not to leave my body. On the day when Mac had been critically wounded, I'd seen everything happen as an observer, like an apparition not connected to physical form. It was months before I could piece together memories with more substance than a bad dream. The doctors had told me not to worry, that the need to create distance was a protection mechanism meant to save the conscious mind from circumstances too difficult to process. But far from protecting me, my corporeal separation had left me weak, foggy, and unable to navigate the events that came after. I wouldn't let that happen, not again.

Stopping just outside a circle of neighbors and emergency responders, I knelt next to a confused Buck and hugged him. I whispered into his big soft ear, "Don't worry, Buck. We still have each other. We'll get through this." Taking slow breaths in and then out, I told myself the house and everything inside was only stuff. Great stuff sure, but all replaceable. When the body shakes began to subside, only one thought remained: the jewels.

Marco had been watching me with Buck, staying near while still giving me space. I thought he might want to comfort me but held back fearing I wouldn't accept the kindness. He was probably right. When I shot to a standing position from my crouch beside Buck, I must have frightened Marco because he jumped. "There's some stuff in that house I absolutely need. Let's go." Marco didn't argue.

I couldn't find Tiffany in the crowd. Pushing through the throng of concerned neighbors, I gazed at what was left of my home. The roof was gone, even though most of the walls I could see were still standing. The fire was out, but one fireman with a hose continued to spray massive amounts of water into my home, destroying what was left of my belongings.

Moving with purpose, I intercepted a fire guy talking on a portable radio and wearing a captain's badge. He kept talking when he saw me, and I mouthed while pointing, "That's my house." When he didn't take the hint, I snatched the mic from his hands and said, "That's my damn house. Can you please tell your water boy over there the fire is out?"

I'd so startled the onsite captain, he glanced where I was pointing and then double timed in the direction of the overzealous, hose wielding firefighter. "That's enough," he yelled. "Give it a rest!"

By this time, Sergeant Murphy must have noticed the commotion and moved to stand next to me. We locked eyes. "I'm so sorry, Marnie."

"Yeah, me too. It was everything I had." As hard as I tried, my voice cracked.

"I got here as soon as I could. Your neighbor, that kid Trevor, called the fire department. It appears the arsonist placed some accelerant along the back wall of your home and was interrupted by the arrival of the police. He or she lit up what they could and bolted. If you hadn't called, I'm pretty sure there'd be nothing left. Great idea about the perimeter sensors."

"Tiffany, I need to get in there."

"No can do, Marnie. It's a crime scene. Also, dangerous. There's no telling about the integrity of the structure. The floor could collapse into the basement if you were to walk around."

"Sergeant Murphy, how do I say this? There's some stuff in there I must have before the wrong people find it. It isn't drugs or anything illegal. If you don't let me in, I will sneak back later. Please, trust me, Tiffany. I need to get in there."

She gave me a classic cop scowl. Her eyes bored into mine, probably running through guesses about what on earth I was hiding. She sighed. "Dammit, Marnie. I shouldn't trust you. Let me have a word with the captain. Don't move until I get back. This would have been an easier sell if you hadn't ripped the captain's mic from his hands."

As she stalked away, Trevor and Marco found me. "I'm totally sorry, Marnie." Trevor said. "I heard the cops and like saw flames from my window at the same time. I called 911, but it was still almost ten minutes before the fire department got here. You really have bad luck."

"If I didn't have bad luck, I wouldn't have any luck at all," I answered, trying to smile. "Thanks for being on top of it. Once again, it's Trevor to the rescue."

Trevor considered the smoking rubble that was once my home. "No offense, but I like wouldn't call this a rescue."

"No, I guess not."

Marco, Trevor, Buck, and I stood silently watching the police and firefighters cleaning up their equipment and packing up to go home. A couple of neighbors I'd seen around stopped near to utter encouragement or to tell me they'd pray for me. A rheumy eyed woman, at least eighty, had come from her dilapidated ranch-style home across the street and offered me a bed for the night. Her generosity to a near stranger moved me deeply. For the first time that night, I'd felt tears welling in my eyes.

I could see Tiffany making her way toward us. She waved for me to join her. With our heads bent together she said in a low voice, "Marnie, Captain Shaw can't let you in there. If something happened, he'd be responsible and liable. He told me they were packing up to leave now, and there was some possibility a pole to test the structure might be inadvertently forgotten. I'm going to romain here until they're gone to take your statement." Murphy's eyebrows wagged conspiratorially up and down.

"Oh, okay. I get it."

Murphy withdrew a small notepad from a shirt pocket and asked, "So, what time did you depart your home today?" She continued to ask questions and take notes until the taillights from the last firetruck could be seen driving away from the scene. "Wait here, Marnie."

Murphy returned hauling a long pole she'd retrieved from the grass near the driveway. "Marco, help me with this," she shouted.

Together, Marco and Murphy pushed the cylindrical object through a missing master bedroom window and heaved it into the floor in several spots. Marco turned to me. "Well, the good news is the floor seems to be stable. When you walk in, go slow. If you feel any sliding or shaking, turn your butt around and head back out."

"Got it." I commanded Buck to stay and climbed through the window. The smell was nauseating, the damage to my life's possessions even more so. The wood doors to my closet were singed black on the outside but still standing.

Taking baby steps, I crept to the other side of the room and stepped around burned roof pieces. Toward the middle, I heard a shifting sound, and I stopped to center myself before continuing.

As I opened the closet, I let out a groan. Everything was soaking wet. The interior smelled like a wet animal that had made a home near a smoker grill, but the contents had survived the fire. I pulled two suitcases from the closet corner and set to work. Filling one suitcase with jewels, weapons, and ammunition, I used the other for important papers and all the best clothes and shoes I could stuff inside. I didn't know if I'd be able to get the smell out, but dry cleaning was preferable to replacement costs.

On my way back to the window, I yanked some undergarments from a dresser and then, avoiding the questionable spot in the room, wheeled the suitcases across the floor. Marco was waiting for me to hand the luggage out through the opening.

Murphy handed me Captain Shaw's card directing that I call him by noon to provide some information. She emphatically added, "And we need to have a long conversation, Marnie. Tomorrow." Her statement held a note of warning.

After saying our goodbyes, she asked where I would go. "I'll find a hotel somewhere for the night and then figure it out." Murphy glanced at Marco and shrugged.

Suddenly, that itch was back! The hair on the back of my neck stood on end. Turning in a circle, I scanned the streets, trees and cars searching for someone watching. Marco noticed. "Are you okay?"

I whispered in his ears, "Not hardly. I must do one more thing before we leave, and I'm going to need your help."

* * *

The man peered through binoculars from his vantage point across the street. It had taken awhile to escape the police and then double back. While the fire raged, two officers had patrolled the neighborhood searching for an arsonist who enjoyed watching his twisted handiwork. But he'd hidden well, and the officers didn't even glance up. They strolled right past his position on a sturdy branch of an old oak tree. The policemen were very involved in a conversation about a woman they knew in common.

As he'd hoped, Marnie extracted two suitcases from what was left of the burned remains of her house. If she had anything of value in that home, it would be in one of those suitcases.

It appeared the excitement was over for the evening. The fire department had left and finally, so had that cop. Marnie, Marco, and the dog were heading back to her SUV.

He climbed out of the tree and kept to the shadows to return to his car and follow them.

Marnie's SUV lights came on. He let her pass and watched. She turned left down a side street, took another quick right into the alley behind her house, and then stopped. *Strange,* he thought. *What's she up to?*

He didn't have visibility from this position. Sliding from the car, he jogged up the street toward her house, keeping to the trees between the sidewalk and the road. She entered from the back of her property and moved quickly to where her garage had once stood. From there, he couldn't see what she was doing. No more than five minutes later, she reappeared following the same path from whence she came.

Maybe she was hiding something in the burned wreck of her home. Should he wait and check out the garage or follow? He concluded he could always come back and check the garage. Better to know where she slept for the night so that he might have a chance to search her baggage.

The man ran back to his vehicle again with as much stealth as possible and entered his car in the nick of time. Marnie had turned back onto the main road, and he had to duck to keep her from seeing him as she passed. When she drove through a green light on the only major intersection in the area, he completed a U-turn and followed.

Chapter 24
The Kindness of Strangers

"You may be the most stubborn woman I've ever known, and I've known some remarkably stubborn women. It makes no sense to go to a hotel tonight. I have an extra bedroom," Marco argued.

We bickered about where I would rest my head for most of the drive to his apartment, and by the time we arrived, I was so spent, I caved.

His apartment was decorated in the fashion of most single men. A flat screen television and sound system dominated one wall of a small living area—a big dark leather sofa and a chair filled the remainder of the room. Unlike me, Marco had spent a little change on a decent table in the adjoining dining area. The place didn't smell of dirty laundry, which is always a possibility when a bachelor wasn't expecting guests. Marco's domicile was sparkling clean and orderly. He was obviously a man who tended what was his.

"The bed is made, and the sheets are clean. You might want to leave those suitcases in the kitchen. They stink."

As if I hadn't noticed.

"Don't suppose you want a drink?" he asked.

"I do in the worst way, but no thank you. If you don't mind, I'd just like to lie down. A glass of water would be great."

I followed Marco down a narrow hallway, carrying a bottle of water. Buck and I entered the guest bedroom. A double bed and small dresser filled the room, leaving only slim passageways between the walls and the furniture.

As if to explain the feminine bed cover and the lack of a weight set or other single male accoutrements, Marco said, "My mom likes to visit. She doesn't do well on a couch."

Too tired to speak, I smiled, nodded, and Marco left. I thought it would take me forever to go to sleep, and I fully expected the dreams to come once I did. Buck jumped in with me, stretched his body along my backside, and I was out. Sometime during the night, I opened my eyes just as Marco opened the door. "You were yelling. You okay? Can I help?" he asked.

"No, just bad dreams. No one can help." I turned away from the door and he left.

Mac, my protector, came to me before the dawn wearing his full battle rattle, everything except a Kevlar helmet. My dad was with him, only he was resplendently adorned in a Marine dress uniform. I didn't know they knew each other, but I went with it, happy they had finally met. My dad remained standing, and Mac sat on the bed next to me.

I was crying from the joy of seeing him again, and this time he wasn't oozing blood from his scalp. He placed a hand on my cheek, and I wept.

"Marnie, finish your crying. You have much to do. We're here, watching over you, always. Don't give up."

"I've tried," I answered. "I can't."

Then my dad spoke. "Oh, but you can, Marnie. Did we teach you nothing? Strength and courage, where do you think they come from?"

"I don't understand what you mean."

"What I mean is that without terrible hardship, there is no strength. And without fear and pain, there is no courage."

"So, you're saying, if I truly want to be strong and brave, now's the time?"

My dad only smiled. Mac's eyes were sad as he said, "We're always with you, Marnie."

"Please don't go," I desperately moaned, and then my eyes opened on a new day.

Buck was gone, and I smelled bacon. *There must be some connection.*

I put on last night's clothes and then ran my fingers through my hair. After visiting Marco's bathroom, where a new toothbrush and clean towels were displayed on the closed toilet lid, I sauntered down the hallway to the kitchen.

A huge pile of bacon and eggs was already placed on a table set for two. Buck was concentrating on the feast with considerable focus.

"I didn't have any dog food, so Buck gets to eat like us. I hope you're hungry. Did you get any sleep?" Marco, carrying a pot of coffee, moved from the kitchen, and I took a seat at the table.

"I'm always hungry, and yes, I caught some winks. I actually feel much better."

I gulped down breakfast while Marco and I pretended yesterday was just another day. I knew he would eventually ask, and he did. "I'm still wondering what I hid by that alley. Should I be concerned?"

"No, you aren't in any trouble. If someone was watching, I think our ruse worked perfectly. And, it's a safe place. No one will find it."

"I don't know how you do it, Marnie, holding all these secrets in the face of what's happening. It must be awful. I'd like to help if you'll allow me."

"I know, Marco, and I'm eternally grateful, but don't you need to get to work?"

"Roger that. I'll call you later. Stay as long as you need," Marco offered.

I waved goodbye and cleaned up the kitchen. I had a few calls to make. First my insurance company, then the fire department, and finally, Tiffany. I was glad that the call to Sergeant Murphy went to voicemail. I didn't need the third degree.

Something had happened during my sleep the night before. The beginning of a fuzzy plan was in my mind when I woke. To implement, I would need to go off the grid for a week or two. I penned a letter to Marco to let him know, and I left the note on the table.

With two stinky, bright blue bags and a beautiful therapy dog, we loaded in my SUV toward another war. I sincerely hoped it would be my last.

Chapter 25
SNAFU

Special Agents Davies and Cook sat side by side at a conference table where files stacked and strewn covered the fake-wood surface. "What do you want to do?" Davies asked Cook. "Interview them all again or winnow the list."

Cook sighed heavily and threw his humongous hands in the air. "I've had a couple of frustrating assignments, but this one feels like a setup for failure. The spooks won't tell us what they found at the grid coordinates in question. We can't hint during interviews about the information we're seeking. We can't even ask directly whether our interviewees made a call from Iraq to the FBI hotline. This investigation is so black and compartmentalized it's like trying to find the culprit blindfolded and tied, while the big boys lob grenades, wanting it yesterday."

Davies asked in almost a whisper, "What do you think they found at that location in Iraq?"

Cook's eyes flitted around the room as if someone might be listening. "WMD. Why else would everyone be so excited about a one-minute call seven years ago?"

"Yeah. My thought as well, but I imagine we aren't supposed to be thinking."

"Correct," Cook responded with a wry smile. "Tag them and turn them over, that's our mission. Back to winnowing. What do you suggest?"

Agent Davies studied Cook. They hadn't been partnered for long. She wasn't sure whether Cook was the kind of guy that truly appreciated suggestions. Her first partner had always asked and then become angry and defensive if her idea was better than his. She'd learned to come at him obliquely so that he believed any new idea was his all along. *To hell with it,* she thought. *I'll give Cook a chance to prove himself.*

"We have a significant amount of data regarding where these women travelled on the battlefield. If we map those routes, we could narrow down who might have discovered the subject grid coordinates."

Cook replied. "That's worth doing, but we can't discount the possibility the caller may have known about the location from some other source, other than finding it during a mission. They could have heard about it from another soldier, contractor, or Iraqi interpreter."

"True. But we're getting nowhere fast, and we need to prioritize the most likely candidates. If we find nothing by this approach, we can always interview the remainder again later."

"I like how you think, Davies. Sounds like a plan to me. We need a clean copy of an Iraqi map and a bunch of different colored markers."

Davies smiled, relieved that this partner was dedicated and a grownup. "Before we do, I still don't understand why now? That call was made seven years ago. The trail couldn't be colder."

Cook smirked. "That's the one thing the CIA did share with me. It's a whopper of a story, and an example of how one person, one cog in the works, can foul-up everything. Our country is as big, vast, rich, and technologically advanced as any the world has ever seen, and yet we're always just one screwup away from destruction, from the one guy you weren't watching."

"That's fatalistic and somewhat depressing, Cook."

He chuckled at himself. "I do wax eloquent from time to time. But back to the story—a parable of government inner workings. On the day our unknown suspect reached out to the FBI hotline from Iraq, an extremely obese man named Henry Hickey received the call. He'd mentioned to a coworker upon his arrival that morning that he didn't feel well but thought his malaise was due to the stress involved with that morning's commute. A horse trailer had blown a tire at peak commuting time on I-95 north. As we all know, a disabled horse trailer alone is enough to jam up the highway for hours, but somehow the horse had escaped and was running along the freeway. Must've been a commuter's worst nightmare.

"When the female caller concluded a short spiel to Mr. Hickey, she then gave him grid coordinates. According to his log, he tried to keep her on the line, but she hung up. He entered a description of the call and the words 'passed to DOD', with a time and date. Not 'will pass', but 'passed', as in past tense.

"I'm sure Henry had every intention of making that call immediately, but he had a massive heart attack at his desk before he could complete the action and did not survive.

"His busy supervisor reviewed Henry's log and concluded all was well, no loose ends. It wasn't until five years later that our call was identified as unresolved when some IT nerd developed an application to compare tip lines between several government agencies. The homeland security programmer who'd created this comparison algorithm had in mind an ability to find commonalities, discrepancies, and leads between distinct agencies. Over one thousand items of interest were produced from the first pass.

"Since no one had believed there could be that many similarities or issues, the results of Homeland's algorithm were pronounced unreliable. Still, they had a list. If the next monstrous terrorist attack on the homeland could have been stopped by the investigation of just one of these thousand items, there would be hell to pay.

"Like an onerous hot potato, Homeland passed the list to the Justice Department for research. Homeland Defense argued it was FBI business to investigate. The FBI was unable to pass the task on to anyone else, and thus, the list was divided into three parts and given to three agents in addition to their fulltime duties.

"Almost eighteen months later, one of those agents finally worked her way down the list to our call. The complaint was never passed to DOD. She immediately contacted DOD to request they check the location, and DOD passed the responsibility to the CIA for support from an agent in country. In conclusion, here we are seven years later. I haven't come up with the moral of the story yet, but I'm working on it."

"If it wasn't so sad, I'd laugh," said Davies.

"Indeed. Enough fun. Let's go get some coffee and then find some colored markers."

There were six names left on the prioritized list once Davies and Cook had drawn routes on their map. Marnie Wilson was one of those names.

Cook suggested they make unannounced visits to the homes of their six candidates, notch up the pressure in the hopes that one of these women would step forward. Davies concurred.

Chapter 26
The Slip

I found one space left in the visitor's parking lot located at the outermost reaches of the school. I knew in my gut the hunters following my scent were out there somewhere, watching my every move. Whoever had Marnie stalking duty this day, I wanted them to stay glued to my SUV.

Buck and I found ourselves in the main office, waiting for access to Kevin. Jada Jordon, the school's real power broker, looked me over with some suspicion. I wasn't my normal put-together self, at least the Marnie who looked the part of a woman with her stuff all in one bag. The heavy black duffle I was carrying added to an overall troubled appearance. I had to assume that Jada, the one person employed by the school who kept the pulse of everything, knew about my issues. Nothing I could do about that. If she checked the duffle to find weapons and my meager belongings, the police would be called, and the game would be up.

"I really need to see him, Jada. My house burned down last night. Everything I have left is in this duffle," I said with what I believed was a convincing voice wobble.

"Oh, my goodness! I am so sorry. I had no idea. He's on a teleconference now. I'll hand him a note." She glanced at me and Buck with pity before she scurried away. And yeah, that look kind of pissed me off, but what could I do?

Kevin came out almost immediately and stood in front of me. "Marnie. What horrible news. I can't imagine what you're going through."

His wispy, strawberry blond hair was styled in a comb-over to hide a balding pate. Always perfectly coiffed, he was wearing a stylish suit, a crisp shirt, and a good striped tie. I thought his light blue eyes, peering intently into mine, revealed real concern. For a moment, I was embarrassed about enlisting Kevin's help when I knew he liked me. I wished I had a better choice.

"What can we do to assist?"

"Could I speak to you alone for a moment?"

"Of course. Let me help you with your bag."

I hefted the duffle, pretending it weighed nothing, and slung it over my shoulder, the straps digging into my neck. "No need Kevin, I've got it." No good would come from giving Kevin reason to be curious about the bag's heavy contents.

He shut the door when we entered his office and invited me to sit. "Would you like some coffee?"

"That would be wonderful."

Kevin made two cups from his little coffee brewer and handed me a mug. "I don't take cream or sugar, so there's none in my office."

"This is great."

"What can I do for you, Marnie?"

"First, can I have two weeks off? I hate to leave you in a lurch, but I need to find someplace to live. There's all sorts of personal business I must attend to."

"Obviously. Don't worry about that. I can find someone to cover. You didn't need a private meeting to ask me that though."

"Also, I'm hoping you'll do me a favor." Kevin waited for me to continue. "The fire was no accident, and I think I'm being followed."

"My God, Marnie! Are the police involved? Do you know who it is?"

"Yes and no. The police are looking for an arsonist. I believe the break-in, the fire, and the fact that I've been followed are all connected, and I'm not safe. It isn't simply a firebug, and I don't know who's responsible."

Kevin was wearing an expression different from what I'd expected. He seemed excited. Perhaps he felt like someone who'd just stepped into a spy novel. Was it possible Principal Kevin's life was tedious and my problems a welcome diversion?

"I need to hide for a while. At least until the cops have a lead on the criminal pursuing me. My SUV is in the visitor's lot. Everything I have left is in this black bag. I was hoping you could sneak me out of the school and drive me to a rental car place. From there, I can find a hotel room and remain hidden for a while. You're the only person I know who could help me without anyone suspecting your assistance. Also, if you could make sure they don't tow my car, I'll be eternally grateful."

"What shall I say if I'm asked about your vehicle?"

"Just tell anyone who asks that you gave me a lift to the airport to visit my mom, and I didn't have anywhere else to leave my SUV. I think that would cover it."

Kevin was nearly vibrating. Men. Rescuing a woman, especially one they found attractive, and being placed in a tiny bit of danger while doing so—priceless. I hoped it was just an itsy-bitsy dash of danger. Even so, Kevin was a nice man. I didn't enjoy playing on the emotions of any man who desired me where the feelings weren't mutual, even out of desperation.

"Of course, I'll help you, Marnie! I can't take you until lunch though. My car is parked behind the school. No one will see us from the back-access road." I knew about the access road, but kept my mouth shut.

"Perfect. My tablet was destroyed during the fire. I was hoping to use the library computers to do some research." In truth, I'd left my tablet behind. If my nemesis had the wherewithal to bug my house with sophisticated technology, my computer was likely hacked as well.

"Have at it. Meet me at the back doors at 11:45."

On the way to the library, I ducked into the lady's room. In a closed-door stall, I pulled the batteries out of three burner phones. My smartphone battery, like all new smartphones, was permanently attached, and carrying that cell would be akin to live, breaking news on Marnie's escape plan. I deposited my costly cell, still turned on, in the female modesty bucket next to toilet. My smartphone would be safe in that bucket because only a well-paid cleaning crew dared to touch them. If the assholes following me had hacked my smartphone, they'd be tricked into waiting around at the school.

I searched for Command Sergeant Major Williams from the library's public computer. After locating three different people with a similar name, I narrowed it down to a retired SGM Williams currently employed by the government at Fort

Bragg, North Carolina. I needed someone who could fill in the blanks, and he was my best option.

That time between when Mac and I had discovered the WMD and my subsequent departure from Iraq was key to understanding my current predicament and, possibly, who else might have known about the stash. My plan was to surprise the retired Sergeant Major Williams at his office tomorrow. With any luck at all, he wasn't the same guy I'd given a bad rap during my tour in Iraq. Maybe, he was a decent and professional NCO who'd been placed in a bad situation because he'd worked for one of the world's preeminent jerks.

Kevin was waiting, as promised, with keys in hand. He started running to his car immediately after he exited the door, and I had to place a restraining hand on his arm. "Kevin, best we not look like this is an escape attempt."

"Oh, oh, of course not. What was I thinking?"

"You were trying to help." I gave him a sincere smile.

I kept watching to our rear, and Buck did the same from the back seat as we drove along a tree-lined access road. I couldn't be positive, but if my watcher's eyes were trained on my SUV from the front of the school, they wouldn't see our departure. I didn't turn back to face the front until Kevin spoke.

"Do you see anyone following us? Do I need to make some unexpected turns to be sure I throw off a tail?"

"Nope, I believe we're good." His face registered disappointment. When else would an elementary school principal have the chance to lose a tail?

"Hey, I have a thought about where you can stay," Kevin added. He must have noticed my alarm. "Not with me, Marnie. My parents left me a house, and I've been working on it for over a year. It's old and needed renovation, but it has good bones. Anyway, I plan to move in once I get the house into ship shape. It's slow going with only weekends to tend to it. The house is furnished and has a big fenced yard for Buck."

"That's way too generous. I couldn't ask that."

"You could indeed take my generosity. I'd prefer someone be in the home, but I didn't want to take on renters. This could work for both of us."

I couldn't imagine staying in a hotel for weeks. I'd probably find a short-term rental until my house was rebuilt, and a rental contract would mean traceable records. His offer was the perfect way to stay hidden. I hesitated as I considered the implications. "That sounds wonderful, Kevin, and I hate to add conditions on top of your most generous offer, but I have two. First, you let me pay you something, and second, that you not share my whereabouts with anyone. Can you keep it a secret?"

"I have to. The people at school might find our arrangement rather unusual. We can work out an agreeable compensation amount later. Utilities would be fine with me. Okay?"

"I'm in!"

As we pulled into the off-brand auto rental agency, Kevin asked, "Marnie, do you think whoever is after you might find out about your rental car? Rentals all have GPS tracking these days."

Getting into the groove about off the grid, Kevin had astutely identified a colossal crater in my plan. For the novice in-the-wind individual, the landscape was brimming with new-world tracking devices, from cameras to GPS, credit card monitoring, and worst of all, government spying. I didn't know what my pursuers could do to find me or if their access extended to the big guns like NSA and snooping drones. I had to assume the worst case, but I didn't have the cash to do anything other than slow them down. I was already approaching my credit card limit with a cash advance to rent an auto from the only business in the area that didn't demand plastic payment.

"I don't know, Kevin. I need to go on a day trip tomorrow. I thought I'd figure it out when I got back."

"If you'll allow me, I might have another solution. Get your rental, and I'll meet you at my house after work."

I was speechless. This was the same guy I'd cavalierly dismissed as being too needy. *Who's needy now, Marnie?* I placed my hand on his arm and said, "Thank you, Kevin. Really."

A subcompact that could easily be classified as barely roadworthy was all that I could afford to rent. The rear bumper had taken a few hits, and the inside reeked of cigarettes. Buck didn't seem particularly enamored with the afforded space, but he didn't complain. I started the ignition, and the hamsters in the drive train gave their mightiest industry to push us forward. I stopped by a drug store for hair dye, scissors, and cosmetics and then headed to the fire station for my interview.

The interview was painless. The captain assured me they would do everything they could to find the person responsible. Fat chance.

Sitting in my new, old ride in a visitor space near the safety of several fire trucks, I pushed the battery back into the pink tape burner phone and called the one person I most owed a call. Also, the one person I least wanted to speak with. Tiffany answered after two rings.

"Where are you, Marnie?" Her voice was mad and worried at the same time.

"Tiffany, I need to go off the grid. I'm sorry, but I think I'm the only one who can piece this together."

"Don't do this, Marnie. Dammit. I'll put out a BOLO on you if you walk away."

"For what? Failure to give you an interview? It's still a free country, Tiffany. But do what you must. I want you to know, your friendship and support has meant a lot to me, and you're a great cop. Unfortunately, I think I'm the only one who can finish this thing, and that's what I plan to do. I'll call you when I have more." She was screaming wait as I hung up, and I yanked the battery out of the Sergeant Murphy phone. Next, on to my hideaway.

Chapter 27
Duped

He saw the buses lining up and not long after, hordes of children running, shouting, and scampering to their rides, a clue the school day was over. He was tired of waiting. He'd caught a few winks the previous night after Marnie had returned with Marco to his apartment, but since then, this day had dragged on to infinity.

She should have come back out by now. Something was up. The blue bags were still in the SUV. She'd carried a duffle into the school, but he'd seen her hauling unwieldy teacher stuff before, so the black bag hadn't raised any alarms. Here he was, thinking all day that Marnie was a total badass for jumping right back into work after having her life burned to the ground. He knew that's how some people dealt with stress, and he might've done the same thing. Now, he was beginning to believe he'd been duped.

The last employee departed the area at about five o'clock. He engaged the ignition, worrying that with only his vehicle and Marnie's left in the lot, someone, maybe a security guard or cop patrolling the area, might notice him. He pulled around a winding circle and drove to the rear of the school only to find staff parking spaces and the additional access road. Maybe, if he was a professional private investigator, he would have thought this shit through a little better, but he wasn't. She'd made a successful run for it.

Driving around to the front again from the rear of the school, he parked close to Marnie's SUV, jumped out with a crowbar in hand, and pried the back open. Pulling out the two suitcases, he closed the vertical door as best he could and skedaddled. At least he could get some dinner tonight.

Later, at home with a dirty martini in hand, he called his partner in crime. "I lost her at the school."

"How's that even possible?" Gerry Jamison asked.

"She either walked out or had someone drive her and left her SUV parked in the visitor's lot. I was watching the SUV. The good news is I stole her suitcases. The bad news is there was nothing in them but clothes. That might even be good news. It confirms what we've said all along. She doesn't know anything and doesn't have any proof."

"If that's true, why is she running?" Gerry asked.

He was stumped. "I don't know."

"Can't you get a GPS signal from her phone?"

"No luck. I tried when I became concerned she'd given me the slip. The cell is still on, located in a school that's lights out and locked down. She's gone."

"You'd better think of something quick. Question the people at the school tomorrow if you have to."

"Not going to happen. You expect me to kidnap and torture a bunch of elementary school teachers? You're out of your mind."

Gerry's voice was raised when he said, "Then think of something else, because it's your fault

189

we've lost her. Find some leverage and make it happen! The FBI is getting ready for a second round of questioning. I still don't understand why you had to burn her house down."

"We can talk about that later. I might have one angle, but it's a dangerous play. I'm going to need your help here in person."

Gerry was silent as he thought about involving himself again in a direct way. "Send me the plan. I can't be there until late tomorrow. You know this Marnie is still surprising me. She's a good deal cagier and more resilient than my asshole brother thought."

"Why does she surprise you? Because she's got a touch of the PTSD bug, that makes her brain dead and stupid? She saved several of my people's asses in that convoy. I'd hardly call her a lightweight."

"I didn't say that. I simply hoped this would all be easier."

"Nothing's right or easy about this, Gerry."

"Amen. I'll text with my schedule for tomorrow as soon as I have flight details. We'll find her."

"You better be here. I'm sick of trying to smoke out Marnie alone."

Chapter 28
New Digs, New Ride

Kevin's second home was leaps and bounds better than my first home, the place I'd laid my head to rest before it became a pile of cinders. The style was vintage sixties contemporary. A large open kitchen had been lovingly restored by Kevin with warm cherry hardwood cabinets, subdued quartz countertops, and a glass and ceramic backsplash. From the kitchen was a view of a high-beamed gathering area and a wall of windows to a landscaped yard. The yard featured an intricate stone waterfall, complete with a burbling brook meandering over jutting rocks into a pond.

"It's absolutely beautiful, Kevin. Did you do all this?"

"Well, most of it. I like working with my hands. My dad did the landscaping twenty years ago after my sister moved out."

"Call me impressed."

He shyly accepted the praise. "Follow me. I'd like to show you something else that you may appreciate even more." He led me from the kitchen, down a short hallway, through a laundry room, and then to the inside garage entry. With a flourish, he turned on the garage lights. "Tada."

A black, forgettable Chevy Caprice appearing to be in mint condition filled the far half of a double garage. "It's in great shape. My mom didn't get out much the last few years. Only seventy thousand miles on the odometer and serviced three months ago. Ready to travel. What do you think?"

I stared at Kevin, a lump forming in my throat at this man's kindness. "Again, it's absolutely beautiful!"

"No way anyone could connect you to this vehicle. If you'll use the Caprice, I can take you before school tomorrow, and we'll return your rental first thing."

I nodded and smiled. "I'm not sure how I'll ever pay you back."

"I could use an interesting friend. Mine are all deadly dull."

"I can do that, Kevin. Not sure about the interesting part, but I'll give it my best effort."

He laughed. "Are you kidding me? A well-read, attractive, female war veteran, one who knows at least two other languages, and a woman willing to track mysterious pursuers."

"Who says that's what I'm doing, tracking my pursuers?"

Kevin's eyebrows shot up. "Call it a gut instinct."

"Kevin, all I ask is that for your own safety, you don't share information on my whereabouts."

"Got it. My lips are sealed." He did a hokey zipping motion over his lips and then continued the tour of the house, giving instructions as he did so. He handed me multiple keys before leaving and shouted over his shoulder on the way out, "You and Buck can help yourselves to any food in the house."

Buck appeared confused by his new surroundings and wandered from one corner to another, smelling the scents of prior residents. I found two cans of tuna and some saltine crackers to whip up dinner for Buck. He consumed the delightful concoction in a few gulps and licked the bowl clean. I let him outside and prepared a can of chicken noodle soup and a mega bowl of cereal for myself.

Both satiated, I got comfortable in the family area on a navy velour couch, and Buck joined me, laying his head on my thigh. I pulled my collection of burner phones from my purse and set them on my lap. Placing the battery into Tiffany's phone first, I was curious whether she was trying to track me down. No text or voicemails. That was good; at least I thought it was. That was unless she'd become weary of my secrets and had given up on me.

Dan's phone was next. I couldn't think of any reason I needed to check in on him and moved on to Marco's phone. The second the Marco phone powered up, multiple texts and voicemails pinged and dinged, blowing up my phone. Rather than read the long thread of texts, I pressed the call button and waited.

He answered with a rapid-fire string of Spanish frustration. He was angry. "Marnie, how could you make me worry like this?"

"I didn't have any choice. I was sure someone was following me again, and I had to get them off my back."

"Did you see somebody?"

"No, I just know. I'm safe, Marco. I shouldn't have gotten you as involved as I already have. I have a roof over my head, and I don't think anyone can find me here. Have you heard anything back from Anton about the DNA?"

"I called him to check. He thinks maybe they'll have a batch in the next couple of days, but he couldn't guarantee it."

I sighed into the receiver, and Marco heard me.

"He's doing the best he can, Marnie."

"Oh, I know. It's all just so freaking hard."

The line was silent for a time. "So, what are you going to do now?"

"I'm going to go talk with someone I knew from Iraq tomorrow. See if I can fill in some blanks."

"And after that?"

"I wish I knew. Hopefully, I'll learn something that will lead me somewhere else."

"I almost hate to ask, but can I help? Is there a place for me in your plan?"

His words sounded like a question that demanded more than one answer. I really liked Marco, maybe more than liked, but I had no hope to offer him right now. "No promises, Marco, but maybe later."

"I see." He was silent for several seconds. "You be safe, Marnie," he replied with a melancholy tone.

"I'll call you again tomorrow night," I said. With that, he disconnected, and I extracted the battery from the phone.

Given everything, my home in ruins, on the run, confused about who was after me, still, it had been a good day. I had another friend and a roof over my head. Clinging to sanity with my last ounce of will, I'd avoided a full-blown panic attack at the fire scene. I thought again about how action, moving forward, doing something, anything, had dulled the sharp edges of doubt and hopelessness. Stasis was my enemy. Unless stasis existed from total fulfillment and a desire to remain in the same wondrous place, a place that I didn't believe was a real part of the human condition, it created a continual state of agitation. I'd been in the same place, running on a treadmill, since the day Mac left me—always wondering how my actions had caused his death and not believing I had the power to resolve my inner conflict. Waiting, waiting, my head down and buried deep, a victim of fate, hoping that I was so special the stars would align to solve my puzzle and save me from the next bad thing.

I giggled, and Buck raised his head, attempting to turn his eyes to me from his side, his body stretching from near my leg to the other end of the sofa. "Buck, between you and me, I'm full of shit."

He produced a dog moan in sympathy and dropped his head again. "I'm not sure how I got so derailed. Sure, the doctors explained the brain's chemical responses to stress and trauma, but even though I could understand the process, it still feels like I should've had more control." I stroked Buck's ears, and then his ruff, and then on to his muscled shoulders. "They did say the brain could rewire itself to some extent. Maybe that's happening now. Maybe seeing our small world turned into a pile of ash has hastened the process. I just know for all this crap, I feel different, better than I've felt in a very long time."

The scene where I found myself was so domestic and tranquil, I didn't want to move. Outside lights illuminated the rock waterfall. I couldn't hear the soothing melody of water cascading over a stone feature with the air-conditioning on, but I could see the hypnotic movement of liquid spilling into a koi pond. I pulled an old orange and brown chevron afghan from the floor, one probably made by Kevin's mother or grandmother, and draped the fuzzy blanket over my body. I had thought I'd read on my Kindle for a while, but my eyelids were heavy, and I allowed them to close.

Chapter 29
First Lead

With the last of summer's dog days refusing to relent, Cook and Davies stood sweating on the sidewalk in front of Marnie's house. Both agents were dressed in dark suits. Cook pulled a cotton handkerchief from a breast pocket and dabbed his brow, and Davies used the back of her hand. The humidity magnified a burned smell overlaid with the stench of fried manmade products.

Yellow crime scene tape hung haphazardly across the front stoop and what had formerly been a garage entry. "Me thinks this could be our first clue," Davies said.

"Possibly," Cook replied. "Did you notice that teenaged kid on the other side of the street? He's covered the same stretch of sidewalk on his skateboard, back and forth, watching us. Why don't you stroll over and see what you can learn? I'll check around the house."

Davies nodded and crossed the street. She waved at the teenager who'd just completed a daring leap from a curb, catching air before he landed and ably regained control of his board. Davies stepped into the skateboarder's path. "Hey! Hi, do you live in this neighborhood? I was wondering if you could speak to me for a moment."

The broad-shouldered young man leaned back and jumped in a maneuver that rocketed the board from the sidewalk to his hands. His eyes gave Davies the once over. He shrugged and ambled to her location. "Who are you?" he asked.

"I'm Special Agent Kiara Davies, FBI. We're here to talk to Ms. Wilson. Do know when this fire happened or where she might be living now?"

"You're not investigating the fire then?" a guileless face asked and instantly mutated into an expression of suspicion.

"No, we weren't aware of a fire. This is her last known address. We wanted to follow-up with her on some background she provided about her time in Iraq."

"It happened night before last. The police think it was done on purpose. Someone also broke into Marnie's house. I don't know you, and I can't tell you anything else except Marnie's a real nice lady."

"Would it help if I showed you my badge?" Davies pulled her jacket from her hip to display the badge hooked to her belt.

Trevor edged closer to get a good look. "Whoa, you really are FBI, cool. Like, I've thought about being an FBI agent. You like it?"

Davies smiled, "Yes, I do. It's a good and challenging profession. Do you know where Marnie went?"

"A friend named Marco was like with her that night, but I don't know his last name. There was a cop called Officer Murphy here too. She'd probably know something."

"Is Officer Murphy local police?"

"I think so."

"Thanks for that."

"No problem. Just FYI, there's some bad guys after Marnie. You and your partner should be like spending your time trying to find them."

"I'll take that under advisement. By the way, the best way to be an FBI agent is to stay in school and do well. Keep your nose clean."

"That's mostly the case for everything," Trevor replied and mounted his board.

Davies replied, "Well, true," to his back as he slalomed into the street.

She joined Cook investigating the scene in the back of Marnie's burned-out home. His shirt was showing sweat marks across the front, and he'd loosened his tie. "Lordy, it's hot," he said. "If I'd known we'd be visiting a crime scene, I'd have dressed differently. See the way the back side is burned to the ground on this part of the perimeter and the front portion only partially decimated? I'm no fire expert, but my initial impression says an arsonist set the fire here."

Cook rubbed the flat of his hand over the grass and positioned his palm a few inches from Davies' nose. "Smell this."

"Accelerant," she responded. "The kid across the street said some bad guys had been after Marnie, and that we should be spending our time trying to find them. He also said she'd had a break-in. He was very protective of her."

"Hmmm. This not-so-simple case of finding a whistleblower caller from seven years ago Just got a whole lot more interesting. It can't be anything good that has someone breaking into her house and then burning it down."

"The kid also said an Officer Murphy, probably local, was on the scene. I think we should pay her a visit."

"Yeah. Let's do what research we can in the car and then make a call on the local gendarmes.

They probably won't be happy to have our involvement."

"As a teenaged boy just told me, that's mostly the case for everything."

Chapter 30
The Sergeant Major

I'd always loved the drive from the D.C. area to Fort Bragg. Once south of Richmond, beyond the worst traffic, the highway was straight and true, allowing time to absorb the deep green scenery of southern Virginia and the sandy pine forests and farms of North Carolina. It was still hot, and translucent waves of heat shimmered over the blacktop in the distance.

My plan hit a snag first thing upon my arrival at the massive military installation that was Fort Bragg. Since 9/11, most military bases no longer allowed personnel on base unescorted without military or government civilian identification. I must have buried this information somewhere in my pile of things I knew and conveniently forgot because when I arrived at the gate, I had to park and join a long line of people desiring base access. There was no way to surprise the retired Sergeant Major Williams. My only hope was that he was available, remembered me, and was willing to come get me.

Since I didn't have his telephone number, the on-duty civilian found it and called. A pleasant, but harried older woman with long straight hair watched me as she waited on the phone for someone to locate Mr. Williams. She gave me a slight smile to say she was either trying to help or that she didn't believe me to be a possible terrorist. It probably didn't hurt that Buck, with his official dog vest, stood close to my side. She might've even assumed I was one of many wounded warriors who had parted ways from service and had come to see an old friend.

"Yes, hello. Mr. Williams. I have a Ms. Marnie Wilson standing in front of me at the Fort Bragg reception center. She desires a visit with you."

The long-haired woman muttered a few uh huh's, and then said, "She says it's personal business. Uh huh, thank you. Could you please hold?"

"Ms. Wilson, you're in luck. He's available today, but not right now due to meetings. He says he can come by in two hours to escort you. Does that work for you?"

Tremendously relieved that I hadn't made a five-hour drive to Fort Bragg for nothing, I returned a huge smile. "Yes!"

Buck and I went in search of nourishment. I found a chain burger place, one of Buck's absolute favorites. Once you move away from a military area, it's easy to forget the clientele that inhabits the environs surrounding a base: boisterous, fit young men with short haircuts in uniform and sometimes outrageous civilian attire, young mothers with barely controlled children, female soldiers who appear confident, strong, and frequently wary, and older retired personnel who are worn but still spritely. These groups were all on display today against a backdrop of fried beef smells.

I found it sad that too many in our country no longer understood who these people were other than videos on the news or that daughter of a friend of a friend in the military. A world apart, they came from small towns or humble beginnings, willing to put it all on the line for patriotism or the desire for a better life, and most often both. The military had become something that other people do. It's one thing to say I support the troops, another to comprehend fully who it is that's being supported other than Uncle Ed, the family World War II hero. To me it was home. I hadn't realized how much I missed this community.

Buck didn't take any notice and instead focused on french fries and cheeseburgers. One young private first class, who still wore acne on his shaved face, came over and asked if he could give Buck a morsel and a pet. He explained his parents had a dog like Buck back home, and he missed her. My sentimental streak reared its head, and I fought the impulse to shed a tear over what might be a very lonely young man. Buck had no such concerns with sentimentality. He politely accepted the offered slab of burger and swallowed it whole.

Buck and I found ourselves waiting at the reception center with a half hour to spare before meeting time with SGM Williams. He came through the door ten minutes early. SGM, now Mr. Williams, hadn't aged a day in seven years. His unlined black face, slightly graying close-cropped hair, trim figure, and big toothy smile were exactly as I remembered. I could only hope he would judge me to be only half as well maintained.

"Specialist Wilson! Can't say I expected a visit, but I'll have to say, you're a sight for sore eyes. How the hell are you?" He reached out to shake my hand with both of his.

"Please, call me Marnie. You look great Sergeant Major. You must keep a Dorian Gray painting in a closet somewhere."

"Good on the outside, but you should see me hobbling when I get out of bed in the morning. You look wonderful as well, Marnie." He checked out Buck, gave an almost imperceptible head nod, and added, "So, somehow I'm thinking you have a purpose for this visit other than a social call. What can I do for you?"

"Sergeant Major—"

He interrupted. "Please call me Ezell."

"Okay, Ezell, I've had some adjustment problems. With the help of counselors, I've realized there's some gaps in my memory about my last days in Iraq. It would be helpful to my recovery if I could fill in those gaps, and I thought you might be able to shed some light."

The sergeant major's face changed. He was circumspect, guilty, and most certainly guarded. Whatever he was thinking, it was obvious I was right. There was more to the story that I was missing.

"I will do whatever I can, Marnie. How about you take a drive with me to my office, and we can talk."

We loaded up and drove in uncomfortable silence through the base to arrive at his place of work. Buck and I followed him through a labyrinth of cubicles and hallways to a small office. After refusing coffee and accepting a bottle of water, I sat in a chair across from his desk.

"Before we start, Marnie, I want you to know, I felt you weren't treated respectfully after the convoy incident. Truthfully, you were treated like dogshit."

"What do you mean?" I asked.

"I think you have some idea, and that's why you're here. I've often wondered about you, how it all sorted out."

I gulped a breath. I couldn't just dive into this subject and screw it up by getting angry. "Do you remember the night I had the open door with the colonel?"

"I do. I still don't know what happened, but I was pretty sure it wasn't good."

"Colonel Jamison said I didn't deserve a medal, and that it had only been approved because of political correctness—that his bosses wanted a female hero. Is that true?"

"Oh my God!" he said, disgust in his voice. "What a flaming asshole. I've known some a-holes in my time, but Jamison took his status as a first-class jerk to a whole new level. Of course you deserved the award, Marnie. Never have any doubts about that."

I continued to press. "Honestly, the award didn't make any difference to me at the time. I had survived while the people I cared about didn't. What confuses me is who did submit that award recommendation? It obviously wasn't Jamison. It wasn't Mac since he was dead. I don't think it was you. Who submitted the award recommendation for me?"

SGM Williams, wanting to be known now as Ezell now, which was difficult as hell for me because it's hard to change someone's first name, ran his hand over his head in thought. "If I remember it right, it was the company commander for the logistics unit your team was supporting the day of the convoy ambush."

"Do you remember his name? I don't remember a captain in the convoy that day."

"As I understand it, he was supposed to go out with you, but a last-minute briefing to higher headquarters came up. Hold up, wait while I try to remember the name." He looked at the ground. "Dan something. It's not coming."

"Okay. Do you remember what this Captain Dan something looked like?"

"Yeah, nervous guy, fidgety. Medium height, dark brown hair and eyes. Thought he was special ops material as I remember. Submitted two applications during the time he was there in Iraq. I heard about his requests when they came across the colonel's desk."

My heart was beginning to pump harder. This information was completely unexpected. The familiar rushing of blood roared in my ears. The sergeant major's description of this Dan sounded very much like the Dan I knew. I reached down and touched Buck, willing his calm nature to travel from my fingers to my heart.

"Do you know if Dan's applications were ever approved? Is there anyone who would know this captain's last name?"

"To your first question, I don't believe his applications for special operations were ever approved, at least not while I was in the group. I have a sergeant major friend that might know the captain's last name. Sorry I can't remember it. Too many names in my noggin. Hold on a sec, and I'll make a call."

Sergeant Major Williams pulled a cellphone from a front shirt pocket, and I waited. As he was making the normal greetings preamble with an old friend, I thought back on my Dan and wondered if there was any possibility this captain could be the same person. What came to mind first was the day that Dan had sat next to me in the VA waiting room and told me I was being followed, and how I'd lost him after group in the hospital hallways—how that van had followed me home even though Dan made it clear the vehicle had fled once the driver had noticed him. Dan had said he wanted to help, but he hadn't provided anything useful. Mostly, Dan had pumped me for information.

I was vaguely aware of the sergeant major still talking to his buddy. A sick feeling in the pit of my stomach, the one I get when I suspect betrayal, was beginning to spread into a more widespread body panic. If Dan was involved, was Marco too?

There was only one possible course of action right now—denial. Deny the possibility that I had been duped and betrayed until I could prove conclusively that the logistics captain in Iraq and my Dan were the same man. To do otherwise was simply too painful. And, I couldn't believe that Marco and his cousin were involved. No way. That just couldn't be.

"Marnie?" The sergeant major was done with his call and staring at me, concern inscribed on his face.

"Oh, sorry. I was just thinking about some of my buddies in Iraq."

"That happens to me, too. One moment I'm here, and the next I'm somewhere half a world away. The name you're needing is Wojocowski. Captain Wojocowski."

"Doesn't ring any bells. I'll think about it. Another subject. Do you recall why my team's mission was changed from prisoner pick-up and intelligence gathering to convoy protection?"

206

"Best I can remember, the intelligence part of your mission wasn't yielding any results. Not that your lack of success was the team's fault. I thought it was a dumb idea from the get go. The colonel decided your team needed to be fully utilized. He put out the word to use Mac's team in a convoy protection capacity whenever possible."

"What was the impetus for the timing? When exactly did Colonel Jamison make that decision?"

The sergeant major appeared uncomfortable. He shifted in his chair, gazed out the window, and then rubbed his head. "I don't understand what you're getting at, Marnie."

"I'm not really sure. One day we're transferring prisoners, and then with no notice, we're suddenly participating in dangerous convoy protection missions. I'm just trying to fully understand when and why. Did it have anything to do with Mac and me? That day when we went to pick up intelligence for the colonel with just the two of us?"

He began to laugh. "That was a really bone-headed move on Mac's part. I was pissed, but then I spent a lot of my time in Iraq pissed at bone-headed moves. Same shit, different day. If you're thinking I held it against Mac and gave you those sketchy missions, get it out of your mind. It didn't come from me!"

"That's good to know. I wasn't sure if it was something I—well I mean we—caused."

"No, nothing like that. I get how you might've made that connection though. It wasn't long after you came back that day, and I chewed Mac's butt, that Colonel Jamison gave orders to utilize your team in a different way. Hell, it was only a few days—a week at most as I remember."

"Okay. I'm relieved to hear it wasn't you. One last question—the mission where Mac was killed. I heard through the grapevine that everyone was aware of heightened enemy activity in the area that day, and that the logistics resupply convoy we were escorting wasn't mission critical. Is that true?"

Guilt was written in hard lines on the sergeant major's face. "We're entering dangerous territory here." He stopped as if a burdensome internal decision was being contemplated. At last he decided, his jaws locked and set a moment before speaking. "That mission is the one thing—the one damn thing from Iraq I wish I could undo." He stopped. He needed to confess something, and I wasn't about to stop him. I waited. Even Buck, anticipating something, got up from his resting position to watch the man.

"You most likely never knew, but there was an investigation about that mission later, after you left country."

"No, I didn't know." My voice had taken an edge. Rather than get angry and interrupt his train of thought, I waited some more. My heart was beating hard, but I was under control for now.

"I argued with Colonel Jamison, Marnie. I pleaded with him to wait on that mission. It was me that later whispered to a sergeant major in higher headquarters that Jamison made dangerous and unnecessary calls. But Jamison was smart. Somehow, he weaseled out of accountability, casting doubt on everyone, including me. The importance of that logistics mission wasn't cut and dry. He argued all too persuasively it was a commander's prerogative to make that call. In the end, there wasn't enough evidence to go forward with any charges.

"I can only tell you that rumors ruined Jamison's career. Whispers about his dangerous and cavalier judgment, and that he was an overall asshole, did him in. He retired before he was considered for promotion to general officer."

"Somehow a ruined career is of little consolation, Sergeant Major Williams. Some good soldiers are dead. People I cared about."

We locked eyes until he looked away. "Could you please take me back to my car?" I whispered.

We drove in silence to the reception center where my car was parked. I wanted to cry, but I wouldn't let him see me break down. When I showed him where I was parked, he pulled behind the Caprice, his vehicle's engine still running. "I'm so sorry, Marnie. I must live with the guilt of knowing I didn't fight hard enough to prevent the buzz saw that found that convoy and killed good men and women. And we didn't have air support ready to react quickly when things went bad. Whether you know it or not, I've thought about you, Mac, and Zeke more times than I can explain."

His voiced cracked. "Know this, Specialist Wilson. You have no guilt. Unlike me, you did fight hard and bravely in a bad situation. You weren't responsible for what happened. Your actions saved lives that day."

"So you say now," were my last words to him.

Chapter 31
Dirty Work

From the moment Gerry jumped into Dan's car at the Baltimore International Airport, he had begun hammering Dan over a lifetime of missteps and culpability that had led to this day. Stuck in stop and go traffic on I-95 South, the two men had ample chance to accuse each other of all manner of stupid decisions and blame. It was obvious to Gerry that neither of them truly wanted to be involved in what was to come, futilely searching for an answer that didn't involve risking their respective necks.

"Explain your plan again, Dan," Gerry sighed.

"Are you ignorant? I just said, we stake out Marnie's friend Marco's place, take him, and hide him away somewhere until we get some answers. All we need is a safe place to store him for a while, and then we let him go."

"I did hear that, although I was hoping my interpretation of your grand plan was confused. To be more precise, please help me to understand why it's necessary. Why should we involve anyone else and leave a greater trail of destruction to be hanged for later?"

"I know you don't want to hear this Gerry, but for the third time, Marnie is gone. Marco was with her the night of the fire. If we want to find out where she is, he's the only one who might know her whereabouts. Who knows, he might know more."

"What about the cop she's been talking to?" Gerry asked.

"Right, good plan. Go to the police. Be my guest!"

Dan's voice lowered a notch. "Do you know of a place to keep Marco? It's a simple question."

"Maybe, but my brother owns it. If Richard finds out we're holding someone connected to Marnie there, who knows what the psychopathic asshole might do."

"Then make sure dickhead Richard doesn't find out."

"Richard has a house on the mouth of the Potomac River. He gave me the key combination a couple of years ago to use for what he called liaisons, not that I have any. I'm too engaged as his errand boy to have any kind of personal life. Anyway, I don't think he's there much. His airhead wife uses it from time to time, but Richard keeps her on a tight leash."

"No problems getting into Richard's place then?"

"It's a combination lock with a security system. I've got everything we need stored in my phone," Gerry answered.

"That'll work." The traffic loosened up. Dan was heading south to his home to pick up what they would need to capture Marco. He kept his eyes on the road as he began to speak. "Ever wonder whether it was all worth it? Whether the money was worth living with this hanging over our heads? Always waiting to for the ax to drop? Participating in activities you know are as bad as it gets? Stealing when you're poor is one thing, but not this."

Gerry answered quickly. "No. I don't wonder. I know it wasn't worth it. It wasn't my idea to join the Army back in college—it was yours. You wanted to be a special forces hero, and I just wanted to be with you."

"And look how well it all worked out," Dan answered. "I pretend to be a special ops guy at a VA trauma group to get Marnie to trust me, I'm wealthy but have to keep my wealth hidden, and we're both alone. Best laid plans."

Gerry replied with some conviction, "We'll do this one last thing, Dan, try to get this Marco to talk, and then find Marnie. Anything after that, I'm done. Let my filthy rich immoral brother handle any dirty work. I don't think I can kill her if it turns out she knows something."

"Richard isn't going to let you walk, Gerry. He'll drag you down with him kicking and screaming. The only reason I'm doing this is to try to keep you safe. You haven't mentioned me, have you?"

"You know I've never told Richard about your involvement, Dan. But don't pretend your ass isn't in a sling as much as mine if the authorities even catch a hint there was something else in that hole."

"How would I know you haven't mentioned my name, Gerry? In all this time, that you haven't been forced to explain to your deranged brother who helped you?"

Gerry scowled at Dan's profile as Dan continued to watch the road. "If I'd even whispered your name in connection to that gold, you'd probably be dead by now. That's how you know, Dan."

Dan smirked. "Point taken." His attention shifted to a sudden flash of brake lights ahead, and he reacted with a quick stop that threw the two men forward against seatbelts. When the traffic began to move again, Dan continued. "Hey, I'm sorry I said that. It doesn't help our situation to flog each other. Just be aware, Marco is a for real SEAL. He only has one eye, but he's still dangerous. It's going to take the both of us to make this happen. Once we pick up some stuff from the house, we'll start staking him out at his apartment until we get the chance to do a snatch and grab."

"Oh, God. I hate the sound of that. How did we get here?"

"One step at a time, Gerry. One stupid step at a time."

Resigned, Gerry answered. "Lead on."

* * *

The only place to watch and wait for Marco was not in view of his apartment building. After driving over a bazillion speed bumps through the cramped apartment complex, Dan finally yelled, "What the hell? There's no place we won't be seen."

"Great plan, Dan," Gerry replied in return. "Just calm down. Let's park at the end of the main exit street. There were some spaces parallel to the road when we came in. Eventually, he'll drive by. We don't need to have eyes on his apartment. I think the fact that the Army never deemed you fit for special ops was probably a lifesaving event for everyone concerned."

"Screw you," Dan quipped.

The stakeout vehicle was sweltering. Even though the temperature had dropped a few degrees in the last hour, Dan had opened the windows, providing only a trace of a humid breeze. Further making the downtime uncomfortable, open windows allowed every mosquito within the city limits to draw blood on human flesh. Only two hours into the stakeout, Gerry was mosquito-bitten and began to construct excuses for calling it a night. Dan, at first reluctant, was warming to the idea.

It was almost 9 p.m. Most of the snacks and beverages they had carried to the task consumed, Dan turned to his sometimes partner with a wry smile. "How far the mighty have fallen. We used to be miserable much of the time when we were in the Army. Now look at us. Can't even sit for a couple of hours in a car without losing our minds."

"I never tolerated this kind of crap very well." Gerry paused and then asked the question that had been on his mind since he'd learned Marnie had slipped from their grasp and was now on the run. "You know what I don't understand, Dan? Why you had to burn Marnie's house down, and how you managed to get this Marco involved in our business to begin with."

"Hmm, yeah, well let's see. I spooked her at the VA group meeting when I told her she was being followed, and then followed her myself to reinforce the fear. Everything was going swimmingly. She came to me wanting help. But then you let her catch you in the act of breaking into her home. What was I supposed to do?"

"You told me she never got back home before five!" Gerry yelled. "That still doesn't explain about the fire."

"Well, since she caught you, she guessed about the possibility of listening devices and asked for my assistance. If I'd turned her down, she'd have just gone somewhere else. I used Marco because Marnie knew him from group. I thought including a person she knew, like Marco, would make her trust me more. It wouldn't be just me, but more like a group of friends. I didn't plan for his Latin lover shtick. I'm still not sure how they hooked up."

Dan continued, "I don't know. Maybe the fire was a bad idea. We needed something to make her desperate without hurting her. I made sure she wasn't home before I set the fire. Until she slipped the noose, the fire plan was working perfectly."

Gerry felt tired. From the beginning their involvement in Richard's scheme was a setup for failure. He was an engineer by trade and Dan a logistician who longed to be a special operations hero. Dan had always been a far better logistics nerd than he was spy material. They weren't suited for this kind of work. Neither of them had any interest in hurting the innocent, and he would absolutely include Marnie as one of the innocent. How had he ever let his evil brother control him like this? How had he been led down this road?

Gerry was just about to speak when another set of headlights came from the direction of the apartments. His eyes followed the vehicle without much interest, reasonably sure Marco was in for the night, and they were wasting their time. He did a double take when the SUV passed, and he realized the vehicle was the same make, model, and color Dan had instructed him to watch for. "Is that him, Dan?" he shouted.

Dan turned abruptly, and before the SUV was too far away to see the license plates, he blurted,

"Hell yes, that's our man. Start getting the gear ready. We may have to wing this."

"That's what I'm most afraid of," Gerry mumbled. He didn't know what gear Dan had in mind, so he plucked two dark face masks from the pile on the backseat, plopped one into Dan's lap, and held on to the other.

Gerry knew Dan's adrenaline would be surging with the chase. From very early on in their relationship, Gerry was aware that Dan craved danger. He'd almost gotten them thrown out of college twice, once for a stupid prank, and another time when they were caught in an elaborate cheating scandal masterminded by Dan. Risk averse himself, it was that very trait that drew him to Dan. Dan had the capacity for interesting escapades, even if he managed to bungle many of them. Like most relationships, Gerry gladly accepted the parts of Dan he needed and tried to minimize the importance of Dan's failings. At times like this, those failings were cause for considerable concern.

That penchant for trouble was also the reason it was so easy to enlist Dan in his brother's scheme to get the gold out of Iraq. It required almost two years to sneak the gold to Qatar, a bit at a time, under the auspices of a military equipment withdrawal. It was another year to complete transactions to sell the gold on the black market. Dan extended his Iraqi tour for a year and then stayed in Qatar for another eighteen months to ensure the deed was done. The sale of the jewels kept Richard satisfied while the gold money trickled in.

When it came time to divvy up the proceeds, Dan only received a small portion of the wealth earned through his labor, and he didn't seem to care. The challenge of moving gold and the risk involved was more exciting to Dan than the money itself.

As they followed their prey, even Gerry felt that familiar tingle of anticipation in his limbs, for which he was immediately ashamed.

Dan maintained a steady speed, far enough back that it was unlikely Marco would see them. He allowed one car and then two to insert themselves between the pursued vehicle and their own. When Marco turned right toward the huge, brightly lit sign of an all-night gym, Dan howled in glee. "This is perfect!"

Dan continued down the road for a half mile more and then turned around. "We'll pick him up on the way out. Now, if he just parks away from those spotlights."

They saw Marco entering the gym just as they drove in the direction of the frontage road. Dan parked in shadows along the side of the building, away from curious eyes. Both men were purposely dressed in normal clothes that wouldn't immediately attract attention.

Dan directed Gerry to stay at the furthest corner of the building as a lookout, while he went to work. Carrying a gym bag, Dan strolled along the front side of the building and then walked calmly back to Gerry's position. "There're two video cameras about ten feet up. I seriously doubt they're actively monitored. Most likely, they're recording devices to reassure gym members every effort is taken to provide for their safety. It's just a cover-your-butt exercise because video recordings don't stop crimes. Anyway, we don't want to play a starring role in any video if the police investigate later. They need to be disabled."

Gerry watched as Dan pulled from his gym bag a contraption with an extendable pole, an aerosol canister attached on one end. He scooted along the edge of the building a second time. Within seconds both cameras were blinded by a coat of paint.

Next Dan grabbed an interesting metal gizmo with a short antenna from his bag of tricks. He pressed a button on the side, a light flashed, and then one by one, three vehicles within thirty yards, including Marco's SUV, *thunked* open as locking mechanisms were disengaged. The sound was louder than Gerry would have liked. "Where did you get all this stuff?" he asked.

"My work. They give us all kinds of cool shit."

"Sometime, we need to have a conversation about what exactly it is that you do."

Dan gave Gerry a crooked smile, pulled the mask over his face, and then nodded. Gerry responded by donning his own mask and following Dan to his designated position, crouching behind the far side of Marco's vehicle to wait. He heard the lock reengage after Dan boarded the SUV.

Gerry knew Dan had a baton stun gun and a weapon. He waited with a small revolver, a spray bottle of chloroform, a washcloth, and a pocket full of zip ties. They had argued about whether to bring lethal weapons, and Dan had easily won that fight. He assured Gerry they would need something to intimidate a guy like Marco, and it was essential they come packing in case things didn't go as planned. It was that part, the part where things didn't go as planned, that worried Gerry the most.

Neither man could see Marco approach, but Gerry heard the bleep of the SUV being unlocked from a distance. He jumped slightly at the sound and then squirreled himself lower next to the car. The SUV door opened and then shut. Gerry was not supposed to move too quickly. He had to be certain Dan had Marco immobilized before he entered the vehicle.

Gerry waited and waited, and it wasn't until he felt a subtle rocking of the SUV against his shoulder that it occurred to him something might have gone wrong. He peeked into the vehicle from the side window.

Dan stared back at him, helpless. Blood dripped from his chin, soaked into his shirt like a red collar, and was splattered across the back of both seats. His nose, the source of the gushing blood, was lying at a weird angle from where it used to sit. Marco, with a full-handed grip on Dan's hair, was trying to pull him forward into the front seat. Both of Dan's hands were engaged in a heroic effort to loosen Marco's hold and were empty of anything resembling a weapon. Even worse, Dan's mask had been freed from his head, and now Marco knew the identity of his hapless kidnapper.

Gerry thought to himself that if he didn't hurry, someone would come along. Then there would be yet another witness to their felonious acts. He pulled the revolver from his pocket and struggled in his shock to determine a way to subdue Marco without having to shoot him.

He tried the passenger door, but it was locked. He hadn't heard Marco relock after entry, but either by an ingrained security habit or an automatic system, Gerry was shut out. Marco was continuing to pull Dan forward. Dan's head and shoulders were now fully on the center console as Marco pounded the hell out of his face with his left hand. Even at an awkward angle, his jabs were lightning swift and powerful. Gerry winced at the sight of Dan's face being beaten into a bloody mess.

Pulling the pistol from his pocket, with the butt end, Gerry smashed the side window in one quick hard strike. The sound and shattering of glass caused Marco to look up from his frenzy of punches.

Gerry saw Marco's one good eye glaze and his strong fingers release their grip on Dan's head. He wasn't at all clear why Marco seemed to be shrinking into himself, but he didn't have a moment to lose. He reached through the broken glass, unlocked the door, and scrambled inside as he stuffed the gun in his belt. His hands shaking, he freed the chloroform and wash rag, doused the rag with liquid, and fumbled over Dan's unmoving body to smash the cloth over Marco's nose and face. There was stark fear on Marco's face, but he seemed paralyzed by that fear. Marco feebly tried to pull Gerry's hands away

"Shit, shit, shit!" Gerry sputtered to himself as he waited in a full panic for Marco to go limp. At last, he felt Marco's quivering subside. He left the cloth hanging on Marco's face and slid back to the passenger seat to take a couple of deep breaths. "Dan?" No answer. With trepidation, he felt for a pulse on Dan's neck. Nothing. "Oh, dear God," he wailed.

Gerry got out and then leaped into the SUV from the back seat. Yanking Dan by the legs and cradling his head, he maneuvered Dan from his arched position on the center console to the bench seat in the back. Feeling for a pulse one more time, he climbed on top of the only man he'd ever had a hard time living without and began CPR.

Gerry's face, hands, and shirt were covered in blood after an eternity of effort to resuscitate his once lover. He thought about taking him to the hospital, but he knew Dan was gone. His poor beaten and destroyed face somehow managed to stare back at him in death's embrace, accusing him of cowardice.

He had to keep himself together. Gerry left Dan where he was and went again to the front passenger door to pull Marco into the passenger seat. He leaned him forward and secured his hands behind his back with zip ties, and then placed several around his ankles. The chloroform-sodden cloth had fallen to the floor. He picked it up and doused it with more liquid, pressing the cloth on Marco's face for a few moments. He shut the door and went around to the driver's seat.

Before he engaged the engine, Gerry pushed Marco against the passenger door to make it appear he was merely sleeping. He thought about his next moves. Find a secluded place, transfer both men to the back where they wouldn't be seen, get to Richard's house, and then figure out what to do next.

The tears began to trickle as the impact of Dan's loss and his current position up shit creek hit home. He bit his lower lip. Richard would know what to do, but telling him was an even more frightening prospect than dealing with the situation all alone and without Dan.

Chapter 32
Partnership

Cook and Davies sat on the opposite side of a conference table from Sergeant Murphy and her captain, John Ross. Captain Ross' office was stereotypical of many local police captains: one wall of I-love-me photos, awards, and schooling certificates and another wall dominated by a government framed landscape. His view from a corner location was a parking area filled with squad cars. The furniture was well worn, as was the carpeting. The attitudes were similar as well. The immediate reactions to an unannounced visit by the FBI were suspicion and a circling of the wagons.

Captain Ross, a compact man in his late fifties, had a ruddy complexion and neatly trimmed dark brown hair. His comportment said he was nobody's fool. He maintained a poker face as Davies spoke. She explained they were looking to question a woman by the name of Ms. Marnie Wilson, and in the process of their investigation had come upon her home, recently destroyed by fire. "We learned from a neighbor that you were there at the fire, Sergeant Murphy, and we hoped you might know of her whereabouts. It's just a simple courtesy we're requesting. Also, anything you might know about who was responsible for the fire, since it appears the fire was no accident."

Murphy's face, as neutral as her captain's, hid concern the FBI's interest in Marnie might expose her own largesse while handling Marnie's unusual difficulties. She started to speak, but the captain motioned for her to wait.

"Is Ms. Wilson the subject of an investigation or perhaps an informant?" Ross asked.

"Actually no, but because of national security issues, we're unable to provide any information on the purpose of our desire to speak with her. I can only say it relates to her service in Iraq," Davies answered.

"Do you have any reason to believe she's connected to terrorism? Is she a threat to this community?" the captain snapped back.

"Well, no, not that we're aware."

Murphy was watching the exchange, her head swiveling from the captain to Agent Davies. The FBI agents wanted information, but apparently weren't willing to give any in return. She cared about Marnie's safety and her own reputation. Davies' self-serving attitude chafed, so Murphy interjected. "I hate to play fifty questions, but you leave us no choice. Is she suspected of leaking secret information, providing aid and comfort to an enemy, anything like that? Because if not, I'm not sure why you're here."

The captain gave Murphy a down-girl frown, and then added, "She makes a fair point."

Cook answered. "I'm as frustrated as you about why we can't provide more information. Davies and I haven't been given the full story either because of security classification limitations. We were told to find someone. Ms. Wilson was one of several candidates. Now we think she might be the woman we're looking for, and frankly, that she could be in danger."

Murphy waited for the captain to take the lead. He was good at this sort of thing, and he didn't disappoint. Ross jumped in with both feet. "Sounds to me like the government is hiding something they don't want in the public square. I hate to be a conspiracy nut, because believe me, the world doesn't need any more, but what you've just told us is rather strange. And in danger from whom?" the captain asked.

"We don't know that either," Davies lamented.

Murphy's fingers were tapping the table. If Marnie was in danger, and she was certain that was the case, the FBI had far more resources to find her than their small police force could ever hope to amass. "I think you're right that she's under threat, but I don't know where she is. I've tried to follow-up several times, and I can't contact her. The last time I spoke with her, she said she was going 'off the grid.'"

"Why didn't you bring her in for questioning?" Davies huffed.

"On what? She hasn't committed a crime that I'm aware of, a fact she reminded me of when I said I was going to put a BOLO on her. I'm worried about her, but last time I checked, we still have laws in the country that protect its citizens. Although sometimes you'd hardly know it. Look, I'm willing to share everything I know with you on one condition, that you take me along on the search."

"Tiffany," the captain warned. "We need to share everything we know because they'll just compel the information anyway."

Being chastised didn't stop Murphy from giving a hard stare at Cook and Davies. "Marnie's a veteran, and from what I can tell, she's had a hard time. I know her, and I can help. I think she trusts me."

Davies and Cook were communicating silently. Cook nodded. "I think we can work with that. I'll have to obtain clearance from my supervisor about how far I can read you in. Now, about your last call with Ms. Wilson, if she used a cell, we can track her."

"Probably not," Murphy sighed. "My impression was that she astutely removed the cell battery after she finished a conversation. In the short time I've known her, she has changed her cell number once. Marnie's probably using burner phones. Even a novice at escaping detection knows you can't hide if you carry around a charged cell."

Davies responded. "With a time and date, we can track her last known location and start from there."

Cook asked the captain, "Is this okay with you, Captain Ross? Can you afford to let Officer Murphy help us if I get approval from my chain?"

The captain chuckled, the corners of his eyes folding. "If I know Murphy, she'll help in her off-duty time even if I say no. Right, Murphy?"

With a cherubic face, bright green eyes, and frizzled hair, Murphy nearly glowed in response.

"Give me a moment to call home, and then we can get started," Cook said.

Chapter 33
Storm Brewing

It was an overcast morning, and my mood synced with flattened and agitated grey clouds warning of rain in the distance. In my bones, I could feel the barometric pressure dropping.

Buck was restless too. He'd just placed a tennis ball into my lap for the hundredth time. I aimed toward the sliding glass doors and gently lobbed the lime green and dirt-stained object for my buddy to retrieve. "Okay, Buck. We'll go for a run in a few minutes. Just let me finish this list, please."

He scrambled, stopped just short of the door, scooped the ball in powerful jaws, trotted to me to dump again, and returned to his spot in anticipation. I smiled at his persistence and then ignored him. My list wasn't much of a list, more like ideas that were forming and coalescing into improbable and frightening theories about events behind the scenes in Iraq when I was too mentally scrambled to notice.

If the Dan I knew from group, the same one that had warned me about being followed, was the same Captain Dan who had recommended me for a silver star, then he was either part of a conspiracy or trying to protect me from one. Either way, friend or foe, he knew about the gold, the jewels, and WMD before I made my call to the FBI.

I was frustrated that I didn't know my Dan's last name. He'd only been in my group for two months. If he or someone else had mentioned his last name, I hadn't bothered to pay attention. When he'd offered to help, I hadn't even asked for a last name. *Way to go, Marnie, you dumbass.*

Even if these two Dans were one and the same, and he'd found the buried storage space himself, it still wouldn't explain how he knew about me. There was only one possibility that made any sense. Mac had told someone else before his death. My mind travelled back to the night Mac and I had argued about going to Colonel Jamison.

* * *

For three days after we'd found the stash, Mac held his tongue. Zeke was on duty the evening of the third day, and Mac and I were alone in the witheringly hot team operations tent, the din of a blowing fan making communication without shouting an exercise in futility. I'd just won the fifth hand in a row at two-person poker. I remember musing to myself that in any other time or place, we could be playing strip poker rather than betting with cans of Rock Star energy drinks.

He smacked the table with his losing hand of cards before he turned them over. "Damn, Marnie. I guess I should be thankful we can't play for money or I wouldn't have the shirt on my back."

"Or the pants on your butt," I replied with a mischievous grin.

A sly smile took one half of his mouth. "Aw, Marnie. Don't go there."

We stared at each other over a tiny collapsible table, me perched on a cot and him on a folding chair that didn't sit straight. He looked away first and then moved to turn down the fan. "We need to talk," he whispered. "I've given you some time, but

227

we need to go to Jamison. It's gonna seem squirrely if we don't do it soon."

"Hold that thought," I replied and held up a finger.

Shuffling to my personal foot locker, I set the snacks and full water bottles sitting on top aside and rifled to the bottom through rarely used military clothing and equipment. I found the deep-green cloth barracks bag and handed it to Mac. "Open it."

He frowned as he unloosed the knot in a string tie. Reaching inside, Mac first felt the contents, his expression confused, and then grasped a handful and extracted his arm. He didn't immediately understand what he was holding, but when he did, his face went white. "Marnie, what have you done? What the hell is this?"

"Just what it looks like, Mac. Jewels. Probably worth millions of dollars. I had to see what was in those ammo cases, and I found them."

"Get rid of them! Jesus." He rubbed his face.

"Why? No one knows they exist. I didn't do anything that three-quarters of the people here wouldn't have done too."

"Because if you're caught with them after we go to Jamison, you'll be in serious trouble. Is that what you want, Marnie? We can't keep what we found secret."

"Why can't we keep it a secret?"

"Dammit, because of the WMD! You want that stuff used on our troops? That what you want?" Mac was trying not to yell, but his voice was straining under the weight of his passion. "And, reporting WMD is the right thing to do."

I sighed, which seemed to make him more upset. Mac's lips tightened, and his neck jutted forward.

"I just don't see it that way. That space had been closed a long time, and whoever put it down there is long gone. It was probably Saddam Hussein or one of his dead lieutenants. The chance that anyone will happen upon that desolate place again is one in a million."

"And you think it's okay for every soldier sent to this hellhole to risk their necks, for them to go on believing they're participating a huge damn mistake? That WMD in Iraq was a lie?"

"Do those WMDs really prove this war wasn't a mistake?" I asked.

At my statement, Mac turned and stormed out. He was quiet the next couple of days and didn't mention our argument. I'd allowed myself to believe he was thinking about what I'd said and what those jewels could mean to our future. Mac made decisions in his own time and own way. It wouldn't help to nag him or try to convince him of my truth. After a few more days, our mission shifted, and the entire issue of buried treasure and buried weapons of mass destruction seemed less important than staying alive.

* * *

In hindsight, maybe I'd convinced myself of what I wanted to believe, that Mac had let it go— that he'd changed his mind just like when he'd surprised me with a visit to the underground room. But maybe, I was wrong. Could he have confessed to someone? Someone like this Dan?

Buck, dozing on the floor now with his head on his paws, perked up when he heard me stand, ready to follow me wherever I went. "Let's split this joint. It's a nice place Kevin's got here, but we shouldn't get too comfortable."

Without a smartphone or tablet, I was really, truly off the grid. I badly needed to find a computer to search for information about Dan. If an internet search didn't work, I would go see Dr. Santori, our group leader. She'd have access to Dan's background and might help me if I could convince her Dan was posing as someone completely different in group. Then again, she might believe me certifiable if my imaginings were dead wrong.

If I had more cash or could use my credit cards, I'd go buy another smartphone. My cash reserves nearly gone, a public library would be the best bet for computer access. That's what the folks running from bad guys in every mystery I've ever read always did. I hoped free library access to the internet wasn't just fiction, because I hadn't been to a library since I was sixteen.

First a run to calm my nerves and Buck's, and then I'll start my search in earnest. As I stepped out the door, it was sprinkling, but thus far no thunder or lightening. "Maybe we can squeeze in our run before the storm hits, Buck." I chuckled to myself. *That sounds very prophetic, Marnie.*

Chapter 34
Huntress

After a grueling run, I showered and selected one of my three remaining on-the-lam outfits, the only one that was clean. If I had a few dimes to spare, I might visit one of my stores to purchase nearly new apparel that would buoy my spirits in the search for my pursuers. But I didn't. I'd be lucky to continue to buy gas and feed myself and Buck. The role of huntress would have to be performed in plain but classic capris and a white short-sleeved top that my mother might have chosen. All in all, my clothing said, *forget me*, which, given current circumstances, was probably for the best.

I dined on the last of the cereal and milk, and Buck polished off the final cans of tuna. The rain had held for our run, but soft thunder booms in the background signaled that ion-charged electricity would soon change to liquid. The downpour started just before we exited the garage on our way to the one library I held in my memory.

The wet jog between the car and the front library entry was enough to ensure the air-conditioning inside gave me a full bloom of goosebumps. I waited in line with Buck to learn how to sign up for computer usage. An older man working the counter was most helpful. I applied for the mandatory library card, a four-page tome with the requisite warnings and reminders of things I should never do, and dire consequences should I chose to ignore those warnings. When I'd filled in every blank, and yes, the old dude checked, he gave me a number for my twenty-minute session on one of their two computer terminals. *Wonderful, only an hour to wait. Why is nothing ever truly free or easy?*

Using the time productively, I found a stack of interesting fiction novels I could read for free using my brand-spanking-new library card. I kept my eyes glued to the number monitor, and when my number came up, I scurried to replace what appeared to be a homeless woman the second she vacated her seat.

Dan Wojocowski wasn't a popular name, and I found him quickly. I scribbled the name of two relatives, his age, and his most likely current address on a notepad. I did a Google Maps search of his address and then hit street view. *Whoa, the Dan that owns that house has some dough.* The newer home on the screen wasn't huge, but it reeked of expensive construction. Pushing the mouse to get a better view of the neighborhood, I found Dan's house wasn't just a one-off in a bad neighborhood. The other homes in the surrounding area were even more grand, some quite large. Having searched for a home I could afford in every hill and dale in ten counties, I knew Dan's place was rich, upwards of a million and probably more like two.

Where would a special forces NCO like my Dan, or even a logistics captain like the one from SGM William's memory, have accrued that kind of money? Sure, there's always the inheritance route or good jobs and lucky investments, but playing the odds, I knew that kind of luck wasn't likely. I returned to Google and scrolled through every listing that contained both his first and last name.

One business reference cited a Dan Wojocowski as the owner of an LLC called DSki Consulting in Raleigh, North Carolina. Consulting would fit with what my Dan had said about his work schedule, several months of employment followed by months of time off. I made another note even though that information wasn't particularly useful.

I glanced at the clock. Time was running out. Thus far there were no photographs or articles that conclusively connected Dan with one identity or another. I hit photo view and a screen of Dans appeared, none of them mine. The last mention of a Dan Wojocowski was a list of Old Dominion University alumni members. If this were my Dan, it could mean he was a college graduate and probably an army officer rather than enlisted, scant evidence but something. My screen popped back to the main menu, signaling my twenty minutes was up. I moaned and then sighed to Buck, "That's all folks."

The same homeless woman from earlier was standing impatiently behind my computer station leering, waiting to take my spot. Less than five feet tall, the woman of unknowable age managed to cut an imposing figure wearing a bright green, crinkly raincoat, the huge pockets filled with survival gear. Her hair was pinned to her scalp with bobby pins, a few dead bits of leaves caught in brown strands. She reminded me of a short friend of mine and how she'd looked whenever we were on field-training exercises. Even the scowl was familiar. "Did they give you more than one number?" I asked as she tapped her foot. I stood up and moved my butt from the chair so as not to be dislodged by a scoot.

"How else you gonna get done what you need to get done?" she replied. Her eyes turned from mine; her fingers were already busily logging on.

"Thanks for the tip." I filed that information away for next time. If we hurried, we still had time to drive to the VA and beg for a minute of Dr. Santori's time.

Buck loped after me to the quick book checkout. I scanned my card and then the books and waited until a receipt was printed. A library guard, yes, libraries need guards these days, checked my receipt against the books under my arm. We ran like the wind through the rain. While jumping aboard the Caprice, I considered how being flat broke had opened to me a new world of reading enjoyment. I could get free books at the library. Who knew?

Chapter 35
VA Waiting Room, Again

I wondered if Mary, the VA welcome desk attendant, would allow me to sit here until close of office hours and then give me a sad song and dance or an I-told-you-so. She had made it quite clear, "We can't handle walk-ins. If you have an issue that must be immediately addressed, Marnie, call the mental health emergency desk and someone will assist you. I can even walk you down there if you'd like."

"It's not like that, Mary. I need to see Dr. Santori. She's the only one that can help," I implored.

"Are you having a crisis or are you considering taking your own life? I'm sorry to put it so bluntly, but you don't look yourself, and I'm concerned."

I tamped down the growing heat I was feeling from her patronizing tone. "First, it's raining outside, and I'm wet. I have a crisis of information, that's all. Information only Dr. Santori would know. And I'm not considering suicide!" I stopped and swallowed to regain control of my temper. "I'll just wait here in this dreary waiting room and read a book. If you could, please tell Dr. Santori I'll wait, and I only need a few minutes of her time. That's all I ask. If the day ends and she can't see me, so be it. I'll come back tomorrow."

Mary exhaled in frustration. "All right, but no guarantees."

Another trauma group had cycled in and out during the afternoon. As the minutes crept toward

4:30, I was beginning to lose hope. Finally, Dr. Santori's grey wiry curls poked out of the door, and her eyes searched the room for me. I was already standing to catch her attention. "Oh, there you are, Marnie. Please, come in," she waved.

She lightly touched my arm when I joined her. "I'm sorry you had to wait so long, but I had a very full schedule today." Her voice was amazing, deep and melodic, sincere, kind, and all playing in concert with an overriding hint of wisdom.

"I understand. I'm sorry for the drop in, but I needed some information and soon."

"So I was told. Hi to you too, Buck. It's been awhile since you've been around. I miss your friendly face." Buck wagged and grinned.

She motioned for me to take a seat in her small office and then sat next to me rather than behind her desk. I wasn't sure what that meant, probably some psychological technique warranted by my stubborn refusal to take no for an answer.

"We've missed you at the last two sessions," Dr. Santori started and then became quiet. Shrinks always do that to get you to talk. Stop and let you fill in the silence. The technique was so predictable it was almost laughable. I had on occasion waited them out just for fun, even knowing my behavior was kind of mean, but I didn't want to waste time today.

"Some stuff came up. I haven't quit on you though. Here's the deal, Doc. In the last two weeks, someone has followed me, broken into my house, and then burned it to the ground. I'm homeless right now and need some help."

Dr. Santori started with the shocked face, which would be quickly followed by real compassion, and then the always perplexing, "How does that make you feel?" question. How else should I feel? I always wanted to scream, "Like shit!" Rather than go there, I short circuited her routine.

"Please, Dr. Santori, I'm not done. I have reason to believe Dan in our group could be involved in my recent problems. I need to know whether he is a special forces NCO and his last name, which I apologize for not knowing. If you could verify his military record to confirm he is what he says he is and give me his last name, that would go a long way toward taking him off my suspect list."

Dr. Santori recovered quickly after my claim. Certainly, in her business, she had heard more than a few whoppers and was prepared for the unusual story. "Marnie, if what you say is true, that's a matter for the police. And I know you understand our privacy practices. There is simply no way I could give you information about another patient. I'm really very sorry to hear of your recent tragedies, and I'm willing to stay and talk with you about it."

She was a nice lady with a hard job, but my abruptness was necessary. For the first time, a part of me felt ready to dump this morass of doubt, guilt, and pain on another human being. However, now was not the time. I pressed on. "You don't have to tell me anything about another patient. I only need confirmation that Dan is what he pretends to be and his last name. Simple."

"No, it isn't that simple. If Dan is posing as someone else, he has his reasons. It wouldn't be the first time a patient has created an unreal world to deal with trauma. In fact, that happens quite frequently."

"If you don't mind me saying so, that sounds like mumbo jumbo to me," I huffed, struggling to hold my ground and not appear to be in the throes of a psychotic break. "In this case, the purpose of the deceit would be nefarious. Are you willing to take that chance with my safety, Dr. Santori? Would his last name hurt?"

"No. The last thing I want is to jeopardize your safety. Why don't we call security and see if they can connect you with the correct police department to investigate your concerns."

Ah oh. More police involvement was the worst possible outcome of this meeting. Trying to affect the most sane, calm Marnie I could project, I lowered my voice into the I-give-up-range. "I appreciate your help, Dr. Santori. I've been working with the police in my city. I just thought that maybe I could help them find whoever it is that's making my life hell." I gave her the saddest, sweetest smile in my repertoire.

"Maybe if you could tell me why you think Dan is involved," she answered.

This might be a ploy to keep me talking. *I hate to be paranoid, but what if she has a buzzer somewhere to bring the guys with long needles and butterfly nets?* I checked my cell. "Oh, jeez. I have an appointment to see a short-term rental apartment. I gotta run. I'd love to take you up on that talk sometime. I'll schedule an appointment next time. No hard feelings about the Dan thing."

Dr. Santori's lips were pressed together in a what-the-hell-just-happened expression as I all but ran out of her office, and Buck had to hustle to catch up with me.

"Well that sucked, Buck. What now? Just when I thought we were making progress."

Chapter 36
Gerry

When Gerry heard Marco moan, he decided he had to stop. He couldn't allow Marco to wake. Gerry turned off a country road onto gravel and drove into a deserted area of marshes. Clumps of deciduous trees stood atop raised sections and grew at an identical angle away from prevailing winds. The low roar of insects chimed their presence, and a half moon flickered in and out of focus from wispy clouds. Even though it was warm, Gerry felt chilled. He thought the eeriness of the night might have something to do with the dead body in the back of his vehicle, a man he had loved, and the semi-comatose figure of another man he had kidnapped.

He opened the rear door of the SUV. During the journey, Dan's body had rolled, and his face was the first thing Gerry saw as the door swung upward. Closed, mangled eyes and a flattened nose made a gruesome parody of the Dan he knew. For the second time that evening, Gerry stumbled away from the SUV and vomited, this time more acidic bile than chunks of snack food. His stomach continued to contract even beyond the point where there was anything left to expel.

Shaking and forlorn, he pushed his hands from his knees, spit out what was left in his mouth, and then wiped his face with the back of his hand. Only a few miles to go.

After the total evacuation of his stomach contents, Gerry reluctantly moved to the SUV, reached across Dan's already stiffening body, and placed the fruity, chemical smelling rag over Marco's nose. He just hoped he didn't kill him too. Gerry had no idea how much chloroform to use and whether too much could be fatal. So far, the man was still breathing.

He sat for a moment in the driver's seat, trying to slow his mind and control the waves of body shakes. *I should be better than this,* he reminded himself. *I had military training. I served during war. I've seen dead bodies before. Yeah well,* his other side argued, *you were never much of a leader or good in a pinch. Face it, Gerry, you've always been a follower—more interested in pleasing everyone else and not making trouble than taking the bull by the horns on your own.*

He'd always done what Richard had told him because he didn't want to anger him, and that approach was easier than arguing with Richard and paying a price. Gerry didn't tell his mom or dad about the cats or his suspicions, even when Little Boy, his favorite cat, had disappeared. Deep down Gerry was afraid they wouldn't believe him, and Richard would exact revenge.

Gerry went along with Dan's shenanigans because he'd loved him and some darkness inside needed the thrill. He'd always known Dan was a bumbler, imperiling himself at every turn. He'd even roped Dan into Richard's scheme to steal the gold because he knew Dan would do it, and Richard was breathing down his neck to find someone.

Gerry wasn't sure if he hated himself or his brother more. He was only sure of one thing—he had to finish this: get Marco to talk, turn the information over to his brother, get rid of Dan's body, and then run. Run for his life. Take the money that he'd hidden away and find a place where his brother couldn't follow. If such a place existed.

At least Marco hadn't seen his face. Unlike Dan, he'd kept his face cover on in Marco's presence. Gerry was angry that Marco had killed Dan, but he knew Marco had only been protecting himself. In a way, he respected this SEAL for having the wherewithal to fight with such deadly force at a moment's notice. Gerry didn't think he'd have been so ready. If he could get Marco to talk, he could set him free, do one decent thing before he split. Marnie, on the other hand, was a goner. There was nothing Gerry could do anymore to protect her from Richard.

Chapter 37
The Principal

The FBI agents in dark suits stood in wild contrast to harried elementary school teachers and exuberant children. Cook and Davies entered the school office first, while Sergeant Murphy lagged to take a drink from a water fountain. Two little girls began screaming at the sight of Cook and Davies. The children had been waiting for their parents to collect them and being well versed in the perils and procedures of school shooters, they had mistakenly arrived at the conclusion the FBI agents were there to kill them.

Jada Jordon was the first to leap to the side of the frightened children and reassure them that these unsmiling individuals were in fact the police. Sergeant Murphy strolled in to the shocked expressions of her temporary partners and the wailing girls. At the sight of Murphy's police uniform, the children began to calm, and Jada asked her assistant to walk them outside the office until they had calmed down. "How can I help you?" Jada asked. "It might be wise in the future to call first," she chided.

Kevin, having heard the excitement, was already moving with alacrity into the reception area to ascertain the source of the noise. When he saw the FBI agents and a police officer, his heart skipped a beat. "I'm Kevin Prescott, the school principal. Is there an emergency?"

Murphy spoke first. "No, no emergency. We're sorry if our unannounced presence caused such a disturbance, but I'm pleased to see everyone is so aware of strangers, including the children. We were hoping to speak with you about one of your employees."

Certain of the employee they were seeking, Kevin did his best to remain calm. "Of course, please follow me." He led the procession to his office, where Murphy introduced herself and the FBI agents. Kevin offered drinks that were declined, and after everyone sat, he waited for Murphy to continue.

"We're here about Marnie Wilson. I assume you're familiar with her?"

"Certainly. She's one of our part-time teachers. I imagine you know that already."

Murphy chuckled. "Just trying to get a conversational flow going, but you're obviously a guy that likes to get right at it. Ms. Wilson is currently listed as a missing person. We're trying to locate her. The last cell communication she made three days ago came from this building. Do you know anything about that or her whereabouts?"

"I doubt that she's missing, Officer Murphy. She stopped by here three days ago to ask for some time off. She told me that her house had burned down. She was out of sorts—I mean, who wouldn't be? Marnie said she was going to go visit her mother, in San Antonio I believe. Have you phoned her mother?"

"We have, and her mother was quite upset when we told her of the fire. She hasn't heard from her daughter in a week."

"That's not good," Kevin replied. "Now I'm worried."

"How long was she here at the school in total? Do you know?"

"Not long, I would think. After we met and discussed some time off, she asked if she could use the computer in the library because hers had been destroyed in the fire. I told her to have at it, but I have no idea how long she stayed after she left my office. I can ask the librarian to see if he remembers more specifically. Do you expect foul play?"

"Not necessarily."

"Sergeant Murphy, the fact that FBI agents have joined you in your search tells me there is far more to Marnie's absence than a simple missing person."

Because none of the three officers of the law were willing to share information, Murphy changed the subject. "Is there a back exit to the school? We can check, but it will save us time to know. Also, Marnie's car is in your parking lot. She either left on foot from here or someone gave her a ride."

"Oh, the car! I completely forgot. She asked if she could leave it here while she travelled to her mother's home."

Murphy pressed, "Did she mention how she was getting to the airport? Does she have any close friends at the school?"

"I'm sorry, but I didn't think to ask about her mode of transportation." Murphy caught a note of sarcasm in his answer. She wondered if Davies and Cook picked up on it. Kevin continued, "I assumed she would call an Uber or something. As far as friends, none that I'm aware of. She keeps mostly to herself. Marnie and I share a love of reading, and I've traded book recommendations with her, but other than me and maybe Jada, I'm not sure anyone else knows her other than by sight."

"I would like to speak with Jada before we leave, and the librarian."

"Of course, I'll give you the use of my office. Sergeant Murphy, after our conversation I'm really concerned. Will you please let me know if you find her? I'm feeling guilty that I didn't pay enough attention to someone who may have been in real distress."

"I'll let you know," Murphy answered.

* * *

Standing around Marnie's SUV, Murphy said, "There's no luggage in her vehicle, and the back door is damaged. She didn't have her suitcases with her in the school. Unless she left them somewhere else, it would appear her luggage has been stolen from her SUV while it was parked here. Jada mentioned she was carrying a big black bag when she entered the school. Is it possible she was trying to fool someone into believing she would return to her vehicle? That she was attempting to throw off a tail? The forensics team is on the way now to go over her SUV. I'll wait for them if you guys want to take off."

Cook seemed distracted. He was rubbing his foot on the blacktop like something was eating at him. "What did you think of the principal, Murph?"

"Funny you should ask. I got some weird vibes, but I couldn't say why. He appeared perfectly at ease, and he had an answer for everything. Almost as if his answers were too practiced. I also thought he was a bit too cavalier about a missing teacher."

"My take too," Davies chimed in. "Could be nothing but our imaginations. Then again. . ."

Cook shook his head. "Let's do a little digging about Principal Kevin tonight. Is the plan still to meet at nine at the station tomorrow and head to the VA? We need to identify this Marco without a last name. Hopefully, you're right Murphy, and the trauma group leader will confirm Marco is in Marnie's group. The VA should be able to give us his last name so we can track him down."

"Works for me," Murphy answered.

A bad feeling in her gut, Murphy watched the two FBI Special Agents, their heads tilted in conversation, move toward their rental car. *Where the hell are you, Marnie, and what are you mixed up in?* She thought again about the Marnie she'd known only a short time, and she still couldn't believe that Marnie would ever be guilty of betraying her country. *Perfect, no. Flawed, most definitely. Disloyal, no way.*

She'd tried to get Cook or Davies to slip and provide more information, taking turns with Cook and then Davies, peppering them with questions whenever she had a chance. The story they were sticking with was that Marnie had some knowledge of an important event in Iraq, period, and Murphy couldn't get the buttoned-up bastards to divulge anything else. She'd ended up in the same place where she'd started, back when she'd first learned Marnie's house had been searched. Marnie held dangerous insights into a crime, her haunted expression a true reflection of her fear, more than her words.

For all Marnie's quirks and bluster, what Murphy saw underneath it all was a spine of steel and a stubbornness that meant Marnie wouldn't quit unless forced. She needed to find her before Marnie got herself into some deep kimchee—deep enough, it got her killed.

Chapter 38
Mostly a Freebie

As the sun rose on another hot, humid day, I decided a walk with Buck would fulfill my exercise requirement. We drove to Buck's favorite park—his favorite because he loved watching and sometimes harassing the ducks that lived there in a pond situated near one of the walking trails.

I needed to clear my head and try again to contact Marco. Maybe he would remember Dan's last name. We stopped at a bench along the walking trail, and I tried once more to reach him, the call ringing through to voicemail. I thumbed two texts and told him I would call at 7 p.m. and to please be available. I probably didn't have the right to be so demanding since I'd walked out of his life with no warning. We didn't have an official relationship, but I thought my unannounced departure probably stung. He was most likely busy, I consoled myself.

Buck gazed at me and whined. He was wearing his hungry stare. We set off for the car at a rapid clip. I swung by a discount grocery store on the way back to Kevin's place. With only $89.37 left in cash, I chose a ten-pound bag of the cheapest dog food in the store, wondered if I could eat the same thing, and decided I wasn't that desperate—yet. I purchased two dozen eggs and a box of instant pancake mix. A day or two of protein and carbs for under four bucks.

What I really wanted was a smartphone. I needed internet that didn't require a phone plan or a trip to the library. The library computer system was a less than ideal means to gather miscellaneous information of questionable worth, and unfortunately, smartphones were so ridiculously expensive you had to take a two-year loan to pay for them. I didn't know anyone that might have a spare.

On a whim, I dropped by an independently owned electronics repair shop that I had used once for a printer that ate paper. They were good and reasonably priced. Who knows, maybe they had something old, repaired, cheap, and that needed a good home.

These sorts of places were a lot like my clothing resale boutiques, filled to the brim with all manner of stuff, trying to be organized and falling just short of chaos. I saw the shop intake coordinator in the back working with a tiny screwdriver in the guts of an aged computer tower. He wasn't the same guy that I'd seen here before. His head popped up when he heard me, and then, unfurling a six-foot, four-inch bundle of stringy limbs, he strolled to a position behind the counter.

The young man, probably early twenties and skinny in the same way as Zeke, pushed his glasses up on his nose twice before he spoke. I liked him already. His hair appeared not to have been combed in at least two days, and his pallor marked him as someone who didn't spend much time outdoors. Classic nerd, with tattoos on his arms that were both strange and undecipherable.

He had a great smile, and his eyes flashed with a glint that I knew meant he possessed an always ready sense of humor. He reminded me so much of a long-haired, tattooed Zeke, I wasn't sure if I wanted to cry or hug him. "What can I do for you on this fine day?" he asked.

"I have a rather unusual request."

"Hit me with it," he answered.

"So, my house burned down, and I lost my tablet and my cell in the fire. I'm still waiting on the insurance check to come in, and I'm a little strapped for cash. Would you maybe have anything portable and cheap where I could get internet access?"

He checked out Buck and then me more closely. "We don't do a lot of resale business, but if I'm reading you right, you need internet temporarily—something that can't be tracked."

"Well no, I didn't say that at all," I sputtered.

"Right. Hang here a second."

He sauntered into a back room and returned carrying an Apple tablet. "Special deal today, a once-in-a-lifetime opportunity. This is mine, and I don't use it much. I'm willing to loan it to you if you'll consider going on a date with me sometime after you return it to me."

I began to laugh. "You do know that's sexual harassment, don't you? I could turn you in to the owner."

"Naw, not meant that way. I mean this in the most respectful way, but you're a very hot, older lady. Most of the women that come in here have white hair and are hauling computers still running on Windows XP. I'll let you use my tablet even if you say no, but what's the harm in asking?" He charmed me with a guileless smile.

"Word to the wise, using *old* in a come-on sentence is a guaranteed deal breaker."

"Good point. Anyway, the owner's my uncle. Don't bother filling him in. He can't afford to hire anyone else that knows computer repair. Just think about it—the date, that is."

"And you'll let me use this tablet either way? There isn't a camera on here that can spy on me, right?"

Now he was laughing. "Whatever you got going on, this puppy ain't no spying machine. It's slow as hell, too."

"Do you need a name or something? I don't have an address now."

"Nope, just bring it back when you're done. I trust you."

"Thank you?"

"The name's Nathan."

"I'm Marnie. You remind me so much of a guy I used to know." My voice nearly cracked when I said it.

"Did you want to date him?"

"No, but I cared about him a lot."

He picked up on my sadness and cut the cute smile. "That's good enough, Ms. Marnie. Your dog looks hungry." He pulled dog treats from under the counter. "Mind?"

"Not at all." After Buck woofed two decent-sized milk bones, I shook Nathan's hand, thanked him profusely, and said over my shoulder before I left, "I'll return this, I promise."

"I know," Nathan replied.

Chapter 39
Booted

A smile on my face after meeting a good-willed Zeke lookalike, I was armed with an untraceable computer with its very own phone number and Wi-Fi connectivity. We headed to Kevin's home away from home. Somewhere along the way, I'd lost sight of the fact that there were still good people in the world. My spirits had been lifted by another trusting stranger.

A nagging inner voice didn't allow me much time to savor high spirts and reminded me I was getting nowhere fast on my search for the bad guys. I thought about the DNA test results, which led me to consider Marco's cousin, and finally my mind quit circling and landed on Marco. I sincerely hoped Marco wouldn't be another unrequited love situation, although our relationship seemed to be trending in that direction.

Hungry, we rushed into the house. The first thing I noticed was a flashing light on a hanging wall phone in the kitchen. Surprised Kevin had bothered with a wired phone, I considered listening to the message and then thought better. His phone calls were none of my business.

Buck was famished and pacing. I heaped dry dog food into a bowl, set the bowl on the floor with Buck's nose following my progress, and then began preparation of my feast. The side of the pancake mix box made claim that it contained sixteen pancakes. As I dumped half the box into a mixing bowl, my eyes caught the annoying flashing message light again.

What was it about a flashing light that was so impossible to ignore? *Maybe it's something important.* A head slapping moment hit like a thunderclap. *Duh, Marnie, Kevin has no way to contact you; the call could be from him.* Pancakes could wait, I pressed the message button.

"Marnie, it's Kevin. I have some bad news. The FBI and a Sergeant Murphy were at the school this morning looking for you. I lied to them. I said I didn't know where you were. I'm calling from my brother's house just in case they're tracing my phone. They tracked your last call to the school, and that's how they ended up at my door.

"I hate to say it, but I think you're going to have to leave. That house is in my name. If they didn't buy my story, I'd say the police could be there as soon as tomorrow." There was a pause in the message, and I thought he'd said his peace, but then Kevin started again.

"I'm so very sorry, but I can't afford to get caught lying to the FBI. I could lose my job, my career for lying and hiding you, a possible fugitive." I winced at the word fugitive. "Just so you know, I still believe in you. The Caprice is in my mom's name, so keep it and return it later. If you need cash, under the kitchen sink there's a silver polish container. There should be about four hundred dollars inside. Take it and pay me back when you can."

He sighed. "You should probably leave today. I wish I could do more. Stay safe, Marnie and have faith this will all work out." Another pause. "Maybe you should turn yourself in."

"For what?" I screamed at the answering machine. Heat surged, and my heart pounded, sending blood swooshing through my ears. My body hadn't turned on me in that crippling version of panic in several days, not since I fought my demons to the ground at the fire. If I could watch my life go up in smoke, I could surely leave the safety of another man's home. Who gives a damn what anyone else believes? All that mattered now was to learn the full truth. Only then would I have a real future.

Breathing in and out slowly, I turned to my last refuge. "Buck, it's just you and me now."

I added the remainder of the pancake box contents to the bowl. "No point being hungry and screwed. Right Buck?"

* * *

Buck and I were traipsing back and forth in a mall, waiting for 7 p.m. to try Marco again. When the time finally came, I sat in a lounge chair near an indoor children's play area. The children's boisterous laughs and giggles washed over me. I could almost pretend one of them was mine, that Buck and I were waiting for our own special child, enjoying every minute of their antics. Buck was watching one little black-haired boy about two, his head following the child's movements around the enclosed area, wanting to join the fun.

Pressing the battery into Marco's phone, I touched the call button and held my breath. I held my breath for ten rings until my call passed to voicemail. I tried again and then followed up with three quick texts, begging him to answer. Nothing.

Chewing the skin around my nails, I wondered if I should wait ten more minutes and try once more. Maybe he was just late, or maybe Marco forgot, or maybe it was one of those days when he didn't have time to check his phone. That last rationalization was surely not true.

I held myself together for fifteen more minutes. As I people watched, I wondered what sort of worries those who passed me might hold. Were any of them homeless like me? And perhaps only one catastrophe away from utter madness? Were their burdens so heavy, the only thing left was to stroll aimlessly along the temperature-controlled, well-tended interior of a retail facility to the tune of an elevator version of the Beatles' "Yesterday" while dreaming of a better life that might never exist?

One last try. After several rings, someone picked up. "Marco, thank God! I was worried." Silence on the other end. "Marco?" A grunt and a moan, seconds of silence, a terrified scream in the background, more silence, and then a click of disconnection.

As if the phone in my hand had eyes, I yanked the battery from its holding prongs and stood. "Come Buck, now."

We hustled through a large department store and ran to the Caprice. I knew where I was headed for the night, but it wasn't yet dark. Talking myself in and out of borrowing Kevin's money, I had finally landed on yes. There was no other reasonable choice. Total, my cash reserves with Kevin's silver polish stash were $452 and some change. That amount wouldn't last long if I had to pay for a motel, even one where most residents rented by the hour.

When we were well clear of the mall, I drove to a Home Depot parking lot. Using Nathan's iPad to find a phone number to call Marco's cousin, I identified several work-related numbers. Only one number appeared to be personal. I used an application on the Apple and pressed in Anton's personal cell, but the familiar tones indicated a disconnected number. A feeling of dread was spreading. I had the urge to vomit a mound of pancakes.

Would someone be waiting for me at Marco's if I drove to his apartment? If I contacted Murphy from this parking lot, would she go check on Marco or use the call location to pursue me first? Was I blowing hysterically out of proportion what I heard on the phone? Paralyzed with fear and indecision, at the bottom of my soul, I wished that moan from Marco's phone was only my vivid imagination, but I didn't believe it. Marco was in trouble.

If my pursuers had taken Marco to get to me, I doubted Murphy could immediately find him or his kidnappers. My best hope, maybe my last hope, was to obtain those DNA results and pray they would lead me to the people holding Marco. If I couldn't reach Anton or if he didn't have the results, I would make another call on Marco's phone and offer a trade. Find someplace safe for Buck to live and give myself up to the bad guys in exchange for Marco. If necessary, I could offer them the jewels too. I wouldn't have a use for them.

The act of deciding has always helped me. Even if my decision was ultimately uninformed or myopic, I experienced a short-term blast of relief until the results were known. Doubting myself in the interim, between the decision and the outcome, never seemed to serve a useful purpose.

Finally, dusk arrived. I powered down the iPad and turned on the Caprice. By the time we arrived at the Coffee Roaster, they were closed and locked up tight. I turned into the alley where I had first taken refuge, on that day when Dan had informed me I was being followed, and I squeezed the SUV between a dumpster and a wood fence in the back of the coffee shop. No one would know we were here.

Completely confused, Buck's beautiful face stared at me, wanting to know what to do next. I climbed into the back seat and called to him. He jumped over the hump and cuddled next to me. I stroked him as I read by flashlight until my eyes would no longer stay open.

I didn't know if the dreams would come. *Let them find me if they must.* I had completely given myself over to ending this waking nightmare, and on a warm, late summer night, hidden behind a dumpster with my dog, that was enough. The tears I shed were only a symbol of the journey and the nearness of the end of my quest.

Chapter 40
Truth Seeks the Surface

Murphy and the FBI duo didn't have to wait long for an audience with Dr. Santori. When Mary, the desk matriarch, first noticed Sergeant Murphy's police uniform enter the visitor's lounge flanked by serious companions, she gathered them up like contagious plague carriers and rushed them through to the warren of back offices and hallways without asking a single question. Having arrived at a group meeting room, Mary herded them inside and shut the door after her. "Sorry about that. We treat individuals with trauma here, and it wouldn't do to have police authorities hanging about. For some, your presence might be disconcerting. What can I do for you?"

"We'd like a moment with Dr. Santori," Murphy answered.

"She seems to be very popular these days. Let me go see if I can retrieve her. If she's in with a patient, you'll have to wait until the session has ended."

"Got it," Murphy said. "Thanks."

After Mary left, Davies shared with Murphy what they'd learned about Kevin the previous evening. "There's not much to tell. He's clean as a whistle. Not even a speeding ticket. He owns two homes, one that was part of his mother's estate. If he helped Marnie, he could have offered her lodging at either of these homes, but—"

Dr. Santori opened the meeting room door, witnessed the gathering, and entered, her forehead creased in concern. "Whenever the police arrive, it's normally bad news about one of my patients," she said.

They stood, introduced themselves, and Murphy began. "We're here about Marnie Wilson."

"Oh my God. Did something happen to her?"

"We hope not. She's been missing for several days, and we're trying to find her."

Dr. Santori sighed, outwardly relieved. "She was here yesterday! She hung around all day in the visitor's lounge hoping to see me."

The police, also practiced in the art of waiting for an interviewee to speak and fill in silent spaces, stared at the doctor as she stared at them.

"This isn't getting us anywhere," Murphy chuckled. "Let's all take a breath and a seat. I know about medical privacy restrictions, Dr. Santori, but can you tell us anything that will help us find her? Also, we're interested to learn the last name of one of her groupmates. He may have knowledge about her whereabouts.

"Why don't you start by telling us what you can about her visit."

Dr. Santori rubbed her eyes. "I'll just say this: Marnie has been resistant to sharing. I was surprised and curious when she showed up yesterday and refused to leave. I may have misjudged the encounter, believing at the time she was experiencing stress related paranoia. She wanted me to determine whether one of her other group members, a man named Dan, was posing as someone else in group. I couldn't violate Dan's privacy and told her so, offering instead to help her establish a contact with police.

"After she left in a hurry, I got curious and conducted a personnel file review. She was correct about Dan. I ran out of the facility, hoping to catch her and encourage her to talk further, but she was gone.

"Trauma, PTSD, can be a difficult diagnosis to treat. It normally begins with one event—one significant event that results in a physiological change to the brain. After that, without treatment, patients may begin to wrap other events into the trauma. Until everything is untangled, pardon my less than scientific wording, but most people can better grasp that phraseology, it's difficult to determine what's what. Thus far, Marnie has been resistant to outside assistance in her treatment."

Davies replied in a soothing voice. "That must have made you feel terrible."

"It did. I obviously mismanaged the entire encounter while Marnie was in imminent peril and needed me the most. There isn't much that's worse for a doctor."

The three cops nodded sympathetically. "I'm sure you can't provide any details about what Marnie claimed, but can you at least give us this Dan's last name?" Davies added, "Also, we need to verify if there is a Marco in the group and his last name."

The doctor glanced nervously around the room. "I could get into a whole lot of trouble if I give something out that the rules forbid. I could lose my license."

Murphy tipped her head from side to side. "Tell you what, those privacy rules are so complicated, it's hard to know sometimes where the lines start and end when you're trying to save folks. Police have the same problem. We can get a warrant, of that you can be sure, but it may cost time we don't have all while Marnie hangs in the balance. Just give us the last names, and we'll be out of your hair. No one will know where those names came from. I give you my word." Tiffany Murphy leveled her pleading green eyes at the doctor.

"I hope I'm doing the right thing. Dan Wojocowski and Marco Carerras. Now, if you please, I'm late for another appointment. I'll direct you to the back exit. And, if you find Marnie, please let me know."

* * *

Cook and Murphy, huddled over the hood of Murphy's police cruiser, divvying up tasks related to finding Dan and Marco and ultimately Marnie. Davies stood back, a frown hanging on her face. When Cook noticed his surly partner, he motioned her forward. "What's up?"

She was biting her bottom lip in frustration. "I think we're going about this the wrong way. That's what's wrong with me."

"How so?" Murphy asked.

"Our mission was to find someone who made a call from Iraq and turn her over to our superiors. I'm ninety-nine percent sure we've found our woman, but we can't locate her to satisfy the second part of our task. We're chasing our tails in a directionless search, following her bread crumbs a step too late. What we should be doing is looking for whoever it is that's also involved in an obvious conspiracy churning in the background. I know it, Cook, you know it, and Murph, you do too. This all relates back to Marnie's time in Iraq."

"I thought that's what we were doing," Cook answered, unapologetically. "I'm not willing to say obvious conspiracy, but it's a strong possibility. What do you recommend that you think we've missed?"

"Let's focus on Marnie's Iraq connections. Get our hooks into DOD and dig around. Check out this Dan and Marco's service records and any connections to Marnie's call to the FBI. See if there was anyone else Marnie hung with. We can start with our suspect list of whistleblower women. They were in Iraq with Marnie at the same time. Maybe one of them knew her. Get ahead of this thing before it blows sky high or disappears into a vacuum forever and maybe takes Marnie with it."

"Call? What call?" Murphy asked.

Cook glared at Davies. "That was more than we're supposed to divulge," he said softly.

"Are you kidding me! How am I supposed to help you find her if you leave me in the dark? Either you tell me now, or I walk and do this on my own. This is bullshit. I served just like Marnie. Do the right thing for shit's sake. That doctor just did!"

"She deserves to know, Cook," Davies pleaded, and then continued. "Marnie called the FBI hotline seven years ago from Iraq, and she provided a grid coordinate. We don't know what was at that location. It was so secret they wouldn't tell us, but we have some guesses."

"Seven years ago, and you're just now getting around to identifying the caller?"

"Long story," Cook added.

"It would have to be. And whatever was at that site was so secret you, FBI special agents, aren't told?" Murphy's bright green eyes were slits in her round face as she inspected her new partners. She paced in a circle, mumbling under her breath. "What would be so explosive or damaging located at that grid coordinate that it would have to be kept secret? Dead bodies from some war crime? Wait, explosive. No, hold up. Did Marnie find the missing WMD? That's it, isn't it? No wonder she's so damn scared. Someone else is involved, and they want to make sure Marnie keeps their secrets. Oh my God!"

Sarcastically, Davies said, "We can neither confirm nor deny your theories."

They stood in the sun to allow Murphy time to calm down. Finally, she asked, "So how do we get into DOD records, quick, fast, and in a hurry?"

"I can't," Davies responded and turned to Cook. "You've got some contacts. Pull some strings. You can find out whether either Dan or Marco was with Marnie in Iraq and anything unusual about their service."

"I can try."

Davies continued. "Murphy, once we determine Dan's home address, you can check him out, and I'll do the same for Marco. I still have this crappy feeling if we don't divide and conquer and get a handle on what's really going on soon, we'll never know."

"I like it, Davies," Cook responded. "I'm glad I have a partner that keeps me from getting tunnel vision. Work for you, Murph?"

"I'm in. By the way, you guys aren't half as bad as I thought you'd be."

"Faint praise," Cook muttered. "But we'll take it."

Murphy responded. "Let's check in this evening at five."

Chapter 41
The Glass Eye

After wrestling Marco's drugged body inside, Gerry left him for the evening in a straight-backed chair, secured with zip ties and tape. The room-sized closet where he'd stuffed Marco was sufficient to prevent any screams from being overheard. After using the last drop of his inner reserves, Gerry had slept hard for eight hours in the fetal position.

He'd begun the following day with his captive in the most humane way, talking plainly to the once Navy SEAL. Repeatedly he'd promised, "Tell me where Marnie is, and as I soon as I have her, I'll set you free." Marco had laughed. The handsome SEAL had laughed in his face.

When reason didn't work, Gerry performed small incisions with a fillet knife that he'd found in the kitchen. Nothing that would cause permanent harm, just something to get Marco's attention and make him realize the seriousness of his predicament. That approach, though seriously gross, had Marco listening if not cooperative.

The whole affair was so gruesome and cruel, Gerry's nervous system had overloaded and short circuited several times, causing his body to shudder and shake. There were only two things Gerry wanted, neither of which were currently possible—to sleep until he woke up from this nightmarish escapade, and to run until he was safe from his brother and the law. During breaks, Gerry mostly grieved over Dan's loss and retched.

Worse than Marco's stubborn refusals, his glass eye had seemed capable of autonomous pursuit, like eyes that follow from the inanimate brush strokes of a masterful oil portrait. Gerry knew Marco's prosthetic replacement was incapable of vision or movement, yet the accusing glass eyeball had tracked him as he paced during breaks from his ghoulish task. Each time he would begin anew, the eye had found him, burrowing into his being and devouring what was left of his soul.

During the time he'd spent with Marco that day, which seemed hours instead of only short bursts, his all-encompassing fury and loathing for his brother had possessed him. How could he have allowed pure evil like Richard to corrupt him, changing him from the warm and caring person he was meant to be into a man who was currently gliding the sharp edge of a knife along the skin of another?

As Gerry's hatred of his brother had grown, so had his burning rage. He'd been used, manipulated, and twisted, his life now in ruins. With no place to go, the malignance of hatred poured from Gerry and sought a target. The target was an easy find—a malevolent glass eye.

The ringing of Marco's phone had startled both the torturer and his victim. The cellphone sat on a shelf next to a pair of outrageously expensive women's boots and sang a bar of light reggae. Earlier, Gerry had begged for the password to Marco's phone and had been denied, even as Gerry had threatened to slice a cut from his inner thigh to his knee.

Gerry grabbed the phone too late as a message with Marnie's worried voice began recording. Waving the knife in Marco's general direction, Gerry signaled to his victim that he must answer the next call. Marco glared at Gerry and then closed his one good eye. As the phone was ringing for the second time, Gerry carried out his threat on Marco's inner thigh. Shaking his head and breathing into the pain, Marco moaned but still refused.

Gerry slipped the phone into his pocket and sped out of the closet, heading to the bathroom to regurgitate more bile. Rinsing blood from his hands, Gerry caught sight of his reflection in the bathroom vanity mirror and gagged at the smudge of dry and crusted blood on his cheek. Gerry hadn't been able to eat all day. Each time a vision of Marco came to mind, the man's glaring contempt and his pitiful moaning made Gerry's stomach seize, and a gag reflex swiftly followed.

He wiped his face, replaced the hood he continued to wear, and then strode to the kitchen to collect a metal nutcracker he'd seen in a drawer.

Upon his return, Marco's eyes were open, the gimp eye snarling in Gerry's direction. "Look dude," Marco started. "You can torture me until I'm a bloody pulp, but as I've told you a thousand times, I can't tell you where she is. She left me a note with a goodbye and nothing else. I'm still pissed off about the fact she left me high and dry. I'm not going to help you find her either. Isn't there a way to work this out? You don't act like this is any better for you than it is for me."

"You can start by pointing that evil eye in another direction," Gerry complained.

Marco chuckled. "You do know it doesn't point at all, right? It's glass. The only reason I have it is to cover a gaping hole."

The phone reverberating in Gerry's pocket precluded him from a caustic response. "Talk to her or I get rid of the eye."

"Dude, you are seriously screwed up," Marco said.

Enraged, Gerry whipped the cell out of his pocket, swiped the phone on, and prodded Marco by tapping him in the face with the cell. Lips tight, Marco became rigid in defiance. The last of Gerry's patience and perhaps his sanity fled. He transferred the phone to his left hand, grabbed the filet knife from the floor, aimed the knife point at the corner of Marco's eye, and flicked the offending orb out of its resting place.

Marco moaned and gasped. With a sharp bang, the glass ball hit the wood floor, bounced a couple of times and rolled near Gerry's foot. Gerry let loose a bloodcurdling scream.

Marco withdrew into himself. This was the second time Gerry had witnessed a curious turtle-like response from Marco. Maybe it had something to do with Marco's PTSD and not because he'd blown a gasket and ripped out the man's prosthetic eye. He hoped so.

Gerry stumbled from the closet and headed for a bed. He wept until sleep found him and lay comatose, this time, for over ten hours. He woke wondering where he was for only a moment. Too quickly, the previous day all came flooding back. Surprisingly, the unhinged panic of the previous day had been replaced with a profound sadness— sadness at the man he'd become and the greater guilt he would now have to carry.

At least that accursed eye has been dealt with, he thought. Gerry resolved to try again at reasoning with Marco, to stay calm and thoughtful.

Other than losing the love of his life to Marco's deadly hands, an instinct of survival on Marco's part, he had done nothing to Gerry. Marco didn't deserve any of this.

Gerry's stomach held down some food and feeling more settled, he entered the closet again. Marco was awake and somewhat worse for wear. The scarred cavity on the left side of his face where the prosthetic had once lived was an ugly reminder of Gerry's cruelty. Several superficial cuts had scabbed over, but they were red and swollen. Marco stank from piss and sweat.

He swallowed and began the speech he'd written in his head over bagels. "Marco, I'm sorry about the eye. That was uncalled for. Let's start again. I realized this morning that I believe you. I don't think you know where Marnie is. Also, I don't have it in me to torture you until you help me find her. I think I'd have to kill you before you'd help me lure her in. So, what can you tell me? Give me something, anything helpful, and we'll call it a day. I'll blindfold you and drop you somewhere far away. You haven't seen my face. I've kept this itchy mask on the entire time. And I doubt you'll be able to find Marnie because I'm keeping your phone."

"Why should I believe you?" Marco asked in a tired voice.

"No good reason. Just know, if you don't, I'll hold you until we locate Marnie and then when my boss gets involved, I guarantee you, you won't survive this. I haven't told him I have you. There's still time. Give me something."

Marco's good eye narrowed. "There might be one thing. The night of her house fire she hid something. I know where it is."

"Do you know what this thing might be?"

"Nope, a fireproof box with something in it. That's all I know."

Gerry became suspicious. "And why should I believe you?"

"No good reason," Marco answered. "Other than I like living, and my options are extremely limited. Take it or leave it."

"Give me the location. If you're telling the truth, I'll come back and set you free. This might be exactly what we've hoped for."

* * *

He'd waited long enough. Marco was mostly certain the crazy fuck who'd been torturing him was gone. Marco was angry. Angry that he'd been tied to a chair by a whack job terrified of a glass eye. Angry that he had thus far been powerless against amateur hour at a residential house of horrors. What the hell had Marnie gotten herself into?

Marco hadn't wanted to tell that fruitcake about the box, but he didn't have any other choice. It was, after all, only a box, and its loss alone wouldn't hurt Marnie. What would hurt her is if this moron or his so-called boss got their hands on her. He needed to find a way to free himself, and the only way to do that was to have some quality time alone.

Marco tested his restraints. *Too bad.* The one thing his tormentor had done right was pay attention to how he'd fastened his victim to a chair.

Marco didn't have clear memories of the drive to this place, but he'd burbled up to consciousness a couple of times. It seemed as if they'd driven for some time. He might have a few hours to attempt to get free.

At least that traitor Dan was out of the picture. He'd seen to that.

Marnie was in big trouble, of that he was certain. His fear at present was more about Marnie and how she was running out of time. She needed him. "Get to it, Marco," he yelled to himself in the empty closet.

Chapter 42
Pay Dirt

At first light, Buck and I left the coziness of our home away from home and wandered around the shrubbery for a morning release. I rummaged in the trunk for Buck's dog food and water bowl, filled them, and then watched him lap and crunch as I nibbled on a couple of cold, dry pancakes.

Dogs were so weird sometimes. At first confused, Buck had taken to homelessness like a fish to water. Since the sun had made its appearance this morning, he'd pranced and danced and otherwise reveled in the joy of sleeping closer to nature. His sunny disposition and natural exuberance soothed the sting of my surly countenance when I checked my face in the rearview mirror.

Most of all, I needed coffee. To avoid questions regarding my choice of an overnight resting spot, I moved the Caprice and parked along the street. The Roaster's front signage flashed on, a not-so-subtle sign the coffee was ready, and we wasted no time heading for the warm, welcoming embrace of a cup of java.

On the dot of 6:30 a.m., Buck and I entered the front door and were the first customers of the day. I was greeted by a barista named Megan. "Marnie, Buck, morning! The usual?"

"Yep. Nothing fancy. One mongo big coffee and lots of sugar. Buck is off the caffeine."

She chuckled and then became serious. "I shouldn't say this, but you look kinda rough this morning. You okay?"

"That's right. I haven't been in here since my house burned down. Buck and I are in transition."

"Oh my God, Marnie. Like, that totally sucks! I am so, so sorry. No one's here yet, coffee is on the house. And I'll throw in a croissant for Buck."

"You don't have to do that. I'll probably just hang here for a while and use your internet."

I left her in tip the price of a coffee and croissant and chose a seat in the corner. I needed to call Anton, but he probably wouldn't be at work yet. I tried Marco instead, just to be sure. The phone rang through to voicemail. I ended the call without leaving a message and quickly extracted the battery. The pancakes in my gut were starting to turn.

The Coffee Roaster was filling with loyal patrons. A group of old retired dudes who arrived at the crack of dawn daily, gathered around the table next to mine. They waved, asked me to join them, and then began their loud conversations about politics, yards, sports, and worrisome vehicle noises. The last subject resulted in several different diagnoses about the source of an automotive issue. Their conversations would provide cover for my next call.

At 7:30, I dialed Anton only to learn from the person who answered that I had the wrong desk. He gave me a different number to try within the organization. This time, I got a woman who sounded as tired as I felt, and she patched me through to yet another office. Finally, I hit pay dirt.

"Anton speaking."

"Anton, Good morning. It's Marnie."

"Marnie! I'm glad you called. I have the results. I tried to call Marco, but he isn't answering, which isn't like him. He always responds."

"I haven't been able to reach him either. I was planning to go over to his place if I don't hear from him soon." Blood was rushing. My heart pounded in my chest, and I swallowed as the edges of the coffee shop blurred. "Did you get a hit?"

"I did. Two results. One result is an exact match, and another is very close, probably a sibling. The DNA you gave me matched a man named Gerry P. Jamison. The record says he was an engineer captain when he left service. Do you need the social security number?"

"Please," I whispered, and then typed the number and full name into the iPad. "And the other name?" Holding my breath, I knew in my heart what he'd say.

"As I said, the degree of similarity in the second match indicates a close relative, most likely a sibling. The second name is Colonel Richard T. Jamison, retired."

I didn't answer when Anton asked if I wanted the social. I couldn't speak. It was like stagnant gears in my head began to turn, at each groove a perfectly fitted prong locked in place. The loose ends and questions that had kept me in the wilderness for years, blaming myself for the uncontrolled trajectory of my life, coalesced into a picture of conspiracy that left me dumbstruck. I couldn't deny my part in the saga no matter how witless, but what came after was the doings of faithless and greedy men.

"Marnie, are you there? Do you know these guys?"

After I collected myself enough to answer, my voice was surprisingly steady and deadly calm. "Colonel Jamison was the group commander where I served in Iraq."

"Oh, man. That's not good," Anton answered. "Do you know what it means?"

"I believe I do. Listen Anton, thank you again. You've saved my life. I hope this favor doesn't come back to bite you in the butt."

"Naw, I'm covered."

"I have to get going. I'll call if I hear from Marco."

Without wasting time, I searched the alumni link where I'd found the elusive Dan. Gerry Jamison was also on the list, an alumnus at the very same university as Dan Wojocowski. Amazing. Not proof positive, but enough for me. Next, I searched for a work number for Richard Dickhead Jamison. It came as no shock that he was employed as the CEO for a large defense contractor. He must have had one hell of an angel investor to go from colonel to the majority owner and CEO of a billion-dollar enterprise.

I dialed. "ATSIG Corporation, Mr. Jamison's office, this is Kelly Yang. How can I help you?"

"Yes, hi. My name is Colonel Samantha Meeks. I was wondering if Mr. Jamison had any appointment time open today?"

"May I ask the purpose of the appointment, please?"

"Yeah, I just retired. I was in Navy intelligence. Anyway, Gerry, Mr. Jamison's brother, told me I should call and talk with Richard about employment."

"Mr. Jamison normally doesn't become involved in individual hiring. I can give you the number for our human resources department. We're always searching for qualified applicants."

"Yeah, I know. Mr. Jamison's a big deal, but Gerry said he'd talked to him, and that Richard had agreed to speak to me."

"Well, I'm afraid he's leaving in a few hours for a weekend away, and he doesn't have any other open time on his calendar. If you'd like, give me your number and I'll get back to you with a time, perhaps as early as next week."

"That's okay. I don't know about my schedule next week. I'm still juggling a multitude of interviews. I'll call back."

"And your name again, please?"

I pressed call end. The devil was in, and I needed to catch him before he left. Who knows, he might lead me straight to Marco. A guy like Richard probably wouldn't want to get his hands dirty, but if my take on him was correct, for me he might make an exception. With my best friend Buck lounging by my feet, the old dudes chattering on about woodchippers, and the palliative smell of roasted beans, I dove into the ethernet to locate my nemesis.

Unlike his accomplices, Gerry and Dan, Richard Jamison thrived on the limelight. At the end of two hours, I'd compiled a timeline of events that comprised his success for the last seven years. Every scrap of information that could lead me to him and make him pay was copied and pasted on a spreadsheet. My only question as I reviewed the evidence was: how had I not seen this?

The beginnings of a rough plan forming in my head, there were two more tasks to finish first. One would be easy. The other, heartbreaking.

Thankfully, the box was still there, shallowly buried and nestled between the power conduit and the fence. I dusted away dirt and shook the contents. The heft and sound were right, easing my fears that someone had found the evidence. Wrapping the metal box in a shirt so it wouldn't rattle, I placed it under the spare tire in the trunk.

I watched Buck mark the area for safekeeping and choked back a sob. *Keep it together, Marnie. You know what you must do.* I knelt beside him and enfolded my arms around his strong neck. I inhaled his scent—a scent of home, and welcome, and belonging. The scent of an enduring friendship that had been my bridge over troubled waters when I had most needed one. I wanted to tell him how much I loved him, but I couldn't speak without losing it. My eyes were already filling and on the cusp of running over. It didn't matter anyway that I couldn't say the words, Buck only needed my touch to know. I'd learned that a dog is built to see beyond human wreckage to our better angels. Or maybe it was their loyalty and unswerving devotion that allowed our better angels to swim through the muck to the surface.

I stood, swallowed hard, and then gritted my teeth, reminding myself again that Buck was in my care, and I owed him my best. "Let's go see your good friend Trevor, Buck."

Standing on Trevor's doorstep, I prayed he was home from school. An eye appeared in the peephole, and the door was yanked open. Buck's tail beat wildly at Trevor's arrival. "Whoa, Marnie! What's up? I've got a lot to tell you. There were some FBI—"

"Yeah, I know Trevor. Hey, I don't have much time. I need to ask a big favor. Could you watch Buck for a while? I can't find anywhere to stay that allows dogs, and I don't know how long it will be until I have a permanent home."

His smile dropped. "Are you okay?"

"Not really, but I'll be better knowing Buck has a safe place to stay with someone who'll take good care of him. Do you think your parents will give the green light to a longer-term situation?"

"Well, yeah. I mean like, they like Buck too. But won't you miss him?"

"More than I can explain, Trevor." I forced a smile. "It's for the best for him." I withdrew a wad of cash from my jeans pocket and offered it to Trevor. "This is $375 dollars to pay for food and whatever else you need."

"You don't have to pay me now."

"I do. Take it, please." I needed to cut this short or risk a meltdown, complete with weeping hysterics. "I've got to run."

Gritting my teeth, I tried to jog to the Caprice without glancing back, but my eyes willfully found the pair before I climbed into the driver's seat. They were both standing on the doorstep watching me, a good boy and a good dog. I turned completely and allowed the sight of them to warm me. Buck's black and tan face was regal, kind, and knowing. I seared a picture of him into my mind to sustain me. This time, I had done the right thing.

Chapter 43
It's Personal

As I drove slowly through my neighborhood, pain wracked my body from fear I might never see Buck again. I glanced ahead to an oncoming vehicle and saw him—the man that I'd chased through the alley, the one I'd seen in Iraq, Gerry Jamison, the younger brother of a vile demon.

Clinging to the steering wheel as he passed, I pretended to be texting and dropped and turned my head away from his white Suburban. He didn't slow or change course. Hopefully, he hadn't seen me. I was driving a different vehicle, my hair was shorter and a medium brown color, and Buck wasn't sitting in the front seat. If I'd turned away soon enough, there was no reason to think he'd have noticed me.

This might be just the break I deserve. My time in the military had taught me many important lessons. Perhaps the most important was that the operational situation can change in an instant, and I needed to be nimble enough to react to that change—flexible enough and humble enough to trash a plan and develop another in light of new information. There was only one reason Gerry Jamison would be lurking around near my burned-out house. Gerry Jamison had Marco, and Marco had been forced to tell him about the hidden box. "You are going to be so disappointed!" I screamed, as I watched in a side mirror while he made the turn toward the alley behind my house.

Continuing forward to a community bank on the corner, I pulled into customer parking with a view to the road. Only five minutes later, Jamison made his way back to the main intersection and hung a left. I had no firsthand experience on how to follow a moving vehicle covertly. So certain was I that Gerry Jamison would lead me to Marco and possibly his older brother, when he zoomed away, I piloted the Caprice from the bank to make chase. *How hard could it be*?

It was a law of nature that whenever I was in a hurry, traffic lights conspired to give me their yellow middle finger. I nearly lost him three times until we cleared city streets. I ran two lights that were fully red by the time I entered the intersection. If corresponding traffic cameras patrolled the areas of my driving indiscretions, Kevin was going to be major league unhappy when my tickets arrived.

Once the Suburban entered I-495 south, my challenge was to stay far enough back, with vehicles in between to avoid being seen. It occurred to me that it was far easier to make this happen in books. Each time I managed to drive comfortably behind a group of cars screening my presence, one of them would foolishly decide to exit or pass Gerry's vehicle.

The white Suburban exited to the east, and I slowed enough that I wouldn't be right up his butt, hoping like crazy he didn't hit a red light at the end of the off ramp. He sailed through on green, and I got the yellow warning light, of course. I chose to sit through on red rather than be smashed to smithereens by impatient northern Virginia drivers.

Surging forward on green at a speed that was even more recklessly dangerous than was normal for me, I began to panic after a mile that he'd made a turn I'd missed. I finally saw the back end of a white Suburban. As I slowed my heart and my Caprice to keep well back, the traffic was beginning to thin.

A wide, slow truck pulled in front of me, somewhere past the hour mark. It was another five miles before I could work up the courage to pass in a continuous no-passing zone of a heavily travelled two-lane highway. I floored it and squeaked in front of the beer truck to the refrain of horns blaring from drivers who feared a head on collision with my Caprice. Breathing in through the nose and out through my mouth, I thanked my lucky stars I was still alive to continue pursuit. Except, as I scanned the area to my front, I couldn't see the Suburban. Telling myself I would find him, I sped dangerously forward, searching for any signs of my quarry.

Mile after mile, no sightings of the white SUV. "No please, I can't lose him now," I pleaded with my maker, the fate gods, and any guardian angels that might be listening. I continued to surge forward because turning back seemed fruitless. If he had taken one of many country roads I'd passed, my chances of finding him were slim.

"There he is!" Sailing by a quick stop gas station on my right, from the corner of my eyes, I saw Jamison moving toward the main store. Within a half mile, a fruit stand looked promising as a staging area to wait. Slowing, the crunch of gravel under tires, I pulled behind the squat wooden stand, my front end sticking out just enough to see the road.

To avoid questions from the proprietors about my loitering, I hurriedly exited the Caprice, grabbed a bag of peaches, and thrust the fruit and a twenty at a cute, bubbly teenaged girl. She couldn't have been much over five feet tall and something about the way she drawled, "Hey!" in the melodic tones of a true southerner said she wanted to talk. To no good effect, I scowled at her to discourage further conversation.

"You road weary?" she asked. "I always feel that way when we drive up here to sell our fruit. I've got some ice cold, homemade lemonade in the cooler that might perk you up. Want some? It's almost as delicious as the peaches. You know, I wish I was as tall as you. My momma says this is probably all the taller that I'm gonna get. You could be a model. You're so pretty."

On any other day, someone who offered cold lemonade and led with a compliment might entice me to stay and chat, but already as jittery as a cat being readied for bath time, I blurted, "Sorry, I'm in a real hurry, but thanks. Keep the change."

The tiny blonde shrugged her shoulders, a smile still lighting her face as I turned and ran back to my vehicle. The alluring aroma of peaches made me dizzy. I gulped two huge bites, peach juice dribbling down my chin, and then set the peach carcass on my bag rather than stain Kevin's well-maintained upholstery. Tiffany Murphy jumped into my thoughts at that moment unbidden, like an annoying itch that needed to be scratched at the worst possible moment. I'd made a promise to her that I'd conveniently forgotten. I had promised her I would let her know if I got a match on the DNA.

Weighing my options as I kept my eyes on the road for Richard's brother, I knew I couldn't allow Tiffany to stop me. She would surely try if I called. Still, my word was important to me even if not to anyone else. If she beat me to wherever Gerry was leading me, the FBI would take him, maybe, and I might never get a chance to face Colonel Jamison. I wanted—no—I needed to stand in front of him, eyeball to eyeball and accuse him of his crimes.

There were criminals and thieves aplenty in this world, but Richard Jamison was far more than that. He was the personification of true evil. He'd betrayed the soldiers in his care, sending us on missions, purposefully hoping for our deaths, and for what? For gold. I could understand the theft of something forgotten and buried. I knew I'd fallen prey to that same alluring siren's song. But to betray and murder innocents that you served alongside in war to keep those misdeeds a secret? The idea of his depravity stole my breath. His deeds were monstrous. What he had done to me and my friends couldn't go unpunished.

If I were truly honest with myself, I hoped he'd give me good reason to rid the world of a loathsome, greedy, betraying murderer.

In my rage, I was quivering, and then those irritating better angels took flight in my noggin. I could almost hear their wings pounding against my skull. If I failed, no one would ever know. Mac and Zeke's deaths and the deaths of eight innocent soldiers might never be avenged. And then there was Marco. If I couldn't save him, what then? There would be no backup. "Shit," I cursed and yanked the Murphy phone from my bag, sending the half-eaten peach to its demise on the floor mat. Inserting the battery and with thumbs flying, I texted a message:

Me: *DNA match for CPT G Jamison. His brother my commander COL Richard Jamison. I found gold/jewels/WMD in desert. My team ldr must have told the COL. I have jewels as proof. The brothers and CPT Dan Wski stole the gold/jewels. Marco Carreras kidnapped by GJ. Following now.*

My finger hovered over send, and just then, the white Suburban sped by. God help me, I set the phone down, but I didn't press send. There was still time.

Chapter 44
Bad, Badder, Baddest

"Who the hell are you, and why are you tied up in my closet?"

A man Marco didn't know, but he guessed was the boss, leaned over and inspected him. Marco was lying on his side, still attached to a chair by zip ties and engineer tape. He'd inched himself and the chair forward to the closet door, his head nearly underneath hanging shirts. He glared up at the man with one eye and an empty eye socket.

"Fucking Gerry," Richard huffed. "What manner of screw up is this?"

Marco and his chair were heaved to the upright position as the man considered Marco's remaining eye. "I asked who you are. I would strongly recommend you answer me."

Marco continued his one-eyed glare. The man silently turned and left, returning all too quickly for Marco's tastes. In his hand he held a stun gun. He didn't give Marco a second chance to respond with his name. He pressed the gun to Marco's shoulder and pulled the trigger, leaving it on for three seconds.

Marco grunted in agony. He strained against his bindings, his back arching away from the chair, involuntarily spasming too long after the weapon had been removed from his shoulder. The man stood by and watched as if he was totally fascinated by the results of his toy.

"I've never used this before. I'd planned to try it out on a very special friend of mine, but I can see now the device was well worth my investment. I'll give you ten seconds to tell me who you are, or we'll conduct another test. I might remind you my brother undoubtedly knows your name and will provide it to me once I reach him. Other than serving as my test subject, there is no useful purpose to withhold your identity."

"Marco Carerras."

"See, that wasn't so hard. I'm Richard. I assume you know Marnie, and that my brother was haplessly attempting to get information from you about her whereabouts." Richard traced a swollen, barely scabbed cut along Marco's arm. "Tsk, tsk, my baby brother never had the stomach for doing what needs to be done. These are only superficial. Hardly the manner in which a tough guy like you needs to be treated.

"Did you inform my brother where Marnie could be found?"

Marco shook his head. "I don't know where she is. She left a note saying she was going off the grid."

"Perhaps. Do you know where my dear brother might be then? He seems to be ignoring my calls."

"He went to get a box I hid for Marnie."

"Wonderful. That sounds like hopeful news! I'm most curious to find out what's stored in that box. I'm betting some jewels. What do you think?"

Marco drew himself in, embarrassed to speak a word to this creep. He thought this must be the guy Gerry called *the boss*. Interesting to learn the boss was Gerry's brother and a whacko just like Gerry, but in a whole different way. This cat was different in a dangerous way. He was consoling himself there was no point to be tortured over information that he'd already provided when his body convulsed again, the stun gun digging into his chest.

"I find it most effective to set high standards from the onset. That way, there's no guessing about what will happen if you fail to cooperate."

Richard waited until Marco had recovered from the surge of electricity jumping from neuron to neuron, crippling his nervous system. "Do we understand each other?"

Marco locked his teeth, stared, and then he laughed. "Amigo, you're just going to kill me anyway. You've let me see your face, so there's no possibility you'll let me leave alive."

"True, but you'll be useful when the real prize arrives. If you'll excuse me, I have some business matters to attend to. We'll talk soon."

Chapter 45
Puzzle Pieces

Special Agent Davies, her laptop open on the table to her front, was flanked by Murphy and Cook to each side. Bent together, three heads were examining information on the screen. Davies led them through Marnie's Army connections and a conspiracy theory that, if true and made known, would shock the world.

"I eliminated Marco Carreras almost immediately. He had no association to Marnie in Iraq and was assigned to Afghanistan at the time. The VA trauma group was the only intersection between the two. Given Marco's presence the night of the fire, I've listed him as a recent friend who got caught in the web of conspiracy because of his association with Marnie."

Murphy added, "He's still listed as missing. Right now, we don't have any leads. A friend of his from work said that Marco was a gym rat and worked out most nights. He was seen at the gym the night before last. I've got someone now going through security tapes and checking the parking lot for any clues."

Davies continued. "Next up—Dan Wojocowski. He was in Iraq at the same time as Marnie." Davies touched his name and a picture appeared on the screen, data on his military service underneath.

"Dan was a captain at the time, commanding a logistics company. His unit was involved in the ill-fated convoy where Marnie survived, and her team was killed. The other connection is his participation in Marnie's VA group. His curious misrepresentation of his background to the VA indicates he was involved in the conspiracy, but not how.

"I then researched the events surrounding the convoy and made an interesting discovery." She placed a finger on another icon. A picture of Colonel Richard Jamison showed on the screen. "COL Jamison was Marnie's group commander. He was investigated for a command failure regarding that same ill-fated convoy, but the investigation didn't substantiate a wrongdoing claim. He's now the CEO of a major defense contractor with hooks into security contracts throughout DOD. More concerning, I had one of our accountants review his rise, and they couldn't determine where the colonel received the original infusion of cash to purchase his company. He didn't come from money.

"Turns out, Jamison has a younger brother, Gerry, also in Iraq at the same time." Gerry's face joined Dan and the colonel on screen. "The only connection Gerry had to the convoy incident was his friend, Dan. They both graduated from the same ROTC department. They knew each other."

Murphy asked, "What do you think it means?"

"My theory?" Another graphic appeared, this one displaying arrows, faces, and assumptions. "There was something else in that hole besides WMD. If someone in Saddam Hussein's regime hid WMD, logically they would also hide a means to make an escape if everything fell apart. Dan, Gerry, and Richard stole it, and the colonel tried to cover up loose ends by offing persons who knew about the riches buried in the desert—Marnie, and perhaps the rest of her team. When we began investigating the hotline call, they got wind of our search. The colonel's company has contracts within the FBI, so it's not a stretch to think he was tipped off, and the chase was on for Marnie. I'm not sure whether she was involved in the theft, but her call and current financial situation tells me she's not."

Murphy's face was red as she pounded the table with her fist. "Let's find this SOB Jamison and send him to hell where he belongs!" She was about to say more when her phone rang, and she stepped away to answer. "Tell me. Uh huh. The cameras were disabled. No surprise. That's quite a coincidence—not. Hey thanks, good work. I'll get back to you soon."

Lips tight and with steel in her voice, Murphy turned to Cook and Davies. "They didn't find Marco's vehicle, but Dan's car was left at the gym parking lot. Another wild-assed theory—when they couldn't find Marnie, they kidnapped Marco to draw her in."

Cook said, "We don't have much time. Davies, what do you know about the Jamisons to give us a starting point to find Marco?"

"Glad you asked." One last visual aid appeared. "These are the properties they separately own. Of course, Richard's company has many other properties, but the conspiracy seems to be a family affair. I'd recommend we start with their personal holdings. We can also get a warrant to track their phones, but that'll take time. If Murphy can round up more help, and you can get some FBI support, we can cover these ten locations before the sun comes up tomorrow. I hope it'll be soon enough."

Chapter 46
Huntress, Take 2

When the white SUV passed through Tappahannock on Highway 17, following the curve of the Rappahannock River, I was certain he was leading me to Deltaville. In my morning surfing on the internet waves, I'd found property tax records for an address on the Chesapeake Bay owned by Richard Jamison. Google Earth displayed a stately home, shrouded in trees, and a dock with a speed boat waiting for the recreational enjoyment of human excrement.

The good news for me was that the home was not new and didn't reside on a clear-cut parcel. There was enough property surrounding the home to hide an approach. With no need to continue my pursuit, another good thing because it was becoming more difficult to stay hidden in the sparsely populated area along Route 17, I stopped at a local grocery store to wait for sunset and total darkness.

The little blonde was right, the peaches were delicious. I woofed several nearly pound-sized juicy specimens and had to step outside the Caprice to remove the stickiness with a water bottle and t-shirt. When my fingers were clean enough to use the iPad, I reviewed the location of the property, avenues of approach, and identified a safe place to park and walk in. Carefully, I readied the gear I would need in the black duffle. Fearing a curious onlooker might see me, I didn't do anything to check weapons. There'd be time once I arrived at my destination.

Watching the day recede into twilight through the windshield, more than once I turned to the passenger seat to make a comment to my best pal, only to be reminded his seat was empty. I wished more than anything Buck was here now, his furry presence consoling me that I wasn't alone. "Buck up, Marnie," I yelled at myself. "Time to put an end to this madness. Someone must do it, and the universe has picked you."

When it was fully dark, I turned the ignition key and drove from the safety of a grocery store parking area. I thought the stars must be aligned because as I reached the chosen hiding place for the Caprice, the spot was exactly as it appeared from Google Earth. A short turn off led into a home that had burned to the ground like mine, and I could leave the Caprice tucked away unseen. Packed tire tracks pointed to the property's use for teenager dalliances or possibly drug deals, but it would have to do. The area was wooded and allowed me to travel to the goal under cover. With any luck at all, my car would still be here when I returned.

Setting the timer on the iPad, I placed it under a floor mat and stuck the Murphy phone into my pocket. There was still time to hit send on the text to Murph and allow for a conversation with the devil before backup arrived. At least, that was the plan.

I rubbed camouflage paint on exposed skin and tucked my dyed brunette pony into a black watch cap. The harness and utility belt I'd kept from my Army days fit snugly as I snapped it shut at my belly. My dad's 45-caliber Colt 1911 in a holster, and his pride and joy, a Remington 700 bolt-action rifle with a Redfield scope slung over my shoulder, I was dressed for success.

For a fraction of a second, I wondered what the hell I was doing. Was I so bent on revenge, my mind warped by years of cowering, that I would take matters into my own hands unwisely? "Hell yes!" I spoke to the universe. "This is personal."

Car lights on the road forced me to duck behind the Caprice, my respiration beginning to climb with the knowledge of what I was about to do. I urged myself on as I paused to ensure the vehicle had passed. The Jamison brothers would never suspect I would turn the tables and come for them. They had played me and my fear, a puppet dancing on a string, all while they manipulated events and destroyed lives for profit.

Undoubtedly, the Jamisons would also underestimate me. They couldn't know my dad had made sure I was comfortable with weapons from an early age, the Army reinforcing that skill. I wasn't merely a good marksman—I was far better than good. Many was the day after a range qualification that Army instructors and colleagues would see me differently, respecting my prowess behind a weapon sight. Besides, somewhere there was an award citation that said I was brave too, even if I still couldn't remember some of the incident. *I'm ready.* Resolute, I stood and set off.

The forest I crossed was inconsistently dense and easy to navigate. Ambient moonlight helped guide me to the outer fringes of Richard's property. Stopping at a chain-link fence, I scanned the area for any sensors or other surveillance technology. Seeing nothing to cause concern, I climbed over the fence and dropped to my belly to crawl the rest of the way in.

Designed to keep prying eyes away, twenty-feet of overly packed trees and shrubbery comprised the landscaping in front of the fence.

As I crept forward, lights filtering through the vegetative screen gave me confidence the monsters were in residence. Drawing nearer to the line between grass and greenery, a clear view inside the home beckoned all comers. None of the windows were covered with shades or curtains. Good news—the Jamison brothers weren't expecting stalking visitors

Locating a good spot to assess the situation, I crawled between the stumps of a hedge near the corner of the home with a view of a side window and the back. Windows and sliding doors across the entire backside provided visibility to a family room and eating area. Squirming into position and pulling back leafy branches, I slid the Remington from my shoulder and set up to watch through the sight.

I lost track of how much time passed as I waited. Finally, from the side window, a silhouette appeared, entering the kitchen. I couldn't see who it was or what he was doing. *Breathe in through your nose and out through your mouth,* I cautioned myself. *Be patient.*

He reappeared with a glass in his hands, walked through the eating area, and hesitated in front of the sliding doors near the family room. He surveyed the landscaped yard as if he were waiting for someone. I could see the distinct image of his evil face through the scope. The freak show of all Army colonels, Richard Jamison, in living color.

My finger restless on the rifle trigger, it would be all too easy to rid the world of this destructive madman. I studied his unworried expression and wondered how a person becomes like him. Even now, my hatred growing for this sorry excuse of a human being, I couldn't kill him in cold blood. Why should I be concerned with fair play when it was a foregone conclusion someone like him wouldn't give a damn?

Colonel Dickhead's searching gaze never landed on my position. At last, he turned and left. At least I had my answer, and I could begin phase two of the plan. Richard was in the house, Gerry had led me here, and Marco must also be inside. Time to send that text.

Cradling the Remington in my left hand, I felt in my pocket for the phone. A second of panic ensued when I didn't feel the rectangular heft in my shirt pocket, until I remembered I'd tucked the phone into my jeans for easier access in case Murphy tried to contact me. I rolled from my stomach slightly to extract the cell, and a crunching sound came from my right. As I pushed up on my hands to see better, the subtle click of a safety switch told me all I needed to know.

"Don't make a move, Marnie. Nice and slow; push that rifle away from you. Don't get any ideas. I have a clear shot at the back of your head. If I get even an inkling you're going to try something stupid, you're dead."

All I could think about was that I didn't send that text—how utterly screwed up it was that I hadn't sent the SOS already. Bile was climbing up my throat. *Oh shit, I'm such a screwup.* Blood surged into my ears, and with quivering arms, I pushed the rifle away from me.

"Very good," Gerry Jamison said. I knew the voice was Gerry's and not Richard's. The sound of the colonel's arrogant tone was imprinted in my memories. "You know the deal. Scoot back and come up on your knees, your hands behind your head." I did as he asked.

"Now I'm going to search you. Stay very still. I'll have the barrel pressed to your head as I relieve you of your burdens."

A cold metal object pressed against the back of my head. "How did you know I was here?" I asked, as his hands ran down my body, and he removed the Colt.

"I made you just after we got off the highway. You're more cunning than you look, but I'd steer clear of trying to follow someone undetected in the future. It takes some practice. I've been out here waiting for you."

"Shit."

"Hey, ten points for effort. Can't say I blame you for trying."

"Is Marco in there?" Gerry found the phone and removed it from my pocket. I could hear him extract the battery with one hand. He must have heaved the unpowered phone into the woods, because I heard it land.

"He is."

"Is Dan in there too?"

"Nope. He's dead. Your boyfriend killed him." He paused. "Wait, how did you know about Dan?"

"You guys left enough clues around to piece it together. You must think I'm stupid."

"Not stupid, but it is me holding a gun on you."

"There's that," I answered, thinking once again about my foolhardy decision to wait on the text to Murphy.

Oddly, Gerry let me lie on my belly. He stood behind me huffing, as if he had something he needed to say. I didn't care to listen to him, but his consternation, whatever it might be about, could give me some leverage. I waited.

"I just want you to know, before we join my asshole brother, that I'm sorry. I didn't want it to end this way. Me and Dan went out of our way to protect you. Dan was the one who submitted the silver star recommendation. When we realized my psycho SOB brother was trying to kill your entire team and anyone who happened to be in your circle, Dan submitted that award. He thought the publicity surrounding a medal would keep Richard off your back."

I couldn't hold it in. I laughed. "Well played, Gerry. Eight people died, I got a medal, and now you're going to serve me up to your brother on a platter."

Angrily he answered, "Place your hands together behind your back." When I didn't immediately comply, he shot a round into the dirt, far too close to my head. "Do it!"

With one hand, he enclosed my wrists with a zip tie, inserted the end into the groove, and yanked it tight. Prodding my head with the barrel of his gun, he ordered, "Stand up, Marnie."

Gerry backed away slightly as I pushed to my feet. "What about Dan?" I asked. "You're the jerk's brother, so he wouldn't off you. What kept Colonel Dickhead from eliminating Dan too?"

"Move to the house."

"He's going to kill me and Marco, right?" Gerry didn't answer. "Right?"

"I'm sorry. If you could've just left it alone, we wouldn't be here now."

"That's right, it's all my fault. You're a pathetic piece of filth just like your asshole brother, Gerry. You can pretend all you want that you have a conscience but sending me in there is murder. You'll have blood on your hands as much as that monster."

"Move," he said roughly.

Chapter 47
Hard Heads

Richard was waiting as Gerry herded me forward through the sliding glass door. Sitting on a crème leather chair, one leg crossed over the other, a bronze highball glass in one hand, he held the same haughty expression on his face that I last remembered. He was wearing tailored pants, a shirt, and shoes that I knew cost more than my entire wardrobe. The disgust I felt at where and how he'd amassed his fortune was like a live animal inside me, clawing to get out.

"Well, well, our war hero returns. Much the worse for wear I can see. What happened to that striking blonde who pranced around the base in Iraq? Seven years has done you no favors, Specialist Wilson."

If there was a way I could've lunged at him without getting my head blown from my shoulders, I would've tried. But there wasn't. Pure, perfect rage coursed through my body. Every instinct wanted movement, leaving me shaking instead for my inability to do so. Unfortunately, the way that I'd pictured this scene had me holding the gun on him, not the other way around. I knew words would mean nothing to a creep like Richard unless he was in fear for his life. I chose to breathe and stay silent instead.

"Did you search her thoroughly?" Richard asked Gerry.

"Seriously? Of course I did."

"I think I should double check." He stood, walked to face my front, and stared into my eyes. I didn't look away. His eyes confirmed everything I knew of him. Like gazing into an abyss, there was nothing behind his cold grey eyes.

He started with his hands on my shoulders, and then, sliding them over my breasts, he grabbed one, pinched, and whispered into my ear, "Are you excited yet, Marnie?"

I clenched my jaws and continued to stare back at him with all the malice he so rightfully deserved. His hands moved on to my back, over my butt and lingered for a moment to grab. When his hands travelled over my hips and down to my crotch, he bent down, and I spat, "Should've known you were a pervert in addition to everything else."

He reacted as I'd hoped, his head coming up to meet me. With everything I had, I arched my body back and whipped my head forward—for once my timing perfect. The smack of skull meeting face was as satisfying a sound as any I'd ever heard. From the other side of the room Gerry gasped and started running to us, his gun held up and pointed at me.

Richard was stunned. His nose was bleeding, and a gash near an eyebrow was leaking blood into his eye. He rubbed blood off with his hand, drew it back, and smashed his fist into my face.

The crunch from inside my head was my nose breaking. I never knew that expression about seeing stars was true until that very moment. A celestial grouping of dark sparks swam at the edges of my vision. I turned to run and avoid a second hit, but my knees flexed of their own volition, and I fell to the floor.

Richard Jamison used the opportunity to kick me in the back while Gerry screamed, "Enough! Enough!"

"What the hell, Richard?" he yelled and bent down near my face to make sure I was still alive.

"She hit me first," the monster pouted.

"Yeah, well sometimes that happens when you grope a woman without permission. What the hell is wrong with you? We agreed we'd do what was necessary and end this. Period. No funny business or unnecessary violence."

I couldn't see the devil's face from my vantage point on the floor. I could only see his Stefano Ricci alligator loafers stepping away from me toward the kitchen. He stopped. "Just get her ready with the other one. Put them in the dining room and make sure there's a tarp underneath. I can't believe you got blood all over the bedroom closet. You're going to clean up the mess, Gerry."

Chapter 48
It's a Family Thing

Gerry placed me in a chair, each leg tightly secured in two places to a wooden leg, my shoulders straining as my arms were pulled around the chair back, and my hands bound and tied to a spindle. Marco watched from an identical position, three feet to my right, as Gerry finished his handiwork and then left.

"Ah, Marnie. What the hell? You don't look too good. I like the new hairdo though."

"Back at you, Marco. You don't smell too good either. Would it make you feel any better if I said Richard's face looks worse?"

"Absolutely! Hey, don't suppose you've worked out something where the cavalry arrives in the nick of time?"

"Maybe yes, maybe no."

"I'll take that. Better odds than I had a few minutes ago."

"You're the SEAL, Marco. Haven't you come up with something to get us the hell out of here?"

"If I could, you think I'd still be here waiting on you? You're the smart one, Marnie. What's your plan?"

"I have one, but it's a long shot."

"Whatever it is, I'm in. I'll follow your lead."

"Marco?"

"Yes?"

"I'm truly sorry I got you into this."

"I know. You warned me, but I couldn't leave you alone."

"Sucks what they did to your eye."

"It does, but better you see me in all my natural splendor. That way after we escape, you'll know what you're getting."

I was about to tell him about the DNA match, and leaving Buck, and anything to take my mind off what would happen next, but the vile bros entered the room.

Richard came in first. He'd changed into work clothes and gloves, a less than positive sign. Funny that I hadn't had a full-out panic attack since being terrorized and tormented by the malicious Jamison boys. Maybe when your nightmares become real again, some survival instinct inside disables the freak-out switch. Whatever the reason, I needed all my wits, and I was glad for the reprieve.

Richard's eyes were already beginning to blacken, his nose askew. He launched into a yawn-worthy narrative while Gerry stood behind him, his head bowed as if embarrassed—another less than encouraging omen. "We can do this easy or do this hard. What I need from either of you is the location of the lock box. If you cooperate, this will all be over quickly. I would also like to know what you've told the FBI."

Psychopaths like Jamison live to play with people's emotions and cause them pain. Freaks like him get a hard on demonstrating how much smarter they are than everyone else. I didn't believe for an instant he wanted to have this over quickly. He'd want to savor his power and control over me. Maybe I could use that.

I wiped away the hateful expression I was undoubtedly wearing and replaced my cold scowl with resignation. "I'll tell you everything you want to know, but at least explain how you've stayed ahead of me every step of the way. I just don't understand how you've managed all of this."

The devil's head tilted, and he smiled. "I had a goal, the will, and the intelligence to carry out my plan. I possess the ability to see many moves ahead, something someone like you wouldn't understand."

"I can see that now. But, how did you know about the gold to begin with? Was it Mac? Did he tell you about what I found?"

"That's exactly why I'm here and you're tied to a chair. I knew all along the sergeant was trying to protect you. Such a Pollyanna. Yes, he came to me. He shared the location of the gold. When I asked him who else knew, he said only him. It was obviously a lie. People like you and him are too weak to hold secrets alone. That is, after all, why you both shared the secret, is it not?"

"But how did you get all that gold out of country? I mean, it couldn't have been easy. Every shipment was inspected multiple times. Was that Dan's part in the plan?"

The demon's omnipotent expression subtly changed. *Bullseye*. "I heard Captain Dan Wojocowski was a logistician. You would need someone with that expertise to transport gold out of Iraq. That was a boatload of gold."

Colonel Richard Jamison's lips puckered, the first time I'd seen a whiff of doubt. I pressed that button again. "When Dan first came to me to say I was being followed, I bought his story, but there was something about him that felt wrong. Without knowing why, I pushed him away. And then—"

"Shut up!" the monster bellowed. I checked out Gerry. No longer studying the floor, his eyes were round. Stark fear washed over his face, and then, something else.

The psychopath turned to his brother. I couldn't see his expression to be sure I'd hit the nerve I was hoping for. I raised my eyebrows twice at Marco to say be ready, and he nodded.

"You involved someone else without telling me?" Richard asked his brother.

"Of course, I did, Dick!"

Oops, I thought. Everyone knew of the colonel's nickname and that he became enraged whenever it was spoken aloud. Dickhead didn't disappoint. His back to me, I could see his hands clench.

"Never call me that again, Gerry," Richard hissed, "or you will live to regret it."

"Oh, screw you, brother. I'm sick of your threats. Our folks always called you Dick. Not my problem you lived up to the nickname. And as far as a partner, of course I had one. How the hell else was I supposed to get the gold out of Iraq? Are you such a clueless megalomaniac you thought I could do it all by myself? Without Dan, that gold would still be buried in the Iraqi desert."

"And where's Dan now?"

"Goddammit, he's dead! Marco killed him when we kidnapped him, and I blame you for that, Richard."

"It was unwise to involve anyone else, Gerry, but at least Dan's one loose end we won't have to concern ourselves with. You always did have a weakness for a cute male ass—a sickness if you ask me."

The onetime colonel returned to his position facing me and Marco. "Now, where were we?"

I could see Gerry's face. The colonel's comment about Gerry's taste in men had struck like a drill, piercing a molar without anesthesia. He launched himself at his brother so fast, I only had a split second to tuck my chin. I wasn't sure if they would crash land on me or Marco, but I needed to be ready.

Four hundred pounds of male fury barreled in my direction. I knew in that moment what it must be like for a running back who'd just caught the football, unable to get out of the way before being tackled. My chair was thrown back, hitting the floor with an earsplitting crash. I had to duck one punch from Gerry before they rolled away slightly, still locked in mortal combat.

I was seeing stars and shook my head to clear away the fog. The back of the chair gave way when I yanked my hands. I needed to hurry and be discreet enough to keep the fighting brothers from noticing me. Now that the chair back was broken, I easily pulled one hand free and then the other. On my back, the bottom half of the chair still intact, I couldn't move my legs.

Glancing to the mound of writhing, grunting, punching, family dysfunction, Gerry's back was facing me, my Colt tucked into his back pocket-- but barely. During the struggle, straining muscles had pushed the gun almost out of its fabric enclosure.

Gerry heaved and rolled on top of his brother. Free at last, the pistol thumped to the floor.

Gerry looked at me at the same instant that I looked at him. We reacted at the same moment too, both reaching for the pistol. He would have had it first, except that Dickhead seized the opportunity to land a right jab under Gerry's chin.

My fingers straining, I hooked a forefinger on the trigger guard and pulled the pistol toward me enough to get a one-handed grip.

Gerry was shaking off the jab. On his knees, straddling his demon brother, he tried to stand. Richard, still unaware of my recent acquisition, went for a strike at Gerry's balls with his knee. Gerry's mouth was already open, probably to warn the devil I was armed, but all words were cut short. A verbal alarm was replaced by an anguished, "*OOOH.*"

I knew I only had moments before Dickhead understood what had happened. I smashed one chair leg with the butt end of the pistol before Gerry's plaintive wail had reached its crescendo. My adrenaline surging, I hit the wood with such force, the chair leg splintered and freed one leg, even though a piece of the chair was still taped to my calf.

I sprung to my feet faster than if I'd learned of an 85% off sale on designer bags. What remained of the broken chair was still affixed to my other leg, but I was mostly stable. During a fight that spanned less than a minute, I'd been transformed from helpless hostage to superhero—Marnie Wilson, anxiety-ridden survivor, enlisted puke, not so dumb blonde, and lover of dogs, books, and wearable accessories, I stood mostly balanced with a two-handed grip, pointing my dad's Colt at them.

Gerry raised his head from a stooped position, breathing hard and gripping his private region. The devil was on one knee, full realization of his changed fortunes settling in.

If I could bottle the looks on their faces, I would never have need of nor be tempted to steal any jewels again.

I glanced at Marco. He was withdrawn and still. *Must be his PTSD reaction,* I thought. *No help there.*

Gerry moved one of his hands. My eyes flitted back to the brothers in an instant. "Don't fucking move!" Both men went still. "The gig's up, ass wipes. As you said Gerry, you know the deal. Slowly, very slowly, remove the weapons from your persons and slide them on the floor in front of you. And before you get any ideas or decide to underestimate me once again, please know I'm the Annie Oakley of modern times. I will not miss or shed a tear over your loss. Do it!"

A twitch of unspoken communication passed between the bruised and bleeding brothers. This was going to get interesting.

Surprisingly, it was Gerry who made the first move. He turned and ran. *Stupid,* I thought. *Too slow.* I shot him in the back of the thigh, the force of the Colt blowing him off his feet onto his face. Without pause, aiming at his heart, I trained my sight on Richard's malevolent figure. He was now standing, reaching for a weapon from a holster. For an instant, the devil's eye caught mine, and a flicker of recognition said he knew he'd be dead if he didn't stand down. Deliberately, with a two-fingered grip, he slid the pistol from the holster and dropped the weapon on the floor.

"Kick it toward me," I commanded. An angry monster shoved the pistol with his foot half way across the room.

Regaining his senses, Marco moaned behind me. In a raspy voice he croaked, "Marnie, you're a stud! What did I miss?"

"The good part," I responded and continued to inspect my nemesis, his lips pursed into a haughty expression, still unwilling to admit he was beaten. I thought about what would happen to Richard Jamison if I turned him over to the police. The extended time it would take to unravel his financial dealings meant he'd have plenty of money to fight charges. He most likely held a hidden bank account somewhere outside the country—all the ultra-rich crooks keep a stash of cash for emergencies. In our judicial system, money and power begot freedom in too many cases. Nobodies like me and Marco had to be innocent and prove it.

Connecting this villainous ass to the deaths that occurred on a convoy seven years past would be likewise difficult. He'd probably get off on a charge of conspiracy to commit murder of brave soldiers, a wonderful man named Mac, and a kind, funny friend named Zeke.

My face broke as I thought of them. They deserved so much more.

At my back, Marco began to speak, his voice even and velvety smooth, "I know what you're thinking, Marnie. He deserves to die. In your shoes, I'd feel the same way. Sweet lady, haven't you been through enough? Finishing what you most want to do will only make you more like them. You'll live with your actions for the rest of your life. I know you will. Don't do this."

"Just so you know, Marco, no one other than my Auntie Veronica has ever called me sweet."

309

He chuckled. "I bet Buck thinks that all the time. Every time he looks at you, in dog language of course. And I see you. Don't do this."

The last thing I wanted was for the slime bag on the business end of my gun to see me cry, but tears leaked from my eyes anyway, and the rotten traitor had the audacity to smirk. My finger on the trigger, I felt truly powerful, the decision of life or death within my grasp. The pad of my first digit was comfortable where it was, only a little pressure and I could end this for good.

Then, in the distance, the sound of vehicles. Someone was pounding on the door. "Police! Open the door!"

Glass shattered at the back of the house. My finger was still on the trigger when they entered the room and ordered me to drop my weapon. Slowly, I placed the Colt on the floor and my hands over my head.

Murphy ran to me. "Oh, Marnie. Thank God you're okay." She wrapped her arms around me, and my body relaxed for the first time in days.

"How did you find us?" I mumbled.

"Some kid named Nathan contacted me. He said he had an app named Call Home on his main computer and that you were in possession of his iPad. He received a pre-timed message from you asking him to call me and provide your location. We would've gotten here eventually, but it might've been too late."

"I didn't know if the app would work. You're just in time, Murphy."

Chapter 49
Homecoming

The FBI wouldn't let me rest. Two days of interviews and follow-ups drained what was left of my inner reserves. Murphy stayed with me as frequently as she was able, but much of what we talked about was classified. I could tell the search and then the aftermath was taking a toll on her too.

At 3:15 p.m. on the second day, in a small interview room with me, Davies, and Cook, Murphy lost her patience. She pounded on the door and then entered without being invited. "Good God, Cook, can't you see Marnie's about to drop?"

Davies chimed in, "Murph, if you can't contain yourself, you're free to leave. Go home and get some rest."

Cook's hands went up. "Hold up, Davies. I think she's right. We've got just about everything we need, for now." His attention shifted back to me. "Marnie, we'll let you go, but as this investigation develops, we may have more questions. I need to be sure you won't drop off the end of the earth again."

Mimicking an "X" drawn over my heart, I answered, "I promise." Cook and Davies were professional and kind, even if the barrage of questions left me hollowed out and empty.

Murphy had already freed my SUV from the evidence impound lot. My vehicle was waiting for me in front of the station. She escorted me to the door and said, "Don't be a stranger."

"Never. You're stuck with me now. I'll never be able to repay you for believing in me when almost no one else did."

"Hey, if two Army gals can't believe in each other, what've we got? Trevor's home, and Buck's eager to see you. Get out of here."

Without letting the door hit me on the way out, I floored it to my old neighborhood. They were in the front yard waiting. Murphy must've called. I could tell Buck heard my SUV because his whole body was readying for a homecoming before I pulled to the curb. His tail wagging furiously and paws dancing, he strained on the lead and bark-whined. Trevor released him as I opened the SUV. He was there before I could get both legs to the ground. Climbing up my legs to kiss my face, he jumped back twirling in a circle, and then repeated the routine again, all while he squealed in a dog's equivalent of happiness.

"You want to go?" I asked him. He blasted from his haunches, and I had to move quickly out of his way as he scrambled from the driver's seat to his rightful place next to me. His smile said, "Let's rock and roll." That was my interpretation anyway.

Trevor strolled over. "I took good care of him. He missed you though. Every time I let him out, he wanted to go to your house and look for you." He pushed a wad of money at me. "I only needed a little bit for dog food and a bed. Marnie, are you okay now?"

I couldn't recall if a smile had ever come over me like the one I gave Trevor. This smile started in my heart, ran though my arms and legs, and I felt as if an indescribable force was lifting me somewhere I'd never been. "I am, Trevor."

Chapter 50
VIP

I parked my SUV in a lot and rode the metro into the Pentagon. Kevin and I had formalized a deal for me to rent his house for a year, the same period the insurance company said it would take to rebuild my burnt home from the ground up. Barely a full day of rest later and just getting comfortable on Kevin's couch, I received a call from the Office of the Secretary of Defense. That's right, the freaking Office of the Secretary of Defense. The secretary hoped to see me, Marnie Wilson, in the flesh, as soon as possible.

Sadly, my first thought was not what they wanted from me or amazement at how important I had suddenly become, but rather what on earth I would wear. I had a sneaking suspicion about what they wanted, but I was dead certain my sad collection of garments wasn't up to the task.

For the first time in recent history, I had decided to purchase brand new clothing. I felt a little less like a fish out of water in my stylish dress and a pair of matching conservative pumps. A robot announcement gave notice of the Pentagon stop. In unison, most of the riders around me stood to exit the rail car. This was my first time entering the Pentagon. I tamped down nervous energy and tried to pretend I knew where I was going, confident and in a hurry like everyone else around me. I slid the metro pass into the slot, pushed through the turnstile, and plucked the upright ticket from its position. Following the military uniformed crowd to the security area, a staff sergeant saw me and rushed to my side.

"Ms. Wilson?" the hunky, blond sergeant asked.

"That's me." I reached out, and we shook hands.

"I'm here to assist you through security and to escort you to the secretary's office."

"Lead on," I murmured, feeling butterflies beginning to gather in my gut.

The sergeant made short work of security, a herculean task if the size of the lines were any indication. We wound through the recesses of long interconnected hallways, my pumps tapping on the hard floors in rhythm with my heart.

The ambiance changed dramatically when the sergeant held the door for me to enter the sanctuary of the head honcho, the great and wonderful Oz of the world's most awesome fighting force. The plush carpet dampened all sound. I always pictured places like this as being filled with frenetic activity, important people running in and out doing the country's business, but this office was anything but—serene, tasteful, and dignified were the words that came to mind.

A four-star general, who I believed to be the Secretary of the Army, greeted me. More handshakes, and then the man himself opened the door to his inner sanctum with a warm smile. "Welcome, please come in. Do you prefer Ms. Wilson or Sergeant Wilson?" he asked as he ushered me to a grouping of plush chairs.

"Marnie's good."

I declined coffee but accepted water. My mouth was as dry as the desert in Iraq on a hot day.

Another smile from the secretary, this one sad.

"First, how are you doing, Marnie? I've been fully briefed on the incident in Iraq and the events that occurred last week."

"I could complain, but who'd listen," I retorted and then felt like a fool talking to a bigwig like that. *Get a grip,* I reminded myself.

He chuckled. Warm hazel eyes peered into my soul. "Normally, I would say that's a true statement. Today, however, I would listen. The entire Department of Defense owes you an apology. Your chain of command in Iraq failed you in the worst possible way. Not only were you placed in unnecessary danger by a criminal wearing an Army uniform and masquerading as a colonel, you were humiliated and belittled for your bravery in action. I can't imagine the emotional consequences of that sort of betrayal."

That apology came out of the blue, and my treacherous tear ducts began to fill with liquid. I drew a long breath and reined in the urge to emote. I was, after all, an Army veteran, capable of keeping a stiff upper lip, at least until this meeting ended and I could dash to a toilet stall to cry in privacy. "It was very difficult. You probably already know though, my actions after finding that cavern in the desert were less than honorable. I owe you an apology too."

"I'm not going to quibble about that point. You were young and had a hiccup in judgment. Many of us at your age might have been tempted to do the same thing. That's why we have a chain of command, to guide soldiers and train them. Your sergeant, SFC McCray, tried to live up to the standards that we hold dear. Colonel Richard Jamison did not."

The one thing I'd never shared with the FBI and Murphy was Mac's part in my folly to learn what was in that hole. I made it sound like Mac only wanted to know what was buried there so he could inform superiors. And in truth, maybe that was his motivation.

"About your silver star—"

I cut him off. "Feel free to rescind the orders."

The general and the secretary exchanged glances. The general cautioned, "Please Marnie, let the man finish."

The secretary continued. "What I was about to say is that the write-up qualifies for a Distinguished Service Cross, a level higher than the award you received."

"Oh, good God, no! An award like that should be an honor, but that medal caused me more grief than you can ever understand. I might've told someone else about the WMD that me and SFC McCray found if not for that award. I was embarrassed to receive recognition, believing it was my fault we were on those dangerous missions to begin with. How could I tell anyone what I'd done when everyone around me was offering congratulations and patting me on the back? Besides, no matter what you say, I'll always wonder about Captain Wojocowski's motivations for submitting the award recommendation."

"I want to remind you, Marnie, you did try to tell your group commander and then called the FBI hotline. I guess the best thing to do is allow the medal to stand as is. Do you know what the award says, Marnie? Have you read the citation lately? While under fire, you pulled three soldiers to safety. You engaged the enemy and coordinated a counter attack that resulted in nine enemy KIA, providing enough time for reinforcements to arrive. If not for your actions, twelve survivors, including yourself, might have died. You should never concern yourself with the captain's motivation."

I shook my head to indicate I hadn't read it lately. Truth is, other than the confused time when the orders were read during the medal presentation, I'd never read the citation at all. "I know it sounds weird, sir, but thinking about that convoy takes me to a place I have trouble revisiting. You know, come to think of it though, there is one thing you can do."

"Name it."

"The day of the incident, SFC McCray was shot trying to cover me. He's the one that pushed me to save myself and the others while he lay dying. Without him, I wouldn't have survived. I just wish I hadn't been too confused to think about his part in what happened until much later. Honestly, I didn't even know a junior enlisted person could recommend someone else for an award. He deserves that medal, more than me. If you view the actions taken after we were attacked as a series of events, it was SFC McCray's courage and leadership that was key to my part."

"That's the way of it I suppose," the secretary said almost to himself. "Nearly every medal recipient focuses on the team. You write it, Marnie, and we'll see."

"Thank you, sir. Now, when do you get to the 'but' part and the true purpose of this meeting?"

"I wish everyone at the Pentagon had your gift for frank talk," the secretary quipped. "As to the *but* you mentioned, we hope you'll consider keeping the contents of the buried room a secret. As you know, the decision to withdraw from Iraq has been made and implemented. It would serve no good purpose to complicate the issue by informing the public that there was a very small amount of WMD buried in the Iraqi desert."

"And if I say no?"

"I've been advised to threaten you by bringing up a jewel theft and the illegal transport of contraband into the United States, but my instincts tell me a threat would be the worst course of action to take with you. I'm asking, pleading actually. The knowledge of WMD in Iraq all along wouldn't change a thing. It would just stir up a political hornet's nest. We've notified previous president to let him know. He said, and I quote, 'For the sake of the country, keep it on the down low.' Are you in, Marnie?"

"If President Bush can keep the information secret, I guess I can too. There's something more though, isn't there?"

"Yes," the secretary responded and paused. "Our lawyers have reviewed the likelihood we could get a conviction on conspiracy to commit murder against Richard Jamison for his orders to send out that convoy. They feel the chances are fifty-fifty at best. I believe to press charges without a good chance of a guilty sentence would needlessly place the families of loved ones killed in that convoy through hell."

"Also, it shines a light on the Army that would be embarrassing," I added.

"Indeed, it does and with good reason. We've coordinated with the FBI and they've given us assurances that the list of charges to include kidnapping, torture, and money laundering are enough to ensure Richard and Gerry Jamison never see freedom again."

I sighed. None of what he told me about the fate of the Jamison brothers came as a surprise. "Anything else?"

"I do have some delightful news." He handed me a check for $85,000. "The Iraqis were offering a finder's fee for the return of a priceless, two-thousand-year-old ruby ring that you've kept safe for them for the past seven years. We believe you are the rightful recipient of the fee. The ring has been returned to Iraq and will soon be on display in a museum."

I examined the check and turned it over to make sure it wasn't a joke. "The ring was—is beautiful. I'm going to miss it, and this check sure does take some of the sting away from our parting. Even so, this feels a little bit like a bribe."

"Not a bribe at all. We can always deposit that check in the treasury if you'd like."

"Nah, that's all right. The treasury has way more money than me, and I can put it to good use." This time, I was the one who smiled.

"Marnie, that's all I have. Can we count on your secrecy?" he asked. I studied him and then tho general and nodded my concurrence.

"Excellent. If you don't mind me asking, I know you speak three languages. We could use people like you in DOD or at the State Department. Would you be interested in employment with the government?"

"Why? So you can keep an eye on me?"

"No, because you're an extremely resilient, tenacious, and courageous individual. Marnie, you have the heart of a warrior. We can always use someone of your ilk."

"Can I think about it, sir?"
"Of course. Take all the time you need."

Chapter 51
Eight Months Later

The skies are blue, the birds are chirping, the trees and spring flowers are in bloom, and Marnie Wilson has friends. It all seemed too perfect, but for now it was true. I kept expecting to hear the warning notes of calamity; a needle sliding over an old-time album or concussive movie music just before everything goes to hell. Those ominous notes that always come, eventually, but not today.

Eight months of therapy, real therapy, the kind where I participated and didn't play games with the doctors, had helped. PTSD was a strange beast. Unseen and in darkness, it stayed hidden and thrived. I pictured the beast as a hideous creature rooting around in my brain, waiting to spring on me when I was most vulnerable. If I tended to it, placed the gruesome brute in a cage, shined a light on the energy that fed its need, I had a chance. I couldn't kill it, but I could tame the beast, even though the nasty bugger still bit me from time to time. Sometimes, I liked knowing I had a wary beast that lived within me.

Step one to recovery was removal of the concrete slabs of guilt I had carried on my shoulders for seven years. Step two: self-forgiveness. I remained a work in progress on that one. The doctors told me the rest was up to me, and no more hiding was allowed. In line with that, I was waiting for my friends to arrive for a picnic at my new home.

The house was nearly done, albeit some interior painting and flooring to be finished, but the kitchen appliances were in. I set heaping bowls of my world-class salsa and guacamole on a chip tray and gazed at the plates of food I'd prepared for guests, truly enough to feed an army. This was my very first foray into hosting a party, and I was a little bit nervous.

Buck's tail wagged, and he sprinted to the foyer. "Hey, Marnie," Trevor shouted from the open door. "I've got the folding tables. Me and Trish will go ahead and set them up in the backyard."

"Thanks, Trev." I answered. Trish was his new girlfriend. They were currently inseparable.

I watched the two infatuated teenagers from the kitchen window and thought about my own love life. Marco and I were taking our relationship very slow. We both had issues, and we'd agreed to give each other a lot of space. Kevin, true to his word, never pressed the issue of an *us*, allowing room for a real friendship instead. He was seeing a teacher, and they'd both be here for my almost-done housewarming. Nathan, tech guru extraordinaire and the fast-reacting young man who'd contacted Officer Murphy, saving me from doing something I'd regret, settled for a dinner on me at a restaurant of his choosing. I think more than anything he wanted to impress a waitress that worked at the place we dined. He still reminded me of Zeke, and we hung out from time to time.

Marco stepped through the garage entry and wrapped his arms around my shoulders from the back. He kissed my neck. "You look gorgeous, Marnie! New outfit?"

"Marco, it doesn't work if you ask me about a new outfit every time you see me." I laughed.

"Uh, let me think." He stood back and looked me over from top to bottom. "No, I'm sure I've never seen those shoes."

"Nope, I wore them yesterday when we went to eat, and they're sandals."

"Well, they match perfectly with your newly painted toes?"

I hugged him. "Go put the beers in the cooler and help Trevor with the tables. He's distracted by Trish."

"Yes, ma'am. Hey, Anton said he can come, but he'll be a little late."

I smiled at the thought of Anton and what he'd risked helping me with DNA. "Outstanding."

Murphy and Marco nearly collided as Marco made haste to chill the beers and extract himself from the hole he'd been digging. "Whoa, Marco," Murphy said, startled.

"Hey, Murph. Don't say anything about Marnie's new outfit."

"Okay?" she replied with a curious look. After placing two casserole dishes on the table, she joined me to stand side by side with a view of the backyard.

"So, how'd it go with Mac's parents?"

"Emotional."

"It was nice of your bud, the Sec Def, to let you deliver the medal."

"It was. I just wish I'd have made that trip a long time ago. If wishes were fishes, as they say." I sighed. "They knew who I was. They were just so happy to see me. We all cried and talked about Mac. His mom has cancer, and it meant a lot to her that I went to visit and to know of her son's courage. She said Mac had written to her about me, and he said I was special."

"Aww, Marnie," Murphy said and pulled me into a hug.

"I'm not going to cry today, Murph. Don't get me started."

"Right," she chuckled. "Another subject—what about a job? Have you done any more thinking on that? If the Sec Def wanted me personally, I would certainly take advantage of the opportunity."

"As soon as I'm settled in this house, I'll decide. Sheesh, some of the positions they're recommending are way above my experience level. Interesting stuff anyway."

"You'll do great, Marnie, whatever you decide. Check in with me first though before you say yes to anything."

"What, not pass it by my BFF? Never. Hey Murph, Buck's eating from that bowl of potato salad. Could you please go outside and supervise?"

"On it."

There wasn't any reason to tell Murphy about the $82,000 I sent to the McCray's anonymously. That was like bragging about doing something right. They weren't rich people. The money would come in handy for Mrs. McCray's cancer treatment. I would have given them the whole amount if I hadn't already used part of the money to pay off my credit card bill. It felt good to help someone else, just like so many folks were helping me.

I could see a Pete and Tommy from our trauma group had joined Marco in the backyard. Murphy gave Buck an order, and he scampered away from the food table, his tail tucked and mayonnaise clinging to his whiskers. I needed to move away from this window and be with my guests, but the moment was too perfect.

The skies are blue, the birds are chirping, the trees and spring flowers are in bloom, and Marnie Wilson has friends.

I hope you enjoyed Soldier Hero Thief. I'd love to hear your feedback. I can be contacted via my website at www.nsaustinwrites.com or send me a note on my author Facebook page at www.facebook.com/nancyaustinauthor.

Also, please consider leaving a review at Soldier Hero Thief on Amazon's Kindle section. Independent novelists like me depend on those reviews to get read.

I'd like to thank the many people who helped me drag this novel to completion. They include: my editors Adele Brinkley at Pen in Hand, Nick May at Typeright Editors, and Lin White at Coinlea services; my beta readers Christel Taylor, Kel Crist, Mal Everidge, Amritha Ninnar, Christine LeCain, and Sara Sykora; my cover artist Ghislain Viau; and finally, my family for their loyal support.

Most of all a very special thanks to an extraordinarily brave veteran, Maricella Acosta, who shared with me her stories about Afghanistan. Every time I think of her now and what she endured, I still get a tear in my eye. I never served in war, but as much as anyone can feel something they never experienced, she helped me to understand the emotions of a woman in combat. God bless you, and truly from the bottom of my heart, thank you for your service.

Made in the USA
Lexington, KY
02 December 2018